ANNE SCHLEA

ISBN - 979-8-9910399-4-9 (Paperback)

ISBN - 979-8-9910399-5-6 (Ebook)

Cover Design and Formatting by 100Covers.com

Books in the *Fallen* Series

Orphan of the Fallen

Recruit of the Fallen

Soldier of the Fallen

Author's Note: This novel was first written in January of 2024 and reflects the social and political climate of the region at that time.

DEDICATION

It was in a hotel room in Perrysburg, Ohio, that the first bits of Marissa's story came to life. I had just finished the adult stand-alone novel, *The Fallen,* when I realized my favorite part of the novel was three teenagers: Marissa, Nick, and Amy. I wanted more of their story. By the end of the weekend, Tevin and Collin had also been born and *Orphan of the Fallen* began to take shape.

I had been visiting my hometown that weekend for my niece Emmalyn's baby shower, forever linking Marissa and Emmalyn in my mind.

This book is for Emmalyn. She's a smart, driven young lady who loves reading (although she prefers graphic novels), softball, and is learning guitar. Keep doing the things you love, Em. Just like Marissa, I'm know you're destined for greatness.

CHAPTER ONE

Tasha catches a solid landing as she dismounts from the platform. She doesn't wobble and she doesn't second guess herself. A solid recruit, she's going to make a strong soldier in a few months. Acting as leadership for the class has come second nature for her. It makes me wish I'd done things differently months ago.

Turning around, she encourages the rest of her team. She can't physically help them complete the challenge; her words are enough. And when they reach the final platform to dismount, she's got a high five and slaps on the back for each of them. Even Kaia seems to push herself harder under Tasha's leadership.

Tevin would have finished the course and then watched his classmates for weakness he could exploit the next time someone challenges him. His focus had always been to be at the top of the class.

Tasha's focus is how to be the best leader she's able. She encourages. She challenges the recruits. She gives positive feedback. She's a natural leader.

Tevin had done none of that.

Such a dichotomy of class superiors.

It challenges me to lead differently, too. I'd been trained under previous leadership. Follow orders. Question nothing. Do as you're told. This is how I expected my students and recruits to behave.

You lose a couple, attend a couple of memorial services, and your perspective changes.

I'm glad to see positivity coming out of the run on our borrowed obstacle course.

I'm grateful for the opportunity to use the course we're working on today. It's part of an Israeli army training center that we've been given permission to use. They think we're a group of young American soldiers here to guard an archeological site that has nowhere to train. They're partially right. Pandora's Box doesn't have anywhere to really train. But we're not normal Americans.

We're Fallen, a race of angels descended from the heavenly realm over two thousand years ago. Our purpose? To capture the demons who escaped from the prison known as Pandora's Box. Discord. Chaos. Nightmare. Thirteen of the most dangerous creatures to walk the earth. For now, our responsibility.

Soon enough, the rest of the world will know about us. Our leaders have decided to go public with our existence, and the existence of the demons around us. It's too difficult to maintain secrecy in today's world. Already, global leaders and military elite have been brought in on the secret. In the shadows, we work together.

Back home in Hope, our Fallen city hidden in an apartment building in New York City, we have an alliance

with local demons that allows us to live in relative peace. Helping to manage that peace is a special unit called the Division. It's made up of humans, demons, and Fallen, and is a part of the human police force. They'll be the first line, the first of us to see the public eye.

"Good job, Jenn!" Tasha cheers on the last recruit as she passes the finish line. I check the clock and mark down her time. She's slower than the last time we ran this course. I wonder where her mind is.

Jenn pauses by the finish line to catch her breath. She's dirty and sweaty from the twenty-minute challenge. Last time, she did it in eighteen. After a few minutes, she approaches me.

"Shouldn't Marissa be out here by now?" Jenn's always been someone to shoot straight. She doesn't dance around a subject or soften something to make it sound nicer. I appreciate that about her.

"Give her another couple of days. She's almost ready." I look at my clipboard. Marissa. She doesn't have a single time logged in for this course. Or anything else that we've done here in Jerusalem. Not even recreational hours. Since her arrival, she's done one mission and then lived within the four walls of a hospital room. I feel a stab of guilt thinking about it. I should have done something different months ago.

"Collin, it's already been a month." Jenn follows me when I start walking. I don't know where I'm going, other than I want to get away from her and the questions I don't want to think too much about. "She's lost her rank and she's losing her muscle mass. She needs to get back to training. You need to push her; she's not listening to any of us."

I take a few steps and then stop, realizing I have nowhere to go. What am I going to do? Run and hide on the bus waiting to take us back to our own barracks? Besides, Jenn's just going to follow me. She doesn't give up.

I face her. "What happened to Marissa is extremely traumatic. She'll be ready when she's ready."

"Or she'll wash out." Jenn's hands come to rest on her hips as she digs into her argument. "What then? Are you going to send her back to Orasul to wait for the next training class? Or force her into civil service? That would kill her. She's worked too hard to be here to fail now. She needs someone to wake her up out of the depression. You can do that."

I think back to the time I almost let the darkness overtake me. I couldn't get out of bed; when I found out my face was going to be forever ruined. When I accepted that Natasha would never look at me the way I wanted her to look at me. Were there words that could have talked me into getting out of bed sooner? Maybe. No one tried, so I don't know.

It had been General Keagan who'd pushed me back then. He didn't know me at all. At the time, he'd just been the guy who'd taken over for Generals Riley and Maxim when they were sent to find Pandora's Box.

He'd walked into my hospital room one day and told me it was time to go back to work. That I had the potential to be a good soldier, and he needed me. The next thing I know is that I'm teaching high school students. Sometimes I wonder how I got there, and I don't remember. Only that I did as I was told.

Have I treated Marissa that way? Honestly? No. I've treated her like she's broken. Maybe she continues to be broken because that's how we're treating her.

"Fine." I can concede when I might be wrong, and Jenn has a point. "When I see her tonight, I'll talk to her."

"Good." Jenn bobs her head once, satisfied with my response. "She didn't deserve what happened to her."

"We rarely do." I look at my clipboard again. Four weeks. Four weeks of Marissa missing out on training and classes. Jenn's right, I never should have let this go on so long. "Deserve it, that is. Sometimes, life just isn't fair."

I look past Jenn and realize the rest of the class is milling about, waiting for my next orders. This morning has been all about staying in shape physically. We ran, we worked out, and then we completed the obstacle course. Now, it's close to one o'clock and I'm sure the class is ready for lunch.

"Good work. Clean yourselves up and head to the mess." I glance at my watch, considering what I want to accomplish before we go, and what we need to do when we get back to the prison. "We board the bus at two-thirty."

The group of recruits start moving away from me, but Jenn stays. Kaia, Jenn's roommate, gives her a questioning look before she joins the rest of her classmates.

"Thank you." Jenn says softly. "I know it was bad, what happened. And I know you've been working with Marissa to help her get over it. Thank you."

I'd like to say, it's my job, but it isn't, and we both know that. I'm not a nurse.

I don't know why I started spending my evenings sitting with Marissa and it isn't something I want to look too closely at. Only that it felt right. I missed having her in class. I thought I could help.

"You're welcome." I lift my chin toward the retreating group of future soldiers. "Now go eat. I'll meet you in a while."

"You're not coming?" She tilts her head. "You've got to be as hungry as we are."

"I want to run the course myself." I'm honest. I need to push my body some more today. Thinking about Marissa and Tevin makes me feel sluggish, out of control. Pushing myself to better my time is something I can discipline.

"You shouldn't do that by yourself." She raises an eyebrow. "What if you take a fall off one of the walls and break your leg? Who's going to know?"

"You, when I don't show up at the bus." I point toward Kaia. "Now, go. I'll be fine."

She stands there for a minute, watching me with narrowed eyes. Then she slowly turns and jogs after the rest of her team.

Once the recruits are out of sight, I take my time walking to the start of the obstacle course.

I can feel him beside me before my brain conjures the image. Tevin. He's my ghost. Well, one of my ghosts. In moments like this, I can imagine him being here. He would have loved this course. Always out to prove himself better than the rest of the unit, he would have pushed himself to get the best time, every time.

Like I do with his classmate Amy, I can't help the feeling I failed him.

One his first mission, he died. It was a series of circumstances none of us could have expected. Command thought we'd considered everything, every possibility. But Discord had one more trick up his sleeve. We thought he needed to touch you to control you. Turns out, if he has enough time, he can simply speak to you and force you to do what he wants.

Discord escaped confinement and Tevin did what he thought he had to in order to save the rest of his unit.

I guess he did have the makings of a good leader in him.

The end result is a dead Fallen, but Discord safely locked away in his cell.

I've thought over the circumstances a hundred times; gone over the video footage of the event with my superiors. The truth is, I don't know what we could have done differently. What Tevin could have done differently. We'd set up the team with what we thought was an easy first mission.

We were wrong.

From the start line, I look down the course and plan my attack. Speed, strength. Both things I'd gotten lazy at while teaching classes and training recruits. I don't know if I'm going to want to train another class after this. Tevin, and the murder of his classmate Amy, might have broken me. Maybe it's time to go back into the army until I can get a position with the Division. Because that's where I really want to be: home. Hope.

"Ready for this?" Tevin's ghost smiles at me, challenging me. His military black cargo pants and black t-shirt are the same as I always see him. I guess it'll never change now. That's just how I remember him. Ready for war and cocky.

I ready my stopwatch. "Let's do it."

Starting a race at the same time you start a timer is tricky. You don't want to lose or gain time by starting too late or too early. If you want a truthful time, you've got to hit start and run at the same time.

I sprint toward the first obstacle, a six-foot-tall wall that I need to scale. I jump when I get there and pull myself over in one concise movement. This isn't a challenge, the wall is six feet, I'm six two. The bigger challenge will be the fifteen-foot wall later in the course. I'll need to grapple the rope and hoist myself over that wall.

The tire run barely slows my sprint.

I hit the ground next, making myself small to belly crawl under a low wire entanglement. This is more of a challenge. I don't want to snare my head on cables above me, but I need to keep my eyes up enough to watch where I'm going.

Behind me, I can hear Tevin. He's always just behind me, almost good enough to take the lead, but never quite there. He would have been a better soldier than me, despite his aversion to the Fallen going public. He knew how to follow orders. He was strong. He was smart, not the book smart kind of smart that gets you through class. The kind of smart that could keep you alive on the streets in a fight. The kind of smart that would have prepared him to lead strike teams.

There are so many "would have beens" and "should have beens" that all became an "almost" the day Tevin and Discord crossed paths.

I pull myself out of the wire entanglement. I'm covered in dirt now; I'll need to shower and clean up before lunch. I don't care. Maybe by the time I get there the recruits will be done. I don't feel like being social today.

Balance beams line up ahead of me. I think of Marissa when I see them. She taught herself how to fight using balance beams. When I first met her, she couldn't stay upright to save her own life. Her opponent barely had to look at her to knock her over. A few weeks into our classes together, she started getting better. A lot better. It took

me some time, but eventually I stumbled upon her in the training center. She'd been suspended in the air, attached to wires, working on balance beams high above the floor.

I don't know what gave her that idea, but it was brilliant. The balance beams taught her focus, because you can't stare at the floor from twenty feet up, and how to keep her feet underneath her. Over time, her movements in the ring turned into more of a dance and less of a stumble. It was a beautiful thing to watch. She'd been determined to get better, sought advice, and then made the most of it. I don't know many other recruits who would have done the same.

Hefting myself up onto the bar, I move cautiously down the wooden beam. It's six inches across. Not impossible, but difficult to do in combat boots. I take longer than I'd like, jealous of Marissa's fluidity on the beams, and hit the ground on the other side less stable than I should be.

I'm too distracted.

"What's taking so long, old man?" Tevin's voice taunts me from the next challenge. "You should have nailed that beam, what's with the wobble?"

I grit my teeth and don't answer. It's questionable enough that I can see a dead recruit, talking to him is crossing a line I know I can't cross. Instead, I grab the first rope of a rope traversing course and hold on. My shoulders scream from the tension, but I don't let go. I'm not going to let my arms beat me.

I don't think anyone knows it, but my left arm is my weakness. In the same battle that caused the scar on my face, my arm had been knocked out of place. Medics were able to put it back in and it healed, but it's never been the same. I'm careful to pull the heaviest weight with my right, just in case. I don't need the left arm going out in front of the recruits. Show no weakness and all that.

I think I'm going to fall on the last rope. Pushing away the pain in my shoulder, I swing one more time and land on solid ground. Tevin is there waiting for me, a smile on his face. "Not bad. Now keep going."

Up next is a low wall into a water pit. I consider skipping this because I don't want to be forced to change into dry clothes, but then I remember that I'm already dirty from the belly crawl. I forge ahead, startled by the cold water. I shake it off. The median temperature this time of year is fourteen degrees Celsius, did I expect the water to be warm?

I manage the cargo net climb onto the three-story tall tower and easily slide down the rope descent on the other side. Then it's through cement pipes, easy, and across another water pit on a rope swing that I have to jump to reach. I almost slip on that one, my hands still wet from the first water pit, managing to hold on by sheer willpower alone. I'm determined not to fail this course.

The wire bridge on the other side of the rope swing is easy enough as long as you don't slip. The key is to not rush it. At this point in the course, the end is almost in sight. It's easy for soldiers to move a little too fast and slide off the narrow cable under your feet. I've seen too many of my recruits screw up this obstacle; I'm not about to make that mistake myself. Sometimes, part of making smart choices on the battlefield is slowing down. That's what Tevin didn't learn. Slow down. Rushing in might not be the best answer.

After the bridge is a set of monkey bars. Again, simple enough if my shoulder holds out. Halfway across, it starts to hurt, and I wonder if I should have a medic look at it the next time I'm visiting Marissa in the hospital. Maybe there's still something more they can do to improve it.

I finish the monkey bars and sprint toward the end of the course: a rope climb onto a wooden platform. The climb is quick. I jump off the platform and run full tilt at the finish line.

I hit the timer on my watch and lean over to take a breath.

Ten seconds slower than my best time. I shake my head in frustration. I should be getting better, not slower. There's too much going on in my head and it's slowing me down.

A quick shower and a change of clothes later, I'm settling into a quiet corner of the mess. Some of the recruits have eaten and left to do who knows what. At least I know they can't get into any real trouble on this base. They're smart enough not to go out of bounds. The rest are relaxing around tables, waiting to load the bus.

I'm about to start on my tabbouleh when Jenn and Kaia drop into chairs next to me.

I'd planned on eating alone, like always, enjoying thirty minutes of quiet.

"You're going to talk to Marissa." Kaia pins me with her stare. "About time. She needs to get her butt out of bed."

I sigh. This again. Nodding, I take a bite of food and hope it's enough of a response to send them away.

"I was thinking I could pick up the work she's missed. It's four whole weeks of classes she needs make up." Kaia keeps staring at me. "Maybe I can study with her at night, help her catch up. Is there a make up test or something she needs to prepare for?"

I literally stop, my fork mid-air on the way to my mouth. I can't honestly be hearing what I think I'm hearing. "Kaia, you hate Marissa. You've done nothing since you met her except try to get ahead of her in classes and training. Do you honestly think I'm going to put her future in your hands now?"

She has the sense to look uncomfortable. "Tevin was like a brother to me."

"I know. That still doesn't explain why you suddenly want to help Marissa." I hurry and shove a bite of food into my mouth. At this rate, I'm not going to eat any of my lunch.

"What Tevin did was stupid and not her fault." Kaia shifts in her seat. I realize in that moment that I've never seen her cry for Tevin. I'd known them before Tevin met Marissa. Before things got complicated and deadly. Kaia and Tevin had been close. "I'm so mad at him I could spit. She might have been dumb enough to get involved with him, but she shouldn't be suffering because of what he did. I just want to help her, that's all."

I take a breath, remembering how close in age these recruits are to me. Three years. Only three years separate us in experience. Keagan must have been desperate to put someone as young as I am in charge of this class. I can related to all of them, Tevin, Marissa, even Kaia. And Nick? He might have shipped himself back to finish training with the Fallen in Les Gens outside of Paris, but I swear he's my younger self. I shouldn't be making these decisions. "Fine. If I promise to get you her homework, will you leave me in peace to eat my lunch?"

"Yes, sir." Kaia lights up like I'd just gifted her a new weapon. "Thank you, sir!"

She and Jenn jump up from their seats and go back to their original table, leaving me to sigh with relief. How in the world am I to make all of this right again?

CHAPTER TWO

I hesitate outside her door. She's come a long way since the first day I visited her. Before the unexpected battle with Discord, Marissa was a force of nature. Strong. Resilient. But she'd gotten too close to Tevin. They'd formed a bond between them that fused their energies together. When he died, a piece of Marissa had died, too.

For Fallen, it's more than a broken heart. We are physically and spiritually dependent on each other for survival. Sometimes, when one half of a bonded pair dies, the other half wastes away and perishes, too. I was honestly worried that would happen to Marissa at first. She was so tied to Tevin that when he was killed, she went down in the field, too.

I saw it happen; the backup arrived moments too late to save Tevin.

He'd pushed Discord into his cell and slammed the door behind them. Seconds later, before anyone could do anything, Discord snapped Tevin's neck.

A few feet away, Marissa crumbled to the ground, her eyes closed and her body shaking.

It happens, I understand. This is a danger in our world. We need each other to survive, but that very need is sometimes what causes our deaths.

Marissa refused help the first few days after she'd been admitted to the hospital wing. With her spirit as torn as it had been, her energy depleted by the loss of Tevin, she needed her friends and family to rally around her. They needed to spend time with her, give her their energy to help her heal. And they tried. But she would send them away, sometimes screaming until they left.

Finally, I stepped in. As her superior officer, I crossed my fingers that she would do what I said, and I came to visit.

She looked frail on the bed; her brown hair was flat and lifeless, and her brown eyes had lost their sparkle. Everything I knew about her was gone. Barely more than a shell, she lay on the bed, cold from loss. She didn't even lift her head when I walked in.

I decided screaming was better than this. At least there was some passion in her shrieks.

I've been coming back every evening since then. After training and classwork, sometimes after a mission late at night, I come. And she's always waiting for me.

At first, I'd sit close by and read a book while she slept. The nurses told me it was the only time she'd sleep: when I visited. It was because she accepted my support. My energy was helping her heal. She wouldn't accept help from anyone else, not the nurses, not Jenn, not even her own mom who is also stationed at Pandora's Box.

Why me? I have no idea.

Lately, in the last week or so, we've started talking. She wants to know what her classmates are doing. What missions are like here in Israel. What she's missing in class. That's good because Jenn's right, I need to push her more. It's time to get out of bed and get back to work. She's strong enough now.

I take a breath and push the door open.

Marissa is out of bed, standing in her light blue pajamas next to the window looking out on the Israeli countryside. Her hair is pulled away from her face, neat and clean like she'd recently washed and brushed it. This is good. I haven't seen her out of bed without prodding since it happened.

"You're up." I close the door behind me and approach my regular seat next to her bed, my voice steady and even. A while ago, someone got rid of the hard, wooden chair that had been there and replaced it with a recliner that's much more comfortable. I set down the books and the tablet I brought with me and go to stand next to her at the window.

"I miss being outside." Her eyes stay trained on the countryside. She's talking to me, but her mind is out there somewhere.

"That's good." I was going to ease into this conversation, but Jenn's right. Someone needs to push Marissa, and this seems like as good a time as any. "It's time for you to come back. It's been long enough."

That gets her attention. Her head turns and her eyes focus on me. "I'm not ready."

"If I'd have waited after my injury until I was ready, I'd probably still be in that hospital room." Her eyes move back to the window, and I wonder if I've lost her attention. "I think it's time, Marissa. I know you don't want to wash out. You have to finish basic. You need to take hold of your life again."

She doesn't say anything. Staring out the window, she takes in steady breaths through her nose.

Not sure what else to do, I analyze her energy. It's better, it gets better every day. I can feel her pushing against me right now, that's good. That means she cares about what I just said. She might not like it, but that's better than the apathy that I'd gotten for the first few weeks.

"I'm afraid to face my classmates." Her voice is small, barely more than a whisper. "They all know. How could any of them trust me now? Who would want me to fight beside them?"

"What happened had nothing to do with trust." I touch her shoulders and turn her body so she's looking at me again. "The broken trust is Tevin's. When we're close like you were, we can't sacrifice ourselves. When we fight, we fight to survive. He didn't. That's on him. You'll take turns working with different classmates until we find another good match. It's what should have been happening all along, I never should have let you two become so focused on fighting together. That's where my fault is in this."

"It's not your fault." Her eyes focus more on mine. It's the first time we've talked about Tevin and the sacrifice that was made. I've been afraid this conversation would break her. She reaches out and touches my arm. "You didn't know how much time we were spending together out of class. This is my fault. I knew better."

"Let's not place blame." I rest my hand on top of hers. Her fingers are warm against mine. It's another sign she's ready. Until now, she's always been cold. "What's done is done. It's time you move forward."

"I can't imagine moving back to the barracks. I kind of like having my own room." She gives me the ghost of a smile and I realize she's trying to joke with me. It's good. It means she's not going to fight with me about this.

"Sorry, you're going to have to share a bathroom with Kaia and Jenn and the others moving forward." I squeeze her hand and drop mine beside me. "I won't talk to the nurses until tomorrow. You can have your private room for one more night."

"Thanks." Her smile grows a little bit. "I guess I'll have to work hard and become an officer to get my own quarters. If that's still possible."

"It's possible. You're not that far behind yet." I tilt my head toward the chair. "Come on, I brought you some of the classwork you've missed. We should start looking at it to help you catch up."

She follows me to the comfortable chair and sits. I pull up the extra wooden chair in the room and sit across from her. She looks at the textbooks, paging through the things she's missed. "Does this mean you're going to be my tutor now?"

"No." I feel a sting of loss and realize I'd love to be her tutor. I'm going to miss the time we've spent together, even though most of it was consumed by silence. "Kaia is going to be your tutor. She asked me today for permission. I'm going to meet with my superiors tomorrow morning and we'll come up with a plan to get you back to where you need to be."

"Kaia?" Her voice quivers and I feel a rush of cold from her. They have baggage, those two, I should have realized she might rebel against this idea. "Don't you think Kaia will do her best to help me fail? Why not Jenn?"

"First off, Kaia's marks are better than Jenn's. Second, she came to me and asked. She wants to see you back on your feet." I can see she's going to protest so I continue. "I'll make sure she isn't doing something nefarious to harm your scores. Besides, she's bored without you. There's no one left to challenge her."

"Tasha's ahead of her in class." Marissa points out. "You've shown me the class list."

"Tasha's too good of a leader to challenge Kaia in the way she needs." I chuckle. Kaia likes friendly rivalry. Tasha's no one's rival. "If Kaia beats her rank and pulls ahead, Tasha will probably throw her a party and give her a high five. Kaia needs a frenemy to be challenged."

"I don't know…" Marissa hesitates, her fingers tapping lightly on the weapons textbook in her hand. "I already have to live with her."

"Let her tutor you." I take the tablet from the pile and pull up a list of classes Marissa has missed. I'll go over the field training notes another day. No reason to overwhelm her. Besides the obstacle courses she's missed, there are countless other tests of marksmanship, sprinting, long distance runs, and other items she's missing. I never realized before how much material we cover in four weeks.

"Fine." She looks up at me with a wry expression on her face. "But, if I fail, I'm blaming you for picking my tutor."

"You're not going to fail." I lean a little closer and drop my voice. "Your mom will kill me if you fail."

"You're not afraid of my mom." Marissa's expression changes to a soft grin.

"I'm very afraid of your mom." I lower my voice even more to a whisper. "I'm probably more afraid of your mom than I am your stepdad. Between the two of them, I could be busted down and cleaning toilets the rest of my career."

"You have a point." Marissa's stepdad is the head commander of this complex. General Riley is no one I want to mess with. Honestly, I'm surprised he didn't replace me in this job when we found out how close Tevin and Marissa had gotten. It's something that should have been noticed and stopped. "How mad was he when he found out about me and Tevin?"

"I think he was too scared for you to be mad." I lean back in my chair, my voice returning to normal. All joking aside, this whole situation could have turned out so differently. "I'd hang onto that if I were you."

"I don't remember my real dad." She closes the book and looks at the next one, military history volume three. Under that is Battle Tactics for Jungle Warfare and Military Leadership. It's a hefty stack of books. I'll be glad when the last of our textbooks are transcribed into tablet form. "I don't really remember my real mom, either. I wasn't even five when they both died. I'm glad I have Mom and Riley. He acts like I'm his real kid."

"I think you kind of are." In the last weeks, I'd seen their relationship. Marissa's mom might really be her aunt, and Riley may have only been in their lives for the last few years, but they're as much a real family as they could be. Anna had been there for Marissa since her real parents were killed, over thirteen years ago now. "You're lucky to have a family like them."

"I know." Her almost smile returns. "I'm so glad they're here."

I don't know what she's thinking about, but I let the thoughts sit for a few minutes. The silence of the room is comfortable. We've gotten used to each other to the point that we don't need words. Some days, we'd sit in silence for my whole visit, and it would be fine. When I give her enough time, I point to the tablet. "We really do need to work on this."

She looks at me with a hint of resistance in her eyes. "I can't get one more day of a free pass?"

"No." I'm firm, but I keep my voice lighthearted. Ultimately, she knows what's good for her; and if she were truly going to fight about this, she would have gotten angry by now. "Let's at least look at what you've missed so you know what you're getting yourself into with Kaia."

Wrinkling her nose, Marissa runs a hand over the textbooks and looks at my tablet from her chair. Four weeks. She's four weeks behind. It's going to be tough to catch up. We only have four and a half months left here before graduation from basic training. She'll have to work double hard to not only learn what she's missed, but to stay on top of her classes as she moves forward.

And there's a good chance she'll never get her rank back at the top of the class where she was before, which will end her dreams of officer's training.

"Fine." She moves three of the books to the bedside table, keeping the weapons text on her lap. "Can we start with this one, it's the most interesting."

"Sure." I hand her a spiral bound notebook and a pen before I look at my notes. "Turn to page sixty-four. I think that's where we were when…"

I pause, afraid to say the words.

"It's okay, you can say it." She opens the book to the right page. "When Tevin died."

"When Tevin died." I give her a moment to see if she's going to disappear back into herself. She doesn't. There's a wash of sadness that flows over her, but it passes.

She takes a deep breath and looks up at me. "I believe we were discussing human drone technology the last time I was in class."

"Right." I give myself an internal shake. I can't get lost in the memories, either. The "what should have been." Although I swear Tevin is standing in the corner of the room watching us. "Drone technology and large-scale warfare."

We focus on the textbooks for almost two hours. It's a good start, and I realize the more she works, the more alive Marissa seems. By the end of the session, there's some color in her cheeks and her eyes have light to them. Jenn's right. Kaia's right. Marissa needed this today. I look toward the window and realize she needs something else today, too.

"Come on." I take the Leadership text from her hands and place it on top of the pile of books on the bedside table. Carefully placing my tablet on top, I look around her room. Her bathrobe is tossed over the end of her bed. I pick it up and hold it out to her and repeat myself. "Come on. Put this on."

"Why?" Suspicion creeps into her voice and a brief hint of panic steals into her eyes.

"You trust me, right?" I keep holding the bathrobe toward her, willing her to take it out of my hand. I don't know how I know this is the right thing, but I feel it all the way inside of me. She needs this.

"Maybe." Marissa's eyes narrow. "Depends on what you want me to do."

"You said you missed being outside." She looks at me, confusion on her face. I remind her, "It's the first thing you said to me today when I got here. Let's go outside."

"Now?" Her eyes move to the window where the sun is low on the horizon. Sunset is coming soon. "I'm not dressed."

"It will be a little chilly, but you'll be fine." I shake the bathrobe at her. "Put this on and let's go. Consider it an order."

Her jaw falls open and then she closes it again. I can see her brain working, can he really order me to do this? Then she slowly reaches out her hand to accept the bundle of material I'm holding toward her. "I don't want to see my classmates. Not yet. Tomorrow, but not today."

"That isn't my intention." I help her slide the sleeves on over her pajamas. "Let's go outside for a few minutes and then I'll get you back in here in time for your dinner and your visit with your mom. Doesn't she usually come after you eat?'

"What?" Marissa is breathless and I can feel the anxiety coming off her in waves. "Yeah. She's supposed to stop by after dinner."

I lightly touch her back, willing some of my energy into her. I'm not as good at that as the nurses, but she only needs a little bit to understand that I'm not going to let her get hurt today. The stiffness in her shoulders relaxes a little bit. "There's a door at the end of this hallway to the outside. We're going to walk to it and let ourselves out. If it's too much, we'll come back."

"Okay." She nods her head, her eyes unfocused. I understand. The last time she was out of this room, Tevin had been killed. She must be thinking about that.

I keep my hand pressed against her back, letting her know that I'm here, and I lead her out the door. As the only patient on the small hospital wing, Marissa draws unwanted attention immediately. I feel her body stiffen again as nurses come hurrying our way.

I motion for them to stop. "We're stepping outside for some fresh air. I promise we're not going to go very far."

"But the chill." The nurse closest to me stops hard, wavering in place. Thankfully, I've been given a kind of carte blanche where Marissa is concerned. I'm hoping it will extend to taking her out of the hospital for a few minutes. "Let me get her a jacket."

"No. We'll be fine. We won't be outside for long." Past the first nurse, a second one looks like she's preparing to tackle us as we walk by. I glare at her, and she takes a step back. "Give us a few minutes and we'll come back inside. Trust me, she needs this."

They look at each other, skeptical. "Maybe we should check with the medic on staff."

"You do that." I start walking with Marissa again, my hand pushing her a little to keep her going. "Let us know what he says, we'll be outside."

"I'll be okay." Marissa startles them both by speaking up. "It's just a few minutes."

That stops both of the nurses in their tracks. Marissa had been resistant to getting up and walking around; she'd never spoken to either of them as far as I know. I take the opportunity of their surprise and hurry Marissa past them.

Finally, we reach the outside door. I open it and gently hurry her through before anyone can stop me.

The air hits us both at the same time. It's chilly, and I don't have a jacket with me, but I'll be fine. I'm more worried about Marissa. She pulls the lapels of her robe tighter around her. The daytime high of twelve degrees has started to slip toward the low of seven. It's not frigid by any means, but there is a chill in the air.

"Oh!" A sound of surprise escapes Marissa as she looks down the hill the prison is built on.

In the distance, across the shallow valley made by the hills, the sun is descending toward the horizon. The fiery ball of light is bright orange, throwing the world around us into bursts of red and yellow light that reflect off the rocks and the building behind us. Between the beauty of the land and the golden glow of daytime's last stand, I can't imagine anything more beautiful.

"We didn't have sunsets in New York. I thought you should see this." I give her a made-up explanation for taking her outside. "I'd never seen anything like this until I came here."

"It's beautiful." There's a lightness to her voice that hadn't been there in her room. Her back presses lightly against my hand, drawing my attention to look down at her.

Marissa is smiling, her face toward the sun and painted with the glowing light. She looks joyful, jubilant, even. In this moment, the past is gone. There isn't any sadness or grief.

Looking at her, I realize that there might be something more beautiful than the setting sun and the thought terrifies me.

CHAPTER THREE

I have class at eight. Yesterday was field training; today is book learning. We'll be in the classroom all day with an hour-long break for lunch. The first half of the day is Leadership and Military History. After lunch, we have Jungle Warfare and a practicum: building a drone. Of course, the recruits don't know we're having a practicum. That's a surprise. They'll have two hours to put together a machine that flies.

Because I have such a busy day, I find myself outside General Riley's office before seven in the morning. I'd texted him the night before to make sure he'd be available to meet. I used the one word I knew would get me a meeting: Marissa. The man would do anything for his stepdaughter, and I know it. I've never seen anything like what happened the day she went down in the field. Needless to say, no one is going to be messing with her anytime soon.

His administrative assistant isn't at his desk when I arrive, but his door is open and he's waiting. There's a stack of papers on his desk, maps from what I can see, and he's focused on the top one. There are marks all over it, some in red and some in blue. He seems mesmerized and I want to ask what it is; I'm smart enough to know it isn't any of my business. Whatever he's working on is well above my pay grade.

"Sir." I clear my throat and make my presence known.

He looks up and gestures to the seat across from him. "Collin, take a seat."

"Thank you, sir." I perch myself on the chair and get right to the point. "I think Marissa should come back to class. Today. I'd like to check her out of the hospital as soon as I leave here. I've already spoken to her about it; she's ready."

Both the General's eyebrows shoot skyward. I don't know how she's been with her mom. With Riley. It's possible that, while she's been better with me, she still refuses to talk to them. That's family business.

He leans back in his chair and considers my request. I haven't worked with the man long; he has a reputation for being a strong leader. Understanding. There's a rumor that Nick got his transfer by appealing directly to the General. I find it hard to believe the kid had to go that high to get moved to Les Gens, but I guess anything's possible. He was Marissa's friend in high school. He would have known the General before he became the General.

"Do you really think she's ready?" He crosses his arms across his chest. I know this move. I use it with my students. It's to cut off my feelings. He doesn't want to know what I feel, he wants to know what I know. "Her mom said she was tired yesterday."

"She had a long day yesterday." I feel a rush of frustration. I should have known yesterday would be

too much if she were visiting with Major Cazut, too. "We worked on homework for almost two hours and then we went outside for a walk at sunset. It's more than she's done in a long time."

"And you think she can make it through an entire day of classes?" He raises an eyebrow. "I know she needs to get back to work, but I don't want to set her up for failure."

"She's not going to fail." I put as much authority in my voice as I feel is appropriate with the General. "You told me to get her through this. I think she is. She's good. She's ready."

"What if she's not?" He looks me straight in the eyes. In my peripheral vision, I see a picture of Marissa on his desk. It's from several years ago. She's wearing a bridesmaid's dress; it must be from his wedding to her mom. I'm struck for a moment by how young she looks; nothing at all like I see her now. She's maybe fifteen. She's grown up so much since then.

"She is." I reiterate my opinion. "I have a classmate who's asked to help tutor her, to get her up to speed with her class. And, if I may be honest, if we don't start now, she may never catch up."

He's quiet for a while, his head nodding. "I've been afraid of that. Afraid the damage Tevin caused was too much, or that she'd have to go back and start over with the next class of recruits. Do you really think it's that bad?"

"No, sir, but it could be if we don't push her." I shake my head, vehemently. "She's strong, really strong. When I told her what we needed to do to catch up yesterday, she took it in stride. She's not happy about my choice of tutors, but other than that she seemed ready to come back. She would like her own bedroom, though."

The General laughs. "That sounds like her. What's your plan of action?"

"Let me take her back to class today, just the book stuff." I consider the physical practical I have planned for tomorrow and dismiss it from my mind. No need to cross that bridge until we come to it. "Let her go back to the barracks. She'll keep gaining strength just bunking up with Kaia and Jenn. Tasha would be stronger, but her current roommates are strong enough to make a difference. She's ready."

He sits quietly at his desk, considering my suggestions. I've worked with him long enough to know he doesn't move quickly; instead, he considers things from all perspectives. He's probably thinking about how her mom will react and what might happen if Marissa's fails. I know she can't fail right now. She needs as many wins under her belt as I'm capable of giving her. He finally acquiesces. "Fine. We'll try this, but the first sign she's going backwards and we're moving her back to the hospital wing."

"Understood." I expected as much. While the General and Anna may not want to destroy Marissa's dreams, they are her parents. They want her alive and well more than they want her to graduate training with this group of recruits. "With all due respect, sir, I think she's stronger than that. It might be a struggle at first, but she's going to pull through this."

"She's my daughter, Collin." The General closes his eyes and rubs the bridge of his nose. It's the first time I've ever seen him show any kind of emotional weakness since the day she went down in the field. "I don't care if it takes her an extra year and a half to finish basic training. Tevin might have saved his team but did a number on her while doing it. I won't let that happen again."

"So noted." Even though I'm sitting upright in the chair, I try to sit a little higher and repeat myself again. "She's strong. I've been working with her for weeks and I'm telling you that she's strong. Maybe not strong enough for the field yet, but she has to get started somewhere. Let this be the start. Let her go to class today and get her feet underneath her. Honestly, her biggest fear is letting down her classmates. She's afraid they won't trust her."

"This insanity isn't on her; this was all Tevin. He shouldn't have been so careless." The General's vehemence startles me. For a man known for being laid back and calm, that sentiment is powerful. It makes me wonder how his relationship is with Maxim, his second in command. After all, Maxim is Tevin's father.

"I agree." I figure that's the safe response. I don't really care who he needs to blame. I care that Marissa is given the opportunity to get better.

He leans forward on his elbows, his hands folded in front of him. For a minute, he looks at the photo of Marissa on his desk, then he leans back again. "Okay. I'll call down to the hospital wing and give you permission to check her out. But I have one caveat."

"Okay." A feeling of dread washes over me. This is where my rank gets busted. I can feel it coming.

"I don't want another situation like Tevin. She doesn't need her emotions to get wrapped up in her new partner. You will be her main patrolling and sparring partner moving forward." The General pins me with his stare. "Are we clear?"

"Yes, sir." My stomach sinks. I can't describe the way she makes me feel, but it's got nothing on Natasha. I think I'd do anything for her. Crap. I'm in a lot of trouble.

I'm going to be late for class. I'm never late. At least I have Tasha; I texted her to start the lesson without me. She's capable.

I look at the time and wonder what's taking Marissa so long. All she had to do was get dressed.

After my conversation with the General, I'd gone to Marissa's hospital room to check her out. She was up and waiting, her breakfast finished, and her small pile of belongings stacked neatly on the bedside table. There were discharge papers for her to sign. They wanted to push her out of the hospital wing in a wheelchair; I nixed that idea. The whole point of her hospital stay was to get her back on her feet. The wheelchair feels like taking a step backwards.

My initial plan had been to drop Marissa off with her roommates and then head to class on my own. Unfortunately, I didn't take breakfast into account and Kaia and Jenn were gone when we arrived. Rather than leave Marissa on her own, the last thing I think she needs, I wait outside her barracks room door while she changes into her everyday clothes.

I wonder what she's going to do with the pajamas she's been wearing. Part of me hopes she burns them along with the memory of all those weeks in the hospital.

Memory can be a funny thing, crippling at times. After my injury, I'd walked around Hope like a ghost. Everyone thought it was because of what I'd seen in the battle that injured me. I couldn't tell anyone about Natasha, the girl I thought I'd fallen in love with who would never see me as

anything more than a friend. She had no idea I'd gotten so attached to her. She hadn't felt anything once I was gone; all I felt was cold. Somedays, I'd think I was doing fine and then I'd pass her in the halls. Just seeing her like that was a punch to my gut.

Yeah, I understand why Nick left.

When I was offered the job in Orasul, I jumped at the opportunity. I was able to leave Natasha and the memories behind at Hope. The move gave me distance and perspective. I wasn't exactly over it by the time I moved back to Hope for recruit training, but I was able to manage my feelings. Seeing Natasha wasn't as bad. I was able to be genuinely happy for her happiness. She enjoys her job and the work she's doing for the army. And to this day, she has no idea she broke my heart.

We hadn't been assigned to Pandora's Box for long when Tevin died. It's not enough time for Marissa to make too many memories. Hopefully, that will make this easier. I know his empty seat in the classroom will be hard enough to see almost every day.

The door finally opens, and she steps out. If I didn't know better, looking at her, I could forget the last few weeks ever happened. She appears exactly the same as always. Her black t-shirt fitted just right, black cargo pants, boots on her feet, backpack slung over one shoulder. Her brown hair is pulled back from her face. She isn't wearing any makeup, not that I think she'd ever need any. That's when I notice it. The only sign of her nerves. Her skin is pale.

She stops and looks at me from the doorway. Behind her, I can see into her room. Two bunkbeds are against the walls, room for four recruits. One is gone, the victim of a murder in New York.

I wonder if Marissa has the top or the bottom bunk. Everything is neatly put away, the way a barracks room should look. Without being told, I can't tell where her personal items are, or which bed is hers.

"Hey." I touch her shoulder. "You're going to be fine. You're ready for this."

"I didn't expect to be so nervous." She crosses her free arm in front of her stomach like she's protecting herself. "I honestly think I could throw up if I let myself."

"Are you going to?" Visions of her puking in the middle of class fill my brain. That's not the best way to ease back into life. "Do we need to stop at a bathroom?"

"No." She laughs weakly. "I didn't eat that much breakfast, anyway. Nerves."

"Then let's go. I know your classmates will be happy to see you." I give her a little shove and we start walking down the hallway toward the classroom. She's completely silent, making me wonder what's going on in her brain. Her face doesn't give me many clues, her focus is straight ahead like a soldier marching in formation.

"Wait a minute." She stops when we reach the classroom door and turns to look at me. Her hand reaches for my bicep, then she stops midair like she suddenly realizes what she's doing. "I know we're not in the hospital anymore, but do you mind?"

"Go ahead." I stand still, allowing her to put her hand on me. There's a little flutter against the edge of my energy, a tiny pull as she uses me to stabilize her nerves. Most Fallen can't do what she's doing now; the nurses taught her while she was in the hospital. We need shared energy to survive. Most of us subconsciously take and give when we're with others of our kind. That's why living in hives is so important. If we aren't around enough of our own, we start to wither. We start to die.

Nurses, and now Marissa, have been taught to consciously give and take energy. What she's doing now is borrowing some of mine to help her through the next step in her day. My energy will fuse with hers to give her a little more oomph.

While she's concentrating, I find myself looking at her face. The way her eyelashes lay against her cheeks while her eyes are closed. I want to reach up and touch her cheek.

I lock the thought down immediately and hope she doesn't feel my energy shift away from her. It's perfectly normal and natural for Fallen to share energy like we're doing right now. But my thoughts need to stay firmly in the superior officer zone. I'm here to train her, not to get soft feelings toward her. Especially now when she's working so hard to come back from being nearly broken. I'm out of line and I know it.

I look away from her and catch a glimpse of my reflection in the doorway window. With the shade drawn on the other side, it makes for a great mirror. The light falls across my left cheek, making my scar stand out. My skin isn't soft like hers. It's torn and broken, an ugly reminder that I'm not enough. Natasha had been my friend for a long time; she didn't want me. And that was before. Now? I'm hard to look at, a perfect teaching example of why you need to stay alert and on your game in the field. I let my attention drop once and now I'll be forever broken. No one will ever want this.

The tremble of Marissa's energy brushing up against mine fades away and she releases her grip on my arm. I immediately take a step back, forcing myself to smile. "Better?"

"Much, thank you." She takes a deep breath through her nose and releases it through her mouth, a grounding technique. "I'm ready."

Without giving her a chance to back out, I open the door to the classroom and walk in. "Sorry I'm late, Tasha, you can take your seat."

I know it when Marissa enters the classroom behind me because Jenn jumps up from her chair. "Marissa!"

Although I'm sure Marissa would have preferred to slip into class unnoticed, she arrives with fanfare. Most of the class stands to welcome her. Jenn wraps her in a tight hug. Others pat her on the back as she inches toward her seat, studiously ignoring the empty desk that used to be Tevin's. They used to sit next to each other. I should have thought ahead and moved someone else into that seat.

It takes several minutes for things to get settled. I lean on my desk and watch, unwilling to break up the joy of the moment. This class has had its fair share of losses. Amy, a promising young medic, had been killed in New York, the victim of a demon attack. The police force there still hasn't caught the perpetrator who did it. I'm afraid they won't, that he's slipped off into the night and disappeared forever.

I glance at Nick's empty desk. He probably joined the army for all the wrong reasons, but he'd turned into a promising young soldier. His scores were up, he knew how to follow orders, and he was a wiz at the technology part of our jobs. He has a bright future in cyber warfare and security. That future just won't be with our unit. He'd been close friends with Marissa. When he found out how close Tevin and Marissa had become, Nick was devastated. Much like I had, he'd put his heart in the hands of the wrong person.

After Marissa was admitted to the hospital, Nick asked for a transfer and landed in the Fallen unit out of France. Although I asked him to stay in touch, he hasn't. I keep track of him through official channels. He seems to have settled in well and I wish him the best.

And, of course, Tevin. The unchallenged leader of the class. Gone, too soon.

We started with twenty-two recruits. Now we're down to nineteen. The core of the class, Tevin, Marissa, Amy, Nick, Jenn, and Kaia has been decimated, leaving Tasha to step up and take command. I can't imagine how difficult these last few months of training will be for them. They'll have to wonder how things might be different if no one had died. Or left.

"Alright, let's settle down. I would like to teach today." I start calming the class. "Find your seats, please."

"Does this mean you're moving back in with us?" Jenn, still holding on to Marissa, basically ignores me.

"I dropped my stuff off on the way here." Detaching herself from Jenn, she moves carefully toward her desk. I see her look at Tevin's empty seat, sadness in her eyes. "I've been set free. No more nurses or medics for me."

"Awesome." Jenn gives her a high five with a lot more excitement in it than Marissa is showing right now. "It's been too quiet with just me and Kaia in there."

"Welcome back." Kaia, who hasn't gotten out of her seat to greet Marissa, speaks quietly from her side of the room. "I'm glad you're feeling better."

"Thank you." The backpack slides under her chair, her Leadership text open, and her notebook and pen at the ready. The rest of the class might want to talk, but Marissa is clearly ready to move the attention away from her and onto the subject at hand.

"You can all catch up with Marissa at lunch, but now we have work to get through." I see the look on Marissa's face. I'm sure catching up is the last thing she wants to do. Maybe I should let her and Kaia eat lunch in the classroom alone under the premise of study. "Let's do a quick review of last week. What are the four C's of military leadership?"

Tasha's hand is first in the air. "Competence, candor, courage, and commitment. I must be skilled in my duties before I can lead others. I should be open and honest with my unit; transparency is the key to unity. I should not let fear guide me, as a Fallen, it is up to me to stand up against the scary things that go bump in the night. And I am faithful to my unit and the Fallen; I should not let other Earthly matters divert me from the task to which I was born."

"Good." My simple praise makes Tasha beam in her seat. If she sticks with it, she'd be the perfect candidate for officer's training. "Now, open your texts to the section on Strategic Leadership. As you know, the primary military structure is Autocratic Leadership. However, we use different styles of leadership at different levels. Who can tell me the basics of using a strategic leadership style and when that might be appropriate in a military setting?"

CHAPTER FOUR

For the first time in a month, I don't have anything to do after class. This is the time I would usually use to go see Marissa. I need to adjust my schedule and find something else to fill my evening now that she's out of the hospital. She's probably in her room, settling in with Kaia and Jenn. Maybe they'll get her to talk to them. It would be good for her to open up to her friends about what happened. Therapeutic. Maybe it will help her find some peace.

I swing by my own place and drop off my classroom work and change into workout clothes. I haven't been as diligent with my physical training in the last few weeks. It's probably past time for me to get back into the habit of staying in shape. While, as a general rule, I don't spar with my students, I believe I should be in at least as good of shape as they are. As the mission with Discord showed, you never know when things might go south in the field. And I would never ask them to do anything I wouldn't do. If they're in a dangerous situation, I will be, too.

Unfortunately, the last time, I was waiting with the other half of the delivery team inside the prison. We came as quickly as we could when realized something was going very wrong, but it wasn't fast enough. We'd arrived with just enough time to see Tevin cage Discord.

I spent some time working through my feelings on this. At first, I convinced myself that I should have been there with the recruits. Somehow, I could have stopped the carnage. Maybe, if they'd had my leadership, Tevin and Giovanni, a soldier from the French unit, wouldn't have died. I realized quickly that the thought process was hubris. No one man has that much power.

Heading up to the main level of Pandora's Box, I let myself out the back doors, the ones by the hospital rooms. It's a nice day outside and it won't get cold for another hour or two. With limited space in this facility, treadmills in the small gym are a commodity. It's easier to take a run outside along the path that runs the inside perimeter of the complex. It's a couple of miles long with some hills. Just enough to get the blood pumping and the heart rate up.

Outside the building are a few challenges for those of us looking to stay in shape. Two walls to climb, one six feet, one fifteen feet with ropes attached. There's a rock-climbing wall with safety wires. A series of balance beams, each one approximately five feet off the ground. There's a female soldier moving along the beams with no spotter in sight.

I shake my head. Five feet might not be a big fall, but it's enough to hurt you or even break a bone if you fall wrong. The balance beams in Hope and Orasul are suspended more than a dozen feet in the air, but since they're inside, they also have catch wires attached to the ceiling in case of

a fall. Whomever is out here this afternoon really should have a partner with them.

I start to stretch, my own run forefront in my mind, when a familiar tingle runs down my back. I consider the feeling for a moment and then return to my stretches. She wouldn't.

"You know she would." Tevin, his ghostly form leaning against the side of the building, smirks. He leans his head to the right so he can look past me.

No. She couldn't possibly be so foolish as to get on those beams the first day out of the hospital wing. She's barely gotten out of bed for the last month. Her legs can't be that steady.

Tevin goes nowhere, his eyes focused on the female working out behind me.

"Fine." I mutter a few choice words under my breath, and I turn around. The beams are far enough away from me that I can't tell who it is on top of them without walking closer. I'm about halfway across the field when her movements become familiar. I pick up the pace and jog the rest of the way. "What are you doing?"

Marissa doesn't stop. She doesn't even look at me. "I'm thinking."

She's walking along one of the long, parallel beams, her eyes on her feet, her arms by her side. She's taken her tennis shoes off and is using her feet to feel where to step next. I've seen her do this before, back in Hope and Orasul. Somehow, she'd gotten the idea in her mind during high school that mastering the balance beams would help her ground herself while she's fighting. It was a good idea at the time, and it worked for her, but it also eliminated any fear of heights or falling that she might have naturally had.

Personally, I hate heights and avoid the beams with everything I'm worth.

"You need to have a spotter out here." I put my hands on my hips, my voice firm. "If you fall, no one will know where you are."

"I know how to fall properly." She tosses a glance over her shoulder and flips off the beam. She lands on the ground, her knees bent to soften the impact. "See?"

Her bare feet are now on the cold ground. It's January, Marissa is barefoot, and that's all I can focus on. We didn't work so hard to get her out of that hospital bed just for her to catch a cold. "Put your shoes on, it's cold out here."

"It isn't that cold." She rolls her eyes but walks toward her shoes as asked. Not asked, ordered. "It's what, fifty-five degrees Fahrenheit? I really think I'll be fine. At least there isn't snow on the ground like there would be in New York."

"You wouldn't be doing this outside in New York." I watch her slide on her socks and running shoes. "I thought you would have been catching up with Kaia and Jenn. I didn't expect you to be out here. You should take some time, don't put too much stress on your body too soon."

"This isn't stressful, this is relaxing." She finishes tying her shoes and stands up. "The balance beams help clear my mind. I was with Jenn and Kaia for a while, but all they want to do is talk. Well, Jenn wants to talk. Kaia wants to dig into the textbooks and start catching up on my homework. It's a lot of noise and I need a break. I came out here."

"You didn't tell them you were coming out here. If you did, one of them would have come with you." I raise an eyebrow. "Truth?"

"Truth." At least she doesn't try to lie. "I told them I was going for a walk and that I needed to clear my head. I didn't completely lie to them."

I look her over and consider what I'm going to say next. It's good that she knows what it takes to settle the voices in her head. She also needs to not be reckless. She's talented on the beams. Being out here alone is still reckless. "They would have wanted to keep chatting if they came out here, right?"

"Yeah." She looks at her feet. "Amy was the only one who would spot me and be quiet. It's not that I don't appreciate their attempt to make me feel better. It's just sometimes, I want to be alone in my head. Amy got that. She was the only one who got that."

"The problem is that you need time to decompress after class, I understand that. You've been alone for a lot of weeks. It's a lot to jump back into life." I walk toward her, crowding into her space, just to see what she'll do. Marissa looks up at me but refuses to back away. I like that. It shows she's got some of that fire coming back. "Next time, ask me. I'm perfectly happy spotting you and keeping my mouth shut. But don't come out here alone again."

"Is that an order?" She still doesn't move, and I find I'm the one getting uncomfortable. We're almost touching we're so close to each other.

"Not officially because I don't want to write you up for being out here alone." Could I really write her up on discipline for being out here by herself? Probably, but I wouldn't. It would be a waste of disciplinary actions when she's technically on her own time and there aren't any real rules against working out alone. Some of the senior officers do it all the time. Heck, I did the obstacle course alone just a few days ago. "Don't test me. I might make it an order the next time."

"Yes, sir." Finally, she steps back, and I feel like I can take a breath again.

I look at her and realize she can't have been out here very long. I'll bet if I let her go now, she'll just find something else to do to avoid going back to her room. She needs to study, Kaia is right about that, but I can also appreciate the need for a little bit of quiet before she jumps back into the social action of studying with friends. "Are you tired yet?"

She considers the question for a minute and then shakes her head. "No. Honestly, I feel like I could do anything right now I'm so glad to be out of that hospital."

"Alright, let's go." I gesture toward the running path.

She hesitates. "Where?"

"There's a running path around the inner perimeter of the fence." I forgot; she hasn't lived here long enough to discover all Pandora's Box's secrets. "Let's take a jog. I promise I won't talk."

At that, she smiles. Then she looks toward the path and around the area like she's mentally measuring the distance. "How long?"

"A couple of miles." I shrug it off like it's no big deal; like she can make that run without a problem.

"If I get tired and need to walk, are you going to make fun of me? Or go all drill sergeant and yell at me to keep running?" Good questions. I hadn't considered that she might not be strong enough to make the whole run. She keeps talking. "I got a little fat and lazy in the hospital. I need to get back into shape."

"I won't yell. Or make fun." She's right, muscles lose definition fast. I'm sure she does need to get moving again. "And I'll walk with you if needed. Are you up for it?"

She considers the question for a few more seconds and then she nods her head. "Yeah. I'm up for it."

I successfully reunite Marissa with her roommates after our jog. Running proved to be too much for her; I slowed my pace to a jog to give her a chance to keep up. We completed the three-mile track around the prison in a reasonable time. If I'd been alone, I would have pushed myself to do it faster, but I didn't want to make her feel bad. I gave up and came inside when we finished, admitting hunger. I told her that she needed to eat, too, and instructed her roommates to take her to the mess for dinner right away.

I follow my own orders and make my way to the mess, too, not bothering to go to my room to change. It's not like I'm trying to impress anyone. Who cares if I'm a little sweaty from the jog?

When my tray is filled, I search the room quickly with my eyes for an empty table. I spot one in a corner and head it's direction. I have some acquaintances in the prison complex I could sit with, but I feel the need to be alone right now. Marissa is heavy on my mind. I need to think about what my next move with her is.

I'm her instructor. I might find her attractive and smart and courageous and independent, but I'm her instructor. Just having thoughts is all kinds of wrong. Add in the complication of being her patrol partner and I'm way out of my depth. As her superior officer, it would be inappropriate to get involved.

Can I remember that all of these signs point to no?

Not to mention that the poor young woman just suffered a catastrophic loss. The last thing she needs is another male getting interested in her.

"Hey, Collin, mind if we sit down?" A feminine voice grabs my attention away from the cheeseburger they're serving for dinner tonight. I'm glad we have mostly Americans on staff, and therefore we often have American food. There's nothing like a good cheeseburger to end a tough day.

Looking up, I do my best to keep my face straight. I guess it could be worse. Marissa's parents could be taking two empty chairs at my table.

Mia, Marissa's step-aunt who also happens to be General Riley's little sister, is balancing her own tray and waiting for a response. Behind her is her patrol partner, Kurt. They're both part of the elite Razbonic warriors and outrank me by more than I can properly calculate in promotions. The point is, I can't say no.

"Sure." I motion to the three empty seats at the table. "Take your pick."

Mia is very young for her rank and her placement among the warriors. I don't know much about how that happens, other than there's a mystical choosing process that picks them. It isn't a regular promotion; you can only be named among the warriors if the priests say you can. There were generations where there were none. And then, suddenly, a few years ago, we got six. They went on a quest, battled some bad guys, and found us a prison.

And now here we are.

The thing is, if Orasul and Hope hadn't split into two cities, I would have been in school with Mia. If I remember

correctly, Mia is my age and Kurt is about ten years older. I'd been eight when the cities split, which means I must have been in primary school with Mia. Like most kids, I don't remember much from those days. We could have sat next to each other in school for all I know.

What I do remember is the confusion and fear I felt when my mom told me we were leaving Orasul. All my friends were there. And for eight years I'd been told we couldn't leave, that we needed each other to live. I thought at first that we'd all die outside of the mountain. I was so scared.

But then Maxim showed us a city within a city; it was a new way to live. Something so different from Orasul, yet at its heart, it was the same. We were still together, the Fallen, keeping each other alive.

"How is she?" Mia drops into the seat next to me. I can't help but notice the tattoos that run down her arm: the markings of a warrior. The Fallen are forbidden from having tattoos of any kind. Unless you're a warrior, then the priests mark you to show your rank. And once you're named a warrior, you're a warrior for life.

I'm so focused on her arms that I don't hear her question at first.

"Yes, they're crazy to look at." She waves a hand in front of my face. "Again. How is she?"

Did I mention that Mia is my General's little sister? It's probably not a good idea to upset her.

"She's actually pretty good." I slide my tray a little to the right, centering it at my chair. "She came to class today. Afterward she spent some time on the balance beams and then we went for a jog. I'd say that's a win for the first day out of the hospital."

"No joke." Mia looks impressed. "If I just got out of the hospital, I'd be milking it for all it was worth. I'd be taking a nap in the afternoon, not going to Military History class."

"Weapons practicum." I correct her. "They had to build a drone this afternoon."

"Did she pass?" The facial expression turns to one of pain. "Are you going to let her make it up later?"

"I offered to let her do it at a later date, but she refused." At the main door to the mess, Marissa and her roommates arrive. There's a little noise and a lot of people look her direction. I know she hates the attention. What she really wants is to just blend in and be forgotten. Being notorious because your partner got killed isn't the kind of attention she wants. I bring my concentration back to our table. "She was a little slower than the rest of the class, but she did it."

"That's good." Mia nods and pokes her salad around in its bowl, mixing the greens up with the dressing and other toppings. "She needs a few wins; it's been a rough year for her."

My fault. She's lost three close friends in just a few months. None of it should have happened and it all happened on my watch. Mia doesn't say it, but I'm sure she's thinking it.

"Look at her." There's admiration in Kurt's voice. "I probably would have brought my dinner back to the barracks. I don't think I would have been able to face this many people on my first day back."

"That's because you're an emotional wimp." Mia breaks off a piece of carrot and chews thoughtfully. "She's strong. You watch, she'll pull through."

The girls find an empty table on the other side of the mess and sit down. It's crowded enough that I can't see her anymore. That's good.

"I heard you were her new patrol partner." Kurt starts eating his dinner while Mia talks. "That's good."

I don't ask how she heard that. Her brother is my General. It's pretty easy to figure out. "My plan is to rotate her training sessions among the rest of the recruits until we find a good match. But, as far as patrol goes? Yes, she'll be paired with me for a while."

"Maybe if it works out you can make that permanent." Mia suggests. I'm starting to wonder if Kurt gets any words in at all when they're alone. "If you're a good pair, that is. You'll be done training the recruiting class soon. Don't you want to get back out into the field?"

"Honestly, I hadn't thought about it." Not completely true, I'd thought about it a little bit. "I like teaching."

"But don't tell me you don't like being in the field." She waves her fork my direction. "We're Fallen. We live to be in the field."

"Aren't you supposed to be some kind of warrior-scholar-monk?" This subject needs to be changed, and fast. The truth is that I hadn't put a lot of thought into my next assignment. I like this class of recruits and I'm not in a hurry to see them go. "What does 'in the field' look like for you? Being locked in the basement archives of the prison?"

"How do you know there's basement archives?" Kurt leans closer, his voice menacing. "That might be privileged information. We might have to kill you now that you know that."

"Every old, musty, historic building has a dungeon and an old library with lost tomes in it. Call it a lucky guess." I hurry up and take a bite of my burger, realizing that I won't get any food in me if I keep talking to Mia. Her salad has been slowly disappearing as we talk, and I can't figure out how. Is she simply inhaling it between sentences?

"It's a fair guess." Kurt looks at his partner. "We're in the middle of the original Fallen homeland. This is the legendary prison they built to be Pandora's Box after the Fall. It doesn't take a genius to figure out there are ancient scrolls here. I bet he can even guess the languages they're written in."

"Aramaic? Probably Sumerian." I think back to my ancient languages' classes. "Coptic and maybe a little bit of Egyptian hieroglyphs. Definitely ancient Greek and a little Latin. Did I miss anything?"

"Not bad for a field soldier." Mia claps her hands, which draws attention from some of the surrounding tables. They see two Razbonic warriors and they turn back to their own meals.

"I was good in school." I shrug, playing off how good I was. The book part of what we do, specifically understanding cultures, languages, and people, comes easy. It makes me makes me think more that I'd be better off working for the Division one day.

CHAPTER FIVE

I'm able to get a little space from Marissa over the next few days; I only see her in class and training. I feel a little bereft without our nightly hospital visits. I hadn't realized how much I enjoyed them, despite the reason. If I'm honest, we'd started to forge a friendship. It's a friendship I now have to decide if I'm going to continue, or if I'm going to let it die away as part of a difficult time of our lives.

Even without inappropriate thoughts about how beautiful she is, I enjoy Marissa's company. We talked about life in New York, what we miss about Hope, and how living in Orasul sometimes was a struggle. Then we talked about books and movies we both like and she would sometimes share renditions of her favorite songs from musicals; side note, she has a terrible singing voice. She likes fashion, which is also strange because we wear the same clothes every day in the army, and she can people watch for hours.

Although laughter was off the table for those weeks, sometimes she would smile, and it would change the whole room. Even in the worst moments of her despair over Tevin's death, she still had powerful energy. If she can harness that, she'll change the world one day.

I realize that I hope I'm around to see it. When she's at full potential, she'll be a force of nature. And when she masters her gift, no one will be able to touch her. She's the only one with the ability to levitate things, as far as I know.

Our God given gifts are special powers each of us are born with. We start to manifest them in our early teens, and we are each given one. Most of the time, these gifts are tied to an element. Tevin could create fire from nothing. Jenn can move water with her mind. Sometimes, they're tied to the spirit like Amy's was. She had the gift of healing.

Not Marissa. The girl who was raised away from any Fallen city has the gift of telekinesis. If she wants a pencil from across the room, it comes to her. If she wants to levitate the pages of her book for fun, they move. Need a sock off the floor and don't want to bend down to get it? No problem.

Her teachers suspect that she might be able to lift people by the time she reaches her mid-twenties. Like any muscle, the more you work your gift, the more powerful it becomes. Marissa started late because of her unique early years. I started training with mine when I was twelve. I can control wind, which is handy when you're tracking something that you don't want to smell you. Just change the direction of the breeze and you'll be forever upwind of your prey.

Marissa started her training when she arrived at Orasul at the age of fifteen. She already had some control over her powers; rumor had it she'd been strong enough the first day to pick up a sword from the floor of the Council chamber without bending over. It's hard to tell if that story is true, or just a rumor, given how strong she has the potential to be. Now, at nineteen, she keeps her exact skill level under wraps. Even I don't know what she can do.

For four days after she starts back to the physical part of her training, I keep her at arm's length. It isn't difficult. She's focused on catching up, she and Kaia use the empty classroom at night to study in. During training sessions, I pair her with a rotating cycle of different classmates. She doesn't do a stellar job with any of them. The matches all seem to be…off. Like neither of the pair is completely comfortable. It's like she's starting all over again as a high school student. I realize it's because she rarely worked with anyone except Tevin, and they had their own language. When they moved through the arena, they didn't need to speak; it was like they were two parts of a whole.

Even Jenn proves to be a difficult match. I give them a bo, a long staff used in Asian fighting arts, and ask them to spar against Thomas, a recruit who'd all but mastered the weapon. He should have been able to handle a double advance from the girls without a problem. Three minutes into the session, Jenn is on the ground with a bloody lip. Not from Thomas. From Marissa. While trying to work together, she'd managed to slam her bo into Jenn's face. Jenn had been behind her at the time.

Now it's day five and it's time to take her out on patrol.

Today's lesson will be a catch-up lesson for her. We'll be visiting the Division headquarters for the Jerusalem area. All of Marissa's classmates have already met Benjamin, the head of the local Division, when he came to class to introduce himself. As part of the staffing at Pandora's Box, it's important we know the locals, but we won't spend as much time with them as we did in Hope.

The class of recruits will be exposed to a variety of jobs in and around Pandora's Box. This includes the local Division. In a few months, they'll make their requests for a full-time position. It's important they know and understand all the options.

One of our local Israeli military hosts meets us at the garage entrance to Pandora's Box. Nathan will be our driver into Jerusalem. He'll help us get through the army checkpoints and into the downtown area where Benjamin's office is housed. His credentials, along with our American military badges, should be enough to get us to our destination.

If not, we'll abort today's patrol and head back to the prison.

"Are you ready?" Nathan looks us over with a critical eye. "You know this isn't the safest time to be doing this."

"We've been warned." I cast a worrying eye on Marissa. I'm more concerned that she's not ready. "You good?"

"I'm good." Slung over her shoulder is a small bag that contains Marissa's military id. We have standard military issued identification cards, obtained for us through the Division. And, a recent addition to our wardrobe due to unrest to the south of us, we have dog tags that we wear under our shirts. That way, if something happens to one of us, the locals can get our information back to the Division in the states.

It's a step toward the total declassification of our entire race. The army might not know *what* we are, but they know *who* we are.

"Are you sure you're ready for this?" I ask once more as Marissa quickly opens the door on her side of the dark sedan we're taking to get back into the city. "This could be dangerous."

"How far are we from the fighting?" She hesitates like she hadn't thought about the fighting happening in Gaza.

"Jerusalem is about seventy-six kilometers from the main area of disruption." Nathan replies from inside the vehicle. "We're coming in from the west. The fighting is to the south. You'll find the city mostly quiet. Most countries are currently discouraging travel to Israel right now. There have been rocket attacks near Tel Aviv. The safest place to stay is inside the compound of Pandora's Box."

Standing at the door, Marissa allows herself to be lost in thought for a minute. Then, she slides into the car. "This is my job. Let's go."

"Seventy-six kilometers is about fifty miles." I interpret the distance for her. When she nods her head, I change topics to the mission at hand. "There are no Fallen in the Division here. The only Fallen who live in Israel are here in the prison. For centuries there was a small Fallen city nearby, but it has been moved due to the instability of the area. The residents picked up and relocated to Ankara in the 1950s. It's close enough that Fallen from that city can reach the this area quickly if necessary. Although, in truth, Hope is a bigger city. Demons are just as unsettled by the uncertainty of region and tend to avoid living in this part of the world."

Marissa's eyes widen at the word demon, and she glances forward at Nathan who already has the car in gear and is headed toward the first checkpoint to exit the compound.

"No need to be concerned." He meets her glance with his own in the rearview mirror. "I've been briefed, and I know what you are. I'm human, but I'm a safe human."

"Good to know." She murmurs a response then directs her attention at me. "How in the world did we get into the country on a commercial flight if security is this tight?"

"I have no idea." For that question, I'm at a loss. Not only did we manage to fly into a country that has travel warnings up, but we did so under the guise of a student group. "I thought we'd be flying in with a military transport until Mia told me otherwise. The commercial flight and the tour bus were a surprise to me."

Four military checkpoints later, Nathan is finally stopping the car in front of a building in the city of Jerusalem. I can't imagine what Marissa is thinking; even I'm shocked at the level of security going in. The white brick building is surrounded by a tall iron fence. There's a small parking lot outside the fence where Nathan pulls into an empty spot. There's what looks like a guard tower on top of the building, and I have to assume inside it is at least one sniper in case of trouble.

An entrance has yellow and red signs, written in Hebrew, with a guardhouse and a gate stopping you from entering without permission.

Unlike police stations I've seen in New York, this one seems to dissuade anyone from walking in. My Hebrew is terrible, I can't read the signs, but the security alone screams, "Go away!"

"Come on. Follow me." Nathan locks the vehicle and then leads us to the gate.

I don't know if it's the part of town we're in, or if all of Jerusalem is this quiet. There's no one on the streets around the building. The traffic we encountered on the way in seems to have subsided, making the city feel lonely and isolated.

"I wanted to see some of the holy sites when I got here." Marissa's voice is barely more than a whisper while Nathan talks to the guard. "The police station wasn't on my list."

"I don't imagine it was." Nathan motions for our military id's and we hand them over. Inside the guard booth is a young woman. She types our names into a computer and waits. "What was on your list?"

"Bethlehem. The Church of the Holy Sepulcher. Maybe walking the Via Dolorosa." She turns to see if anyone is coming down the street behind us. There isn't. It's as deserted as it was when we first arrived.

"Christian pilgrimage locations." I'm a little surprised. We have our own religion and our own practices. I realize I've never asked her if she attended chapel or was particularly faithful. Maybe when she was in the hospital, I should have offered to have a priest visit.

"Mom sent me to a Catholic school before we came back to Orasul." She looks embarrassed. "I kind of liked it."

"We're in." Nathan interrupts us as the gate clicks open. The woman in the booth smiles our direction and indicates we should walk through the gate.

On the other side of the gate is a metal detector. Nathan removes his service weapon and hands it to the guard who tags it and places it in locked storage until we finish our business. We walk through the metal detector and get our first glimpse of the inside of the police station.

If more people were speaking English, you could have convinced me this building was anywhere in the US. It's well lit, with plastic chairs in a small waiting room. Another woman and a man are seated behind a tall desk, hallways go off in several directions and the phone is ringing. The man answers it at the same time the woman waves us forward.

"We have an appointment with Superintendent Benjamin." Nathan switches to English and ushers us forward.

The woman types something into her computer and waits a moment. Then she raises her eyes to study Marissa and me. "The Americans?"

I'd been told most cultures picture Americans as blond-haired, blue eyed, pale skinned people. If that is her image of us, I can see why she's confused. Marissa and I aren't technically American. We're Fallen, which means we have tanned skin and dark features. My green eyes are the lightest thing about either of us.

"Yes, the Americans." Nathan's smile is more forced as she continues to scrutinize our appearance.

Finally, she points to the waiting area. "He's expecting you. Wait there."

We shuffle over to the area she indicated and take seats.

"Friendly." Marissa keeps her voice low.

"We aren't in America and tourism is all but gone here." Nathan also keeps his voice down. "We must be cautious. There are many people who would consider blowing up a police station an act of heroism. Besides, you are dressed as the military you are. Perhaps if you had worn regular street clothes you would have attracted less attention."

An assessment of my clothing proves he's right. Marissa and I are wearing matching black shirts with cargo pants and combat boots. We should have changed.

"Captain, it's good to see you again!" Benjamin, the human in charge of Jerusalem's Division, appears out of the door to our left. He reaches out and briefly shakes my hand before he bows to Marissa. Remembering proper protocol, Marissa smiles and drops her head. "Thank you for being willing to come into my territory, I'm excited to show you what we've been doing."

"The drive was a little anxious, but we're glad to be here." I gesture toward Marissa. "This is Marissa Cazut. She was not able to attend your lecture when we met last."

"Ah, the young lady whose partner was killed." Benjamin's brow furrows in a frown. "Please accept my condolences for your loss."

"Thank you." Marissa bows her head again, locking her hands in front of her.

"If you will put these on, you may follow me." We're handed visitor's passes that we hang around our necks.

Nathan declines his, gestures back to the seat, and pulls a worn book from his back pocket. "I'm just the driver and I came prepared to kill time. I'll wait here."

"As you wish." Benjamin opens his arm toward the doorway. "Captain, Marissa, if you will come with me."

The first time I met Benjamin, he'd driven out to Pandora's Box to meet the class. There are too many recruits to fit into his small office. He's a focused and friendly guy, I'm grateful to get this second opportunity with him.

We don't go far down the hallway before he turns and opens the door to the conference room. There are two other police officers waiting inside. They both stand and greet us when we enter.

"This is Simeon and Barbara. Constance is out handling a situation; she sends her apologies." Benjamin motions for us to sit. "This is my entire team."

"It's so small." Marissa takes her place on one of the conference chairs. "I'm sorry, I don't mean any disrespect."

"None taken." Simeon reaches out to shake my hand in greeting. Like Benjamin, he gives a little bow toward Marissa. "We have very few problems with demons here in Jerusalem, so our need is not for a large department. The military has a larger number of soldiers who know about you. Many of them work with you at Pandora's Box. Our problems here in the city are mostly of human nature."

"We exist mostly to support Pandora's Box." Benjamin takes his place at the head of the table. "We keep an eye on things here, make sure demon activity doesn't suddenly rise. There are a handful of demon families who live here, but mostly they avoid the Holy Lands. Too much unrest."

"Then why have a Division here at all?" Spinning in her chair slowly, Marissa looks around the table. "I understand why we need the Division in New York. There are hundreds of demon families and Hope. But, if you don't have any of that here, why exist at all?"

"Pandora's Box." Benjamin smiles gently. "In the interest of cooperation, there are demons living out there and working with you in the prison. Yes?"

"Yes." She hasn't worked with them yet, but she has seen them around the site. "Wouldn't they fall under Fallen jurisdiction at the prison?"

"Some of them will choose to stay here when their term of employment is completed." Pointing to a map of the city, Benjamin indicates a section that is highlighted in blue. "Some of them are already bringing their families here. In this area, the area in blue, we have a dozen families residing there already. You may not see it now, but this is a beautiful and wonderful place to live when we have peace."

"You're all human. How do you get them to trust you?" Marissa thinks about her question. "Although, I guess they're more likely to trust you than me."

Simeon laughs. "Constance is not human. She is our liaison until they get comfortable with us."

"We also know there are a few demon families who live outside of the city in the smaller neighboring towns." Benjamin points to several areas on a larger map of the country. "Once knowledge of your people becomes commonplace, we will be responsible for them as well. Our job right now is more about preparing for the future than addressing the present. Jerusalem and Israel will be an important piece of the worldwide puzzle as your world expands. With Pandora's Box so close, we expect many more Fallen and demons to come through our city than have in the past."

"Let me show you a little about how we operate, how we support local families." Simeon stands from his chair. "Come with me to my office."

"Really?" Marissa's eyes light up.

"Really. Come on." He guides her out of the door and down the hallway.

"She's different than the others." Benjamin watches her go. "Much more interested in what we're doing."

"I think she likes being at the prison because her mom and stepdad are there." I consider my next words carefully. "She had an aptitude for working with Aria in New York with the New York Division. I think she could be good at this if it's what she wants."

"I'm afraid she's going to get a little more time to explore our city than expected." He looks at the desk and spins his cell phone around. "I received notification just before you arrived that there was a roadside explosion on the route back to your prison. It will take at least twenty-four hours before you can navigate home. We'll have to put you both up for the night."

I feel my stomach drop. I'm going to be stuck here in the city overnight with Marissa? We didn't bring go-bags, we don't have anything with us to get us through the night. And what about my training session tomorrow? I'm scheduled to lead the recruits on a fifteen-mile run.

Then, the big reality hits me.

What if we'd been driving through when the explosion happened? Marissa could have been killed.

"I see your concerns on your face." Benjamin stands up and comes over to my side of the table. "Don't worry, we're not going to turn you out into the city alone. We've reserved you two rooms in a safe hotel with a restaurant that will provide you both dinner tonight and breakfast tomorrow. It's in the Old City. Perhaps tomorrow you may visit a few of our sacred sites before you leave with your driver. The road should be open again after lunchtime."

"What about Nathan?" I wonder about our driver.

"His parents live here in town, my administrator spoke to him and he said he'd be happy spending the evening with them. That will leave you alone with your recruit. I hope that is okay." Benjamin frowns again. "I just realized I don't know your customs. Is it inappropriate for you to be alone with Marissa? Do you need a chaperone?"

It's only inappropriate because I think she's both brilliant and stunning.

"No, as long as we're not in the same hotel room, we should be fine." I want to take a deep breath and let it out

slowly to clear my head. Instead, I do my best to stay calm. "Thank you for your consideration, we'd be quite lost for the night if not for your help."

"It's the least I can do."

CHAPTER SIX

Vacations aren't something the Fallen do. We live in our cities, work for the greater good, die, and spread our ashes. Being stuck overnight in Jerusalem without the rest of the recruitment squad is exciting. Staying in a hotel overnight is something I've never done and eating in a human restaurant is a nice change from the mess at Pandora's Box. We'd had human restaurants near Hope, of course, but that was weeks ago.

I wonder if Marissa has ever been on a vacation. Her life is different from the average Fallen. Her mom raised her for ten years outside a Fallen city. Marissa went to a human school and had human friends. It's possible that she's seen the beach or been to Disney World.

When I tell her the change of plan, Marissa takes it in stride. Her only concern is not having anything, including a toothbrush, for the night. Nathan volunteers to take us to a shopping center to pick up a few necessities. I forgot how much Marissa likes to shop; the trip takes a little longer than anticipated. Her necessities turn out to include something to sleep in and a change of clothes to wear to dinner. She even picks up a pair of shoes.

"If I don't have to wear combat boots to dinner, I'm not going to." Her resolve is set. Neither Nathan nor I want to argue with her, so we wait outside while she picks out the things she feels she needs and pays. Thankfully, the sales associate at the counter speaks English, which prevents Nathan from being forced to translate for her.

She's also a fast shopper. In and out in under thirty minutes. I imagine she'd normally take longer if given the opportunity. Especially here. We rarely get off the compound that is Pandora's Box. None of us have had a proper night off since we left Hope. We're tied to the base; nights off mean an evening alone in our rooms, working out in the small gym, or gathering in the game room to see if anyone wants to play cards or video games. Shopping is a thing of the past except for the small exchange at the prison; and that is filled with necessities.

A short time later, Nathan is driving us through the Old City to our hotel for the night with our shopping bags in the trunk of the car.

Marissa is excited. Even if I couldn't feel the energy coming off her body only a foot away in the car, I can tell by watching her face. Our polite conversation had died away as we passed a mix of beautiful buildings, old and new. Her entire focus is outside of the window, every now and then breathing in quickly as she sees something that thrills her.

I look out my window, too, and notice other things. I notice there are people out and about in this part of town.

They're walking and we pass cars on the street. It seems here, life goes on. It's not as crowded as I imagined it would be. Lack of tourism is likely the culprit for that. But Benjamin assured me, hotels are still open, and restaurants are still serving. Pilgrims, determined to visit their holy sites, continue to come to the area despite being advised not to.

Nathan pulls in front of our hotel, an old building that looks like it was originally built a couple of hundred years ago. Sandstone colored bricks give way to arched windows and doors. The building is large, but it blends in with the other buildings around it, and I can't quite see where it ends.

"I'm going to go in with you to make sure there are no problems with your check in." Nathan steps out of the car. "The Division has put you in a nice hotel for the night. You should be very comfortable. Leave your bags in the car until we check you in."

I'm unable to tell much about the hotel from the outside.

Inside, Marissa and I follow Nathan to the front desk. I'm able to focus on what Nathan is saying, but it takes a lot of effort. The inside is nothing like I've ever seen in person before. Beautifully tiled floors in colors of cream and tan, expensive-looking furniture that contrasts in jeweled tones like orange and green and purple. Through a window, I can see that outside there are two open stories with doors leading off a rectangular walkway. Small tables are in the courtyard.

Everything looks new and beautiful.

Nathan finishes talking to the front desk and then turns to me. "You have my phone number."

"Yes." He'd put it in my phone while we were waiting for Marissa to finish shopping.

"I'll call you after lunch tomorrow and confirm your pickup." He hands us each a piece of plastic that looks like a credit card. There's a sticky note on it with a number and he gives me another cream colored card I can't read. "Your room number is on the note, and these are the keys to your rooms. You're next door to each other. The room is paid for, here's a voucher for dinner in the restaurant. Breakfast is included, served early so don't miss it. Most of the sites you may want to visit will be open early tomorrow. If you're not sure about anything, ask the concierge at the front desk. He'll be happy to help you; everyone here speaks English. You should be fine."

"Thank you for your help." I accept the keys and the voucher from him. We return to the vehicle, grab our bags from the back, and say our goodbyes. We'll call in the morning to see what time he plans on picking us up to leave.

I'm overwhelmed. I've never stayed in a hotel before, I'm not sure how to find our rooms, or what I'm supposed to do with the voucher we have for dinner. I realize in the moment how little the Fallen know about life outside of our cities.

"You look like you're freaking out." Marissa steps close to me, her voice low.

"I'm not freaking out, just getting my bearings." I adjust my grip on my bag and look around. Room number 211. If I can find a doorway, I can determine which direction we need to go.

"You're freaking out." She takes one of the keys from my grip and looks at it. "This is probably on the second floor. Let's head to the stairs."

"How can you tell?" I follow her through the lobby to a staircase that leads upward.

"One hundreds are usually first floor, two hundreds second floor." She frowns and stops at the bottom of the stairs. "You've never stayed in a hotel before, have you?"

"No." I begrudgingly admit. I've always lived in a Fallen city and never had a reason to travel until I came here. "Have you?"

"I went to the beach with a friend from school when I was young." She points to a sign at the stairs. It says rooms two hundred to two twenty are on the second floor. "Mom only let me do it once because I got really sick while I was away from her. It was probably something I ate, but she still never let me do it again."

We take the stairs to the second floor and then out a door that leads to the covered walkway. Marissa leads me to the left and finds our rooms.

"This one is yours; the next one is mine." She indicates the next door on the walkway. "I'm willing to bet there's a shower in there where I can take as long as I want without someone complaining I'm using up all the hot water. I'm going to use it. Want to meet back out here in an hour for dinner?"

I look at the clock on my phone. We'd spent several hours at the police station, but it's still early. There's time to kill.

"Sure." I note the time and wonder if I should set a timer. "One hour, right here."

"Awesome. See you in a bit." Marissa uses the keycard to swipe her way into the room.

The door closes behind her and I'm left feeling overwhelmed again. I look at the card, notice the little arrows, and copy Marissa's actions. The lock to the door clicks open and I'm able to get inside. Good, one challenge complete.

The inside of the room is just as expensive looking as the foyer down below. A tiled floor is covered in a tapestry-like carpet, there's a double bed, and a desk with a plush chair that takes up most of the room. It's twice as big as my room in the barracks back at Pandora's Box. If nothing else, I should be comfortable for the night. There's a small refrigerator tucked under one side of the desk and a flat television mounted on the wall. Decorative green pillows on the bed match the desk chair, the rest of the bedding is stark white. There's a door. I step through it to find the bathroom and shower Marissa had been so excited about.

I set my small bag of supplies down on the bathroom counter, I don't need much except the basic bathroom necessities, and then I wander back into the main room. One hour. What am I going to do to kill one hour?

It turns out an hour can pass quickly when you've got to call in to your boss and explain why you're not coming back to work. I worked my way through the chain of command until I got a substitute trainer for the morning's run, thus making sure my recruits are covered. Then, almost as soon as I hang up the phone, it rings again. This number isn't familiar to me, but I answer anyway in case it's one of my superiors at the prison.

"This is Captain Smith." Tired of pacing the room, I drop into the chair at the desk.

"This is Anna Cazut, Marissa's mom." A female voice states into my ear. "Tell me where you are with my daughter."

I know who Anna Cazut is. She's one of the top brass who runs Pandora's Box. She's a Razbonic warrior, just like General Riley, her husband. And she's not someone I would ever think about messing with.

"The Division put us up in a hotel for the night. Marissa is in the room next to mine." I feel the urge to stand at attention while I talk, like Major Cazut can see me. "We're perfectly safe and will be on our way back to the barracks tomorrow. They expect the road to be cleared sometime after lunch."

"That doesn't tell me where you are, Captain." Her voice isn't sharp, exactly, but it's demanding. She will get the answers she wants. And, if she doesn't like the answers I give her, I can see myself packing up and moving to another hotel with Marissa.

I clarify, wishing I knew the name of the hotel. "We're in a nice hotel in the Old City, the Jewish district. The area seems safe. We don't have to leave the hotel for dinner."

"Why didn't you return using a different route?" I can't sit anymore, so I stand and pace again. Thank God I'm not around the Major very often. The last thing I need is her picking up on the softness I feel for Marissa. Major Cazut is empathic, she can feel and sometimes manipulate another person's emotions. It's a similar gift to what Amy had, only more latent.

"Benjamin, the head of the Division, said he didn't trust the side roads we'd have to take. While there is no fighting in this area, there is no reason to not be cautious." I reach up and rub the bridge of my nose. This is the third time I've given this explanation in the last hour. "The main road has checkpoints and security. He thought it best we wait for that road to open again."

"Hmmm." She makes a noise on the other end of the line.

"It's just a day, ma'am, I'm sure we'll be fine."

She starts to respond, but I don't hear her because there's a knock on the door. I realize my hour must be up and it's probably Marissa. Keeping the phone to my ear, I open it.

Immediately I wish I'd taken the time to grab some civilian clothes. Marissa is wearing a slim pair of khaki pants and a lightweight black sweater. She has soft, slip-on, flat shoes the same shade of black as her shirt. Her hair is worn down around her shoulders. She doesn't wear her hair down very often, normally she pulls it back to keep it out of her way while she trains or works.

Yeah, she's beautiful.

When she notices the phone, she cocks her head to the side and mimics holding a phone to her ear.

I mouth the word, "mom," and point at her.

Her eyes get big. She points to herself. "My mom?"

I nod.

Before I can stop her, Marissa grabs the phone out of my hand. "Mom. What are you doing?"

I have enough sense to take a few steps back. I shouldn't listen to their conversation.

Marissa follows me into my room and closes the door behind her. She listens intently to what her mom is saying. "No, I'm in the room next door. I'm here to meet Collin for dinner. I don't…"

I look for something to do, straighten the bed sheets. Fold towels. Anything.

"Yes, mom, I know better." She pauses. "Of course not, but I'm not going to spend the evening locked up alone. It's just dinner. He's my commanding officer, you have nothing to worry about. Please relax. I'll be back in the morning."

I'm relieved when the Major's volume lowers. It's easier to ignore what they're saying when she isn't so loud.

"It's part of my job, you know that." Marissa smiles. "I know. I'll make time to see you tomorrow when I get back. I promise. Love you, too."

Marissa hangs up the phone and tosses it back to me.

"I'm sorry, I tried not to listen." I put the phone in my pocket. "It made it kind of hard when you walked into the room."

"She's afraid I'm going to fall into another unhealthy relationship." She throws her hands in the air. "Like I didn't learn anything the first time."

"She almost lost you. It scared her." I consider my reaction to how nice Marissa is dressed, and I secretly admit the fear isn't irrational. Marissa is beautiful and vibrant. Males are going to be attracted to her.

"She also understands that I have a job I'm training for." Her hands drop to her hips. "We're built for war. She can't freak out every time I'm in a little bit of danger."

"Hunting demons is one thing. We mostly fight fair." I think about what is happening not too far from us. "They have rockets and grenades and missiles. It's different."

"We're going to have to adapt." Marissa makes a good point, a point that many in the military have been saying since the announcement that we're going public. We'll have to learn to fight like a human. "Isn't that why we're studying things like drone technology?"

"Humans can destroy entire cities without even being on the same continent." I step closer to her. "We won't ever do anything like that. We study human technology to understand it. Mass destruction isn't our job. We're more like their snipers; we're sent in to take out single targets. Or, like the Division, their police. I don't know exactly how the world is going to change, but you're right. We'll have to adapt."

"Exactly." She looks triumphant and I realize I just sided with her over her mom in some imagined disagreement. On one hand, awesome, she has my support. On the other, oh, no, I just took a side against one of my commanding officers. I need to change subjects, and quickly.

"I'm not completely sure what I just agreed to, but I recommend we move this conversation to dinner." I gesture toward the doorway. "I, for one, am hungry."

"Me, too." She takes my lead and turns toward the doorway. "I feel like lunch was forever ago. I learned so much at the Division headquarters. I can't believe they gave us so much access."

I quietly respond, wondering how I'm going to get through dinner. In such a short time, Marissa came back to life. Her sparkle and vibrancy are intoxicating. I'd noticed it before, while we were in Hope, and now I see it ever more clearly. I want to spend time with her, and I feel like a creep for wanting that. She just lost Tevin for goodness sake.

I let her take the lead once we're out of the hotel room. She all but skips down the walkway to the staircase and down to the first floor. This time, I'm less overwhelmed and take better note of my surroundings. The entrance to the restaurant is to our left.

The menu is a bit difficult to navigate. It's written in both Hebrew and English, that isn't the problem. The problem is my unfamiliarity with Middle Eastern foods. In the mess hall, either at the Israeli base or at our own, I eat what I'm served. I don't pay much attention to what it's called. Now, here I am sitting in a restaurant staring at a menu with no idea what I like.

Once again, Marissa saves the day. When the waiter comes by to offer us water, she asks him about the menu. "I'm an American and I'm not sure what to order. What would you recommend?"

The waiter happily explains his favorite dishes to Marissa. Internally, I sigh with relief and listen closely. When he's finished, we're both able to order something that sounds delicious. I order lamb dolmas with apricots and tamarind. I don't think it's anything I've had before, but I like beef so I guess lamb shouldn't be that different, and I know apricots are good. Dolmas are common in Fallen festivals, although I've only had the vegetarian versions.

As I hand the waiter back the menu, I realize how right Marissa is. As a species, if we're going to live among humans, we have to adapt. It's probably a little easier for those of us who live in Hope. We already interact with humans. While I've never stayed in a hotel before, I have ordered food in a restaurant and shopped in a human store. There are Fallen in more remote cities like Orasul who have never left the city they've been born in. Their food, clothing, shopping, everything is provided within their city.

How impossible would today have been if that were my story?

Marissa finishes her order, hands the waiter her menu, and he leaves us noticeably alone.

I find myself shifting in my seat; I wonder how we're going to get through this meal.

"Don't get all weird because of what my mom said." She admonishes me while she unfolds her napkin and drops it in her lap. "It's not like we're in a romantic restaurant on a date. We're just a couple of coworkers."

She's right about one thing: we aren't on a date. As for the restaurant? If she doesn't want to call it romantic, I'd still call it…cozy with its dark woods, jewel toned seats, and candles on the table. I latch onto the truest thing she's said. "You're right, this isn't a date. We've spent the last few weeks hanging out, this isn't any different."

"Exactly." She smiles and nods her head. "We've just upgraded the location. This is much nicer than the hospital room. And it smells better, too."

I chuckle. It wasn't that *she* smelled bad in the hospital room, but that entire wing has an antiseptic, too clean smell.

I know we need to have a conversation about something. I go back through the day in my mind until I grab a thought I'd stowed away for later. "Why a Catholic school?"

CHAPTER SEVEN

"Catholic school?" Marissa's face lights up. I see I've hit upon a good topic.

"Yeah."

In the hospital, we talked about mostly benign topics. Training. Books. What we liked most about living in Hope. I'd avoided more personal subject matter because I didn't know what would trigger her into a depression. My job had been to make her better, not worse. "I don't know anything about being Catholic, other than it's a human religion. What made your mom choose to send you to one of their special schools? What was it like?"

"I asked her that once. The why part. When we moved back to Orasul, when I was fifteen, I got this super-fast education on what it meant to be Fallen. Part of that was about chapel and the religion of the Fallen." Marissa's nose scrunches up while she thinks. It's adorable and I struggle to concentrate on her words. "I thought at first, she did it

to keep me connected to God. That, since we couldn't go to Fallen chapel services, she did it as an alternative. When I asked her, she gave me a much simpler answer. Demons avoid the church. She sent me there because she felt it was safer than public school."

"What was it like?" I can't imagine going to a school full of humans. As a Fallen, you couldn't be yourself. Marissa would have begun to manifest her gifts by fifteen. She would have had to hide what she was from everyone around her. "And what about now? Do you go to chapel?"

"That's two questions." She picks up her fork and twirls in between her fingers slowly. She's thinking. I learned that about her while we were in the hospital. She likes to fidget while she thinks. "The school was amazing, I really liked it there. The teachers were incredible; Latin is still my best language. I had friends, human friends. As long as she met them first, and probably scoped out their building, I was allowed to go to sleepovers and birthday parties. I was sad when I left them behind, but I knew I was different. I wonder now that I know our world is going to be public if I can reconnect to them some day. If they would remember me. To them, I just disappeared one night in the middle of the night."

"That must have been tough." Leaving everything you know behind in the middle of the night? It must have been impossible for a teenager. I would be hard for me right now. I don't have a lot of close friends in the prison, but I do have relationships. I wouldn't want to drop everything and go. "You didn't tell them anything?"

"No. Nothing." She drops the fork in favor of the butter knife. "Mom called the school and told them we had to leave the country for a family emergency. Someone at Orasul forged transfer documents and everything. But I wasn't allowed to call my friends, or text them, or anything. It was really okay; I knew I was different, and I'd known it for a long time. I figured the day would come when I had to leave. And then it did. I didn't have time to think much about it. We spent one day travelling to get back to Orasul and one day getting settled into our apartment. The next day, I was in school there. I was so excited. These kids were like me. I didn't have to hide who I was any more."

"Amy and Nick made it easier. They kind of adopted me into their friendship on the first day. They didn't give me any time to be lonely." Her face falls a little as she talked about her old friends, now gone. I worry this is where our conversation will stall, but she keeps going. "As happy as I was to be around other Fallen, I was even happier when Hope and Orasul started working together to teach their students and train their recruits. I got two things that were very important to putting me on this path. I got a connection back to New York and I got you. You were the best teacher I'd had since I'd come to Orasul."

I try to ignore my heart skipping a beat when she lists me among the best things that happened to her since she joined the Fallen. I know she doesn't mean that statement in the way my body is reacting to it. "I heard your first teacher was pretty crappy."

"He was terrible." She sighs dramatically and drops the silverware on the table. "He'd stand around and let us do whatever we wanted. I don't think he stepped into the ring himself the entire time he taught us, and I'd had him for over a year before you came."

"When General Keagan recruited me, he indicated that your education to that point hadn't been up to standards." I remember that meeting. He'd basically come in and tell me to get up, get myself together, and get to work. "You said you were happy to have a connection back to New York. Do you miss it?"

"All. The. Time." Marissa emphasizes each word. "I liked Orasul, and I could live there if I have to, but god I miss the city. When I found out that was an option, I thought I'd won a contest. When I think about going home, that's the place I think about."

"There is something special about the city." I lean back in my seat as the waiter approaches with our food. He places the dishes, asks if we need anything else, and steps away. The food looks amazing. "I hope to be stationed there one day. For now, that's my goal."

"With the Division?" She picks up her fork and pokes at the food on her plate. I wonder if she regrets her order, then she takes a bite and smiles. "This is wonderful."

"I'd love to work for the Division, so yeah, I have my application in there. It's so hard to get a position with them that I don't have a lot of hope until they build the department, which won't happen for a few years." I also know there are a lot of applicants in line. I could be waiting a lifetime for that job. "It's just a question of a job opening up at the right time and me having the right qualifications."

"Tevin thought being part of the Division was a waste of talent." My stomach drops at her comment. Tevin is *not* a subject I want to talk about tonight. "I think he was wrong. I think the Division will be more important in the future. I kind of thought it might be a job I'd like one day."

"Submit your application. See what happens." I consider the possibility of working with Marissa long term, back in the city. Then I immediately banish the thought. That possibility takes my mind down roads I need to stay off of. I redirect the conversation. "You never answered my second question. What about now? Does your Catholic background drive you to go to chapel? Or is it too different?"

"Mmmm." She slowly chews her food, considering my question. Her eyes are distant, and I wonder what memories I'm pulling forward. "I went to Catholic church a lot when I was in New York. I had chapel a couple of times a week as part of school and Mom and I would go some Sundays, too. I loved the holidays: Christmas Eve and Easter were my favorite. They were special. When I got to Orasul, I stopped going as much. Sometimes I would go with Nick and his family; they're very devout. I had trouble understanding exactly what was going on, and no one has ever explained it to me, so I don't go much by myself. I don't like going alone, I feel lost."

"If you'd grown up here, you would have had chapel school until you were ten." My mom made sure I went to chapel until I graduated from high school. "Then the priests figure it's up to your parents to bring you."

"Part of the problem was that I was hanging around with Tevin. His dad never made him go to chapel, so he didn't go. Then, I didn't go." She considers this statement for a minute, food forgotten. "Maybe if I'd spent more time with Nick, I'd understand it more."

"I don't go every week, but if you ever want to, you're welcome to go with me." Sometimes I wonder what, exactly, Tevin and Marissa had in common besides being recruits together. Listening to her, I can hear how much she enjoyed the spiritual side of life when she lived in New York. To completely give that up seems wrong somehow. I can tell that from one night and one conversation. I know now they'd been together for months; he should have known. "Unless that would make you feel uncomfortable. With me being your superior and all. And I'm not ordering you, just offering."

"In class, you're Captain Smith." She leans forward. "Out here, you're just Collin and you're my friend. Wait, you are my friend, right?"

"Yes, I'm your friend." Friend. That's not too complicated. We can be friends. I hesitate to ask the next question, but I feel like I have to. "How are you doing? Really doing? It's okay if you don't want to talk about it, but I feel like I should ask. I know sometimes I think I'm going to turn around in class and he'll still be here. I imagine it's a lot worse for you."

"Being back to training is really helpful." She pushes more of her food around on her plate. "In the hospital, everyone left me alone. Well, except for you. It gave me a lot of time to think about him, about what happened and what I should have done differently. I'd been so frustrated standing there, unable to move. I thought that maybe, if I'd been a little bit stronger, I could have shut the cage door with my mind or been able to attack."

"You know you couldn't have done anything differently." My heart breaks for her. This isn't something she should be dealing with as a recruit in training.

"I know that." Marissa sets her fork down and folds her hands in front of her. "The crazy part is sometimes I think

I see him. In class. On the training field. Places I remember him being."

"That's not crazy." I think of the times I've seen him, too. The ghost of a student I couldn't save.

"Anyway." She picks her fork back up and continues eating. "It's a lot better now. I can see things more clearly. We fought a lot. It wasn't a healthy relationship. I know what one looks like; I've seen my mom and Riley together. That's the kind of relationship I want. Don't get me wrong, I'm not happy Tevin's dead, but I'm learning to accept it and move on with my life."

"I'm sorry I brought it up." My dolmas finished, I push my plate away from me.

"Don't be." Raising an eyebrow she lifts one shoulder. "Everyone else is afraid to ask me how I feel. They treat me like I'm still broken. Except Kaia. She told me Tevin was an irrational, selfish, jerk and I needed to get over him because I deserve better."

At that, I laugh out loud. It's enough to draw the attention of diners at the next table. I calm myself and quiet my voice. "That doesn't sound like Kaia."

"She's actually okay, once you get past the hard exterior. She's lost him, too. It makes us the same in a lot of ways." Marissa returns to eating her meal and I see she's right. Marissa and Kaia are very much alike.

Marissa and I sat in the restaurant until late, just talking. Well, talking and enjoying baklava and coffee. It was a little like the days back in the hospital and I wonder what I was worried about. Despite the Major's concerns, it didn't feel at all like a date. The evening felt like two friends catching up.

When we parted ways for bed, I warned Marissa to meet me early the next morning for breakfast. She seemed taken aback. "I thought we couldn't leave until after lunch. Why so early?"

"While we're here, we're going to take care of a few things." I purposefully make my plans sound work related. "We might as well make the most of this trip. You can wear your civilian clothes, no need for the combat boots unless you want to wear them."

"Okay, see you at seven." She gives me a quick, American style salute, and then disappears behind her door.

Hopefully, after we parted ways, Marissa slept better than I did. Despite the big bed with the soft sheets, I tossed and turned for a fair portion of the night. It might have been the lights outside my window when I'm used to a completely dark room. Or it might have been the unfamiliar place, it takes me a few nights to get settled in when I move barracks rooms, too. Regardless, seven came early and even though I'm still tired from the night, I'm determined to enjoy the rest of my morning.

Marissa and I meet as planned, I'm on time this morning, she doesn't need to knock on my door, and we make our way down to breakfast. We find a traditional Israeli spread of breakfast foods waiting. There's no meat, but there are salads, cheeses, spreads, a selection of breads, humus, butter, jelly, an egg dish, and more. While we eat, Marissa tries her best to coerce me into telling her what we're doing this morning, but I hold firm. I want this to be a surprise. I even snuck down to the concierge station last night after Marissa went to bed to make sure my plan would work.

After breakfast is over, I lead Marissa out onto the early morning street. There is more foot traffic this morning than I remember from last night. It seems that even amid times of strife people must go to work. "We're going to have to walk to get to our destination. You good?"

"Yeah." She adjusts the strap on her shoulder bag. "Let's go."

The streets are narrow, and the buildings are a mix of old architecture and new, although the term new is strictly comparative. The hotel we slept in last night would be new, and according to the concierge, it's over two hundred years old.

As we walk, I see the signs of unrest to the south. Markets that should be packed with fruit vendors and shops are mostly empty. While many restaurants, coffee shops, and hotels are open, some are boarded up and closed. The concierge had told me the night before that many shopkeepers have decided to keep their doors closed, rather than take on the expense of opening in the current climate. Tourists are few and far between.

Even our hotel, as elegant as it is, is only half full. The restaurant sat five tables last night. It's a testament to the sad state of affairs right now for the usually bustling city.

"It's a little eerie out here." Marissa looks down one street as we pass. There are a handful of shop owners sitting on chairs in front of their buildings. Most of them sell necessities that the locals would need to survive.

"Tourism brings the main income here." I see soldiers ahead and reach into my pocket for my ID and credentials. "Without it, this area is suffering. The concierge at the hotel told me that last month air traffic into Tel Aviv's airport was down seventy-one percent from last year. It was the worst Christmas season on record. Get out your ID, I think we're coming up on a checkpoint."

Marissa reaches into her bag and hands the soldier her ID. The soldiers are all young, probably younger than she is, but heavily armed. One strikes up a conversation with us. "What has you wandering the streets in this part of town? We don't see many American soldiers out here."

"We're assigned to the archeological site outside of town." I accept my badge and put it into my pocket. "We got stuck in town last night because the road got taken out. We're seeing some sites until the road opens back up this afternoon."

"It's a good time to do it if the sites are open, there isn't much in the way of tourists right now." He checks Marissa's badge, glances in her bag, and then gives the badge back to her. "I heard that archeological site was some kind of ancient prison. It must be important; it's guarded like it is."

"I can't tell you much about it, I'm not a scientist." I play off comment. "I just know we're there to make sure nothing happens to it."

"Well, whatever it is, good luck and stay safe out there." The soldier nods his head in a friendly manner and motions for us to pass.

When we get far enough down the street, Marissa looks at me in a panic. "How do they know what the site is?"

"Who knows?" I make a mental note to let my superiors know the gossip. "It's just a rumor. And the truth will be out there soon enough, anyway. It's nothing for us to worry about."

Marissa's expression is enough for me to understand she doesn't agree.

"I'll talk to my superiors." Doing my best to soothe her concerns, I acquiesce. "Honest. It's not unusual for there to be stories about top secret areas and that speculation is usually based on some level of truth. So what if someone thinks we're guarding an ancient archeological site that happens to have been a prison? How does that disrupt our mission?"

"It doesn't." She agrees with me. "Unless some nut case sneaks onto the base to get a look at the site. You know it could happen."

"In the middle of a war?" This time it's my turn to raise an eyebrow. "There are two guard lines into the complex, both of which have cameras watching the perimeter. If someone were to get through that level of security, then you'd have a whole base full of soldiers you'd have to pass before you made it into the prison. Only then, after all that, would you have a chance at getting a look at what we're containing. I think, for the time being, we've got it covered."

Ahead of me, our destination comes into sight.

"But, what if…"

"Stop." I step in front of her and pause her words with a hand on her arm. Her energy pulses against me, familiar and warm. Immediately, I pull back. "We're here."

"Where's here?" Eyes moving around the buildings near us, Marissa seems to be getting her bearings. "Where are we?"

"We're checking off something on your list." I point forward. "The Church of the Holy Sepulcher."

CHAPTER EIGHT

Marissa stops walking to get a good look at the building in front of us. It doesn't look like the cathedrals we're familiar with. There are no huge, arching windows of stained glass. There aren't any flying buttresses like Notre Dame or towering spires like Holy Trinity Lutheran on the upper west side of Manhattan. From the outside, it looks mostly like the buildings around it. The same cream-colored bricks and round windows with bars. Its roof makes it different; the round, blueish dome with a Christian Cross mounted on the top.

Despite the lack of tourism, we aren't the only ones approaching the building. There are a dozen or more humans walking the same direction we are in various states of reverence. Some, like us, look like they're casually interested in a venerated historic site that dates back almost two thousand years. Others are obviously pilgrims, saying prayers as they approach. There's even a small tour group being led by a guide near the entrance.

"Seriously?" Marissa' eyes stay focused on the building, taking in everything she can. "You brought me here?"

"You said it was on your list and we're in the neighborhood." My eyes study the building; I wonder what she sees that I don't. I simply see a building with historic significance to humans. She's almost glowing with reverence. "Why is this building important?"

"A couple of reasons, if you believe in Christianity." Her eyes come into focus and her attention moves back to me. "In Christianity, the son of God sacrifices himself to atone for the sins of mankind. On his way to crucifixion, he walks the Via Dolorosa, a path marred with shame, humiliation, and pain. The last four stops on that walk are here within this church. Most importantly, this church is said to house the rock on which he was crucified and the tomb in which he was buried. It's probably one of the most sacred site in the Christian world."

"Do you believe it?" I gesture to the building, my voice low as to not disturb the other pilgrims nearby. "The story?"

"I believe it's possible. I mean, we're here." She tugs at my arm until she has my hand in hers. She flips it over, palm up, and presses her thumb in the middle of my palm. My hand tingles where she touches me and I'm glad I don't have to wear gloves to control my gift like some Fallen do. "Look at you, flesh and bone and blood, just like a human. But we're not human. We're one of the angels of their stories and we Fell. Who's to say both events didn't happen? God sends us and a few centuries later, God sends a son."

"You know we have an unfair advantage." Her fingers are still touching my hand, sending shivers down my spine. I dutifully stand still; I don't want to pull away. "We know we're real. These humans around us believe all of this on faith alone. Like you said, they write about our kind in books and poetry, yet here we stand. Flesh and blood."

Something profound, something I can't name, passes between us. It's only there a moment, and then it's gone and she's letting go of my hand. Her eyes drop to the ground and I'm glad. I don't know what secrets I'd give away if she kept staring into my eyes.

"Come on, let's go inside." She turns and starts making her way toward the entrance, following the other pilgrims. I fall into step beside her, wondering what just happened.

We reach the entrance and are guided up a stairway to a beautifully decorated area where there are two chapels. Marissa bows her head and makes the sign of the cross. I look at her questioningly. She nods to a large cross hanging in the front with a man on it. "Old habits die hard."

I'm not sure what that means, I file it away to ask later.

She takes her time in this area, admiring the artwork and brilliance of the room. I'm careful not to rush her, this might be her only opportunity to visit here. Instead, I watch the people. I can hear several languages being spoken quietly, reverently in this poorly lit room and I'm humbled to know that humanity has such a strong belief that even war will not keep them away. It makes me wonder what they will do when they find out angels truly walk among them.

When Marissa gets into the line leading to the main altar, I join her, just because I'm following her. Eventually, we reach the altar, and I see there is exposed rock below it. She kneels and touches it with her hand. I do the same because I'm standing in line, and I want to blend in.

I'm surprised to feel a warmth coming from the earth, much like the warmth I would feel from another person.

It startles me and I pull my hand away quickly. Marissa glances at me, curious about my reaction. "If the legends are true, this is where he went back. The son died here on this rock and returned to the heavenly realm."

"Do you ever wonder if we're going back?" I place my hand back on the rock, taking in the warmth this time instead of being startled by it. The story is possible. After all, as Marissa pointed out, we exist.

"I don't know." She stands from her kneeling position, and we move away for another pilgrim to take our place. "I think we will go back when we die. But will we go back in the flesh? I think there's a lot of work to be done here first."

A second stairway leads us downward toward another area. Here, Marissa explains, is the tomb and a fragment of rock that was used to seal the tomb. Again, we take in the artwork decorating the sacred site and watch the pilgrims as they say their prayers. Just being present here is moving me; I can see it has quite an effect on Marissa.

"Maybe I should start going to chapel." Her whisper is so quiet I dip my head to properly hear her. "Things like this reminds me why we do this. It's not just about the killing of bad guys. We came here with a higher purpose, even if it was twenty-five hundred years ago. I think I'm done here."

I nod, and we start walking toward the entrance. We're almost out of the building when an older woman stops us. She has graying hair that is pulled back into a tight bun, her clothes are dark and non-descript. There's a colorful shawl over her shoulders. The energy radiating off her is one of devotion. She is here because she fully believes.

"I see you for what you are." Her words stop me in my tracks, making my stomach go cold. She seems human, but only a demon should recognize us as something other. "You are here for the greatness of God. May you have many blessings bestowed upon you."

I open my mouth, searching for words, but Marissa's hand on my arm stops me. She shakes her head and takes my hand. Then she addresses the old woman. "Thank you. May God be with you."

"Thank you." If possible, the woman's energy radiates even more strongly. "Thank you."

Marissa offers her a smile and pulls my hand to lead me out of the church. I follow her until we're a block from the building and then I stop, pulling my hand from her grip. "What was that?"

"A church." She stops walking, her euphoric expression dampened by the tone of my voice. "A burial spot. Ane execution ground. It's a lot of things, Collin. What do you want it to be?"

"No, the old woman. What was that?" I temper my anger. Surely Marissa didn't just give away our secret identity.

"Oh, that." She looks at me with big eyes and shrugs her shoulders dramatically. "I don't know."

"Why did you respond to her at all?" I look back at the church, half expecting the woman to be following us. Thank goodness, she's nowhere in sight. "You all but told her we were something other than human. What were you thinking?"

"There was this woman when I went to the Catholic school. She was...different. Special." Her eyes focus on the distant past, like she's trying to remember exactly what the woman looked like. What her energy felt like. "Every time we met, she thought I was an angel. She wasn't wrong, but

I couldn't tell her that. Each week, she'd ask God to bless me. I would say thank you and move on. I don't know how to explain it, other than some humans are more in tune than others. Somehow, she just knew."

"That doesn't make any sense." My phone starts to vibrate. I want to ignore it and continue this discussion, but it could be the prison, or it could be Nathan trying to pick us up. I give Marissa a hard look and answer the phone. "This is Collin."

"Collin, glad I caught you. This is Benjamin." The voice of the local director of the Division drives away any other concern I have. I can return to this conversation with Marissa later. "I was hoping you hadn't left Jerusalem yet. I have a family that would like to meet you."

My first reaction is, why? I'm just a trainer for the recruitment class. Who am I?

"They've never met a Fallen before and they're scared about the alliance. They're afraid of being brought out into the public light." Benjamin continues before I can ask any questions. "I was hoping that, if you meet them, they may feel better about this whole situation."

"Oh." I watch Marissa shove her hands in her pockets, looking at the street around her. I refocus on Benjamin. "Sure. We're out and about in the Old City, we'll have to get back to the hotel to meet you there. And I need to call Nathan and let him know about the delay."

"I'm already on my way to you. Give me your location and I'll direct you to the nearest street where I can pick you up." I give him our location and repeat his directions out loud so Marissa can hear them. I hang up the phone and send a text to Nathan who replies he'll wait for us to let him know we're ready to go after our meeting.

Once I'm done, Marissa starts asking questions. "What's going on? Where are headed?"

We start walking toward the cross-street Benjamin told us to meet him at. "There's a demon family that wants to meet us. From the sounds of it, they're afraid. They've never met a Fallen and they're afraid of the Five-Year plan. I imagine they want some reassurance that we're not going to kill them in their sleep."

"That's terrible." Keeping step beside me, Marissa makes a face. "The integration process had already started when I met Aria in New York. I didn't realize it would be so much different elsewhere."

"There are only a few Fallen cities. In those areas, we've established an alliance and have begun the process of working together." Turning right, we pass through another area that should be filled with bustling shops. It's all but empty. "In places like this, where there is no Fallen city, we've become the boogie man that demons tell their children about. They have a right to be afraid. Just like us, some of them have lost friends and family to Fallen swords throughout the centuries."

"I can't imagine killing someone like Aria just because she's a demon." She shivers, probably thinking about how hard it would be to kill Aria or Aria's girlfriend Sasha. Marissa had become friends with both of them back in New York, they'd gone to the theater together and shopping. "Please tell me we didn't wipe out innocent people like her."

"You know your history, Marissa, I taught it to you." We reach the street Benjamin is supposed to meet us at and we wait. "Not that long ago, we didn't care if a demon had higher reasoning skills or not. We hadn't taken the time to

consider that they aren't all the same. All we knew was their kind hurt and maimed humans and we were sent to stop it. Demons like Discord didn't help. They used our own ignorance against us, helping to perpetuate an unnecessary battle and feed the fear on both sides. It took some brave souls to propose working together."

"And now, here we are, about to help build that bridge." She considers what I said. "Not that long ago, I wouldn't have been able to be friends with Sasha."

"No." I agree. "Not that long ago, within your parents' lifetime, you would have killed her immediately and burned Erik's place to the ground."

One night on patrol, Marissa and Tevin stumbled upon a demon bar in Manhattan owned by a demon named Erik. Although they'd already met Aria, that was the night Marissa met Sasha and a friendship had formed. It's a friendship that would have been forbidden only a few years ago.

She's still deep in thought when Benjamin pulls up in front of us. He motions for us to get into the car. A female is seated beside him. Much like Aria, she looks human enough that she wouldn't stand out in a crowd. Only her energy gives her away as something else.

"This is Constance." Benjamin introduces us as he pulls into traffic. "As I told you yesterday, she's our primary liaison to the demons that live here in Jerusalem."

"It's nice to meet you." We get into the backseat of the vehicle.

"Likewise." Constance has dark brown hair with blue eyes and creamy white skin. She doesn't look like the locals.

Benjamin merges the car into traffic and turns toward our hotel. "We'll pick up anything you left at the hotel first. I apologize if I interrupted your site-seeing. When Constance reached out to me, I thought this would be a good opportunity for some positive interaction."

I watch out the window as we pass more empty shops and nearly empty pilgrimage sites. "No apology necessary. What we're doing is important work that needs a good foundation. We're happy to help if we're able."

At least, I hope we are. I didn't think to ask Marissa if she cared to meet this family, I just assumed.

"What's the family's concern?" Marissa leans forward to talk to Constance.

"The usual." The officer turns in her seat to see Marissa better. "Your defined purpose has always been to stop the demons. What does that mean now? The prison worries them, too, that you'll start rounding up as many of them as you can find to lock away. These are the concerns all of our people have."

"Integrating with humans must be a concern, too." Marissa draws the next logical conclusion. "You have been portrayed as the bad guys in theology for thousands of years. It's going to be difficult to get away from that narrative."

A quick stop at our hotel and we're ready to go.

Marissa continues her quiet conversation with Constance while we drive. Benjamin concentrates on the road, leaving me to my own thoughts. Just like with Aria and Sasha, Marissa is doing well with Constance. She's natural at calming people; at making them feel at ease with her. I'm curious to see how she deals with this family we're going to meet. Benjamin hasn't given us any indication what we're about to walk into, other than this family falls under the alliance and that they're scared.

I'm surprised when we don't leave City Center. After the hotel, we drive a short distance until Benjamin drops us off in front of a collection of shops. Constance leads us to a doorway on the side of the building where she rings the second floor. The door is remotely unlocked, and she lets us in.

Upstairs, we reach a landing between two apartments. Constance guides us to the left, where she knocks. A moment later, the door is opened by a male.

The male looks similar in appearance to Constance: blue eyes, brown hair, average build. He, too, would easily blend in with the city, except for a short pair of horns on top of his head. Maybe he could hide his head with a hat, but it's unlikely he could work in plain sight. I wonder how they afford their apartment.

"This is Matthew, and his wife, Sara. Sara's my sister." Constance makes the introductions.

If Matthew looks similar to Constance, Sara is her younger twin. There's youth in her eyes that Constance doesn't have any more. But there's also fear. I realize with a start that the fear is directed at me and Marissa.

If Marissa picks up on the fear, she doesn't show it. She steps right into the apartment and greets them both. "I'm so happy to meet you. You have a lovely home."

Lovely isn't how I'd describe it, but I can't judge, I live in a single room in the barracks. This apartment is tidy, with well-loved furniture and colorful decorations. There's an open door to a tiny bathroom and an archway leads into an equally tiny bedroom. The kitchen space is limited to a handful of cabinets and narrow counter against one wall with a half size refrigerator.

From the bedroom, a small cry calls out. Constance touches Sara on the arm. "I'll get her."

"My daughter." Sara explains. "I'd hoped she'd sleep through your visit."

"I'm sorry we woke her." I look to Matthew, wondering where we should start.

"You and Constance are sisters?" Marissa jumps in, keeping a respectful distance from the couple, but starting the conversation. "You look different from each other."

"These?" Sara reaches up and touches one of the horns on top of her head. "They grow in when we're toddlers. My parents had Constance's removed as soon as they were finished growing."

"It's a barbaric, horrible tradition, but one our people had to endure for years. It's the only way we could survive." Constance reappears from the bedroom, a tiny baby girl wrapped in a pink blanket in her arms. "It was so hard on me that they didn't do it to Sara. Mom said that I almost died."

"A lot of children do." Matthew gently touches his daughter's head. "That's why some of us simply choose to stay hidden. We don't want to torture our children that way."

"Living here, I'm still able to work." Voice hopeful, Sara takes an ID card off her kitchen counter to show us. "I work at one of the museums, that's part of the reason we live in this part of town. I can walk to work. I wear a headscarf. The people I work for think it is our religious tradition."

"I work for an IT company, from here at home. I watch the baby." Matthew focuses on me. "We have credentials and pay our taxes. We are not a bother to anyone, and we do not cause trouble."

"We're not here to question you." The fear radiating from them both is overwhelming. I try to reassure them, still unsure of what to say. "We're not here to put you in prison or take away your child. We're here to show you that we come peacefully. It's taken us a long time to understand this, but we recognize that just because you're a demon, it doesn't mean you're bad."

Sara and Matthew exchange a troubled look between them. "But what about the Thirteen?"

"He didn't say you're all good, either." Their bodies stiffen as they look at Marissa. "Honestly, I know a few Fallen I'd rather not hang around with, either. There are humans who are murderers and Fallen who are just downright mean people. No one race is perfect, but we do have to learn how to live together. You shouldn't have to hide who you are for your job."

As Marissa talks, the couple begins to relax. I can see she has an effect on them. Even Constance looks more at ease.

"May I?" Reaching for her shoulder bag, she waits until Matthew nods his head. I know what she's doing, going slowly to assure them she doesn't have a weapon to hurt them with. She pulls out her cell phone and scrolls through her pictures until she finds one of herself with Sasha. "This is my friend, Sasha. She lives in New York where she works. When I'm home, we go to shows together and have dinner at this one place that welcomes demons and sometimes we can go shopping together. She's like you."

"She's blue." Sara reaches out as if she's going to touch the screen. At the last minute, she stops, her fingers hovering over the phone. "How can she go outside?"

"In New York, where there are more of you, we have a few places that are friendly to demons. A bar, it's like a nightclub, and a theater. If you were there, you could go and take off your headscarf." Marissa mimics removing a scarf from her head. "The bar is the first time I'd ever seen anyone like you. A male and a female, just having an evening out."

"This is how it is in New York?" Adjusting the baby in her arms, Constance looks at the picture on the phone, her face surprised. "Fallen and demons are friends?"

"This is how we hope it will be." I glance at Marissa. I hadn't known she'd been spending so many of her nights off with Sasha. I guess she still has some surprises for me. "Marissa is unique. Marissa embraces this new world wholeheartedly. Many Fallen are just as fearful as you are. We're asking the world a lot, to accept us as we are."

"But you are stronger than we are." Matthew makes a motion with his hands I assume to be an imitation of Fallen using their gifts. "You have powers. What can humans do to you?"

"We can be killed." No need to mince words. If enough humans, or their weapons, attack us. It would be just as deadly for us as it is for Matthew and his family. "Trust. I know it's a lot to ask. It's a lot for all of us."

He stands there, looking between me, Marissa, and his wife. Finally, he nods and holds his hand toward their small living room, inviting us farther into their apartment. "Then let us talk. Perhaps we can be friends, too."

CHAPTER NINE

Heading back to base in the car with Nathan, I analyze my feelings about the meeting with Matthew and Sara. They're nice people with honest concerns. They told us some demons are moving out of crowded cities in anticipation of human reaction to their presence. I hope Matthew doesn't feel the need to do that. I hope they're able to keep their home and their jobs. Only time will tell.

The clock is ticking down, we're rushing toward public knowledge and we all know it. Demons and Fallen alike are nervous. It's been six months since we told the recruits, and while Marissa is embracing the coming reality, most are still resistant. I'm glad Marissa was with me on this trip, someone like Kaia could have been a disaster.

The most important thing that happened was my conversation with Benjamin just before we parted ways.

Benjamin had waited outside the apartment, not willing to overwhelm the family inside with too many people.

After we said our goodbyes, Constance spoke quietly to Benjamin. He treated us to a quick lunch and then took us to the police station where Nathan was waiting. Stopping me when we got out of the car, he looked me over. "Constance says you did well with Matthew and Sara, and she does not give compliments easily. You impressed her today and you helped calm a very frightened family. It's good work."

"Thank you, sir." I shake the hand he offers. "That means a lot."

"If you ever want to get out of the army, I could use you on my staff." He lifts his chin toward Marissa. "I could use both of you. She's great with people. I know you'd have to live at the prison, which makes for a long commute, but we could work something out. If you're interested."

The offer floors me. Getting out of the army is something I'd considered, but in my mind, I always imagined myself returning to Hope. I never considered another city. "Thank you. Marissa has another few months of basic training and I'm with the unit until then, too. I'll have to think about it."

"Please do." Benjamin smiles and steps back from the car. "You know how to get ahold of me."

"You're thinking about Benjamin's offer, aren't you." Marissa's voice breaks into my thoughts. I shake myself in my seat, look out the window, and realize we're more than halfway back to Pandora's Box.

"I am." I don't know what else to say. I'm still struggling to sort out my feelings. It's an incredible opportunity for both of us if that's something Marissa wants to do. But it's not the assignment I really want. Hope is what I want. Working for Aria in New York. That job isn't available and has a lot of applicants waiting in line for a chance there. This opportunity is a blank slate. "What about you?"

"With the way things are right now?" She takes a deep breath. "Mom might kill me. I mean, it's basically a job in a war zone. Working at the prison would be safer."

"I seem to remember us talking about safe choices versus what you really want to do before." In high school, Marissa struggled with her decision to go to basic training. She had been afraid her mom wouldn't approve; that she'd want Marissa to take a safer option. "What do you want to do?"

"I really like the idea of working for the Division." She makes a noise and shakes her head. "If I don't catch up, it might not be an option. I still have a lot of work that I need to get done from my time in the hospital."

"Hey, don't do that." When I first met Marissa, she had something to prove. Having been raised among humans, she was behind her classmates in a lot of areas. She worked hard and finished second in her class to Tevin. Every once in a while, that old Marissa appears. Someone who's afraid they aren't good enough. That they can't quite do the job. "You've been in a tough spot before and you worked your way through it. You'll do that again. And, besides, the class isn't going to leave you behind. We're a team, all of us. Kaia, Jenn, me, and the rest of the class? We have your back."

"Thanks, I do know that." Her expression changes to one of chagrin. "It's something that's been bothering me since I got out of the hospital. I feel like I've always been second best. First, to Kaia in school. I worked so hard to be better than her and she kept beating me, over and over. Then Tevin. We were close, but he was always one step ahead. One point higher."

"You're judging yourself on Tevin's aspirations, Marissa." Shifting in my seat so I can see her better, I think about Tevin. "He wanted to be assigned to the army.

Specifically, he wanted to be part of the unit that gets sent out to the small town or into the jungle to search out the demons that terrorize people and eat small children. I don't think he was ever going to embrace our new world, not the way you do. But he's gone now and you aren't stifled by his dreams. You're not second best to anyone. You're the best you that you can be, and you were amazing today. Not many of us could talk to Sara and Matthew the way you did. You don't see them as a different species. You see them like you see your classmates. As people. And that is a gift."

"I get that I grew up different." She turns toward me in her seat, and I can feel the energy pulse between us. "But is it really that hard to see someone for who they are and not the label life has given them? Aria was never anything except amazing when she taught our class last semester. And Sasha's…cool. We have so much in common. Why do Fallen like Kaia have such a hard time seeing that?"

"Because they're scared." I breathe in through my nose and release some of my internal frustration. There's part of me that's so happy Tevin is out of Marissa's life. I think she would have went along with his plans just because of their bond. It would have destroyed her. She isn't built for the kill; she has too much compassion in her. "At some point, we're all scared of change. Of something different. I want you to focus on the good. Think about it, does anyone else in your class have a job offer?"

"No." At that she smiles, and it lights up the car. I can feel her energy start to settle, and then a small brush of sadness. "Can I ask you if you've heard from Nick?"

"You can ask." I consider my response. If Nick has chosen not to contact Marissa himself, I owe him his privacy. I know he's been in touch with Jenn.

Nick had been close friends with both Marissa and Amy in high school. When Tevin arrived, the balance of their friendship had been upset until Nick fancied himself in love with Marissa; feelings she did not reciprocate. After a serious conversation, Marissa convinced Nick that she wasn't ready for any relationship and that they should stay friends. Nick held onto her words, believing they would have a chance later on, after basic training. Then, when Tevin died and Marissa ended up in the hospital, Nick realized they had been carrying on a relationship for months. He respectfully asked for a transfer to a different unit, which was granted.

"He's doing well." I decide it's safe to give her basic information. Most of it she already knows. "He's settled into Les Gens, the city outside of Paris, and is getting good marks. Although, the language is a challenge. His email hasn't changed. You can always reach out to him."

"I thought about it, but every time I sit at a computer, I chicken out." She runs a hand through her hair, which makes me focus on the strands. Browns and golds, spun together. When she'd been in the hospital, it had looked limp and dim. Now that she's accepting the energy of Fallen around her it looks bright and beautiful. "I think Jenn's still talking to him. She says he's happy there."

I think about my relationship with Natasha, a female I thought I was in love with, and I realize Nick might not want to hear from Marissa. I know I cringe every time I hear from Natasha. And it's worse when I see her. That would be the only drawback to returning to Hope. She still lives there.

"Would you want to hear from me, if you were in his position?" Her voice is quiet and small. I realize she knows the answer.

"No." I'm honest. It's not about being angry, either. It's about feeling the wound open again and again. "You didn't mean to, but you hurt him. Give him time to heal. He knows how to find you."

"Do you talk to Natasha?" I told Marissa about my relationship a few months ago. I'm surprised she remembers. "That's her name, right?"

"Not if I don't have to." I think about my feelings where she's concerned. "It's not that it hurts any more, she's just not part of my life. I've moved on and I want to focus on healthy relationships and my career."

"So, I should leave him alone." She nods once, firming a belief. "You're probably right."

"Sorry to interrupt, but we're coming up on the outer perimeter of Pandora's Box." Nathan's voice reminds me that we're on our way back to the prison. I look out the front window and see the first checkpoint. "You'll need your credentials in a moment."

"Thanks." Marissa and I reach for our ID's as the car slows down.

We make it through both checkpoints and then reach the garage entrance to the prison. I can see Marissa's mom waiting near the bay doors, her arms crossed over her chest, with several other soldiers including Kaia. I've been told Major Cazut is warm, caring, and an easy person to get along with. I wouldn't know, I've never spent any time with her. All I do know is that right now, watching her from the car, I can't avoid the feelings of intimidation.

Marissa turns in surprise and looks at me. "My mom scares you!"

"You weren't supposed to feel that." I keep the embarrassment out of my voice. "And, yes, she intimidates me."

"I'm sorry, I didn't mean to read your energy without permission." The car slows to a stop and Marissa jumps out.

She doesn't give me a chance to respond, which is fine. I thank Nathan for being our driver, I let myself out of the vehicle, and take our bags from the trunk of the car.

"We're heading out to Brazil to track down something that's terrorizing a small village." Major Cazut is talking quietly to Marissa. "We'll be back in a few days. You'll be okay while I'm gone?"

"I'll be fine." I can hear Marissa roll her eyes in the comment. She hates it when her mom is overprotective. "I survived overnight in Jerusalem. I'm sure I'll be good and busy here. I have work to catch up on and muscles to get back into shape. I don't need you taking care of me."

"I know." Major Cazut smiles and I try my best not to listen. "I can't help it sometimes. You'll always be my little girl."

"Mom!" This time, she does make a face. "Are you leaving immediately?"

"Yes. The transport's waiting to take us to the airport. I made them delay until you got in." That explains the other soldiers milling around. They must all be waiting on the mission. "When I get back, I want to hear all about Jerusalem."

"Yes, mom." Marissa smiles and gives her mom a hug. "You need to get going."

Her mom stands still for a moment, taking in Marissa's face. Then she turns to me. Her whole demeanor changes into one of a superior officer. "We're taking Kaia and Patrick with us. Is that going to be a problem?"

"No, ma'am." Kaia, for her part, is standing with a completely calm face, like she does this every day. Patrick looks like he's going to be sick.

"Good. I want to see what these recruits can do in the field." She picks up her duffle and motions to the rest of the waiting soldiers. "Let's go."

Marissa and I watch as they load up one of the transports that will take them to the closest military base. From there, they'll fly to Brazil and then to their final destination. I remember a time when I would have been dying to go with them on a mission like this. Today, I'm glad I'm not. A visit to Rio would be interesting; marching through the jungles to find and kill a rouge demon is not what I envision as a good time.

From the look on Marissa's face, she must feel the same way.

"Head to your barracks. Grad some dinner. Enjoy your evening." I give Marissa the shopping bags I took from the car, aware of the number of other people standing around and suddenly feeling uncomfortable. "You've had a long day."

"Wait." She stops me with a hand on my arm when I turn to walk away. "What can I share about our trip? What parts are confidential?"

"None of it was confidential." I stand still, very aware of the warmth of her hand. "I wouldn't share the names or location of the family we visited, but if you want to talk about it with your mom or Jenn, I think that would be perfectly acceptable. You found a job that speaks to you. You should talk about that with your friends and family. Everything from the Division headquarters they will both already know."

"Thank you." Her hand drops away from me, and I feel like I can breathe again. "And thank you for a fun evening

and the visit to the church. I know it wasn't planned, but I had a good time."

"Collin! Welcome back!" A new voice calls out from behind me. Marissa smiles at me and steps away, headed into the corridor that would lead her to the barracks. I watch her disappear into the hallway before I turn around.

Mia is cutting a path across the bay, her stride strong and solid as she makes her way toward me. I stand and wait for her, wondering when we became friends. She and Kurt have had meals with me twice now and they treat me like an old friend. I considered if it's because of my relationship with Marissa – if Mia is keeping an eye on me to make sure everything stays professional.

"I heard you got stuck overnight in Jerusalem." She stops in front of me, Kurt nowhere in sight. "Were you locked down in your hotel?"

"It wasn't that bad." No need to tell her how nice the hotel was. Or that dinner was amazing for a lot of reasons. "The Division put us up in a hotel and sent us to dinner. This morning, we went to an ancient church Marissa wanted to see, and then we were called in to do a little work for the Jerusalem Division. Shouldn't you be on a transport headed to the jungle right now?"

"No, that's Anna's detail. She's the one who kills demons, I read about them." Taking in the bag in my hand and what is probably a tired expression on my face, she gestures toward the corridor. "Headed toward the barracks? I'll walk with you. Which church did you go to?"

"Church of the Holy Sepulcher." I fall into step beside her and force myself to keep my thoughts and emotions neutral.

"Ah, Marissa is embracing her Catholic side again." Mia smiles. "She goes through phases. Some days she professes to have no interest in religion, other times she goes to chapel with Nick. Although I guess that won't be happening anymore. I heard a rumor that you've applied to the Division in New York."

"Not a rumor, that's the truth." There are days I can't believe how fast gossip travels in the Fallen world. I thought that transfer request was confidential. "There's a long waiting list for that job. I don't expect to get it. At least not any time soon."

"You want to abandon us out here in the army?" Her voice is lighthearted, so I know she's not actually accusing me of deserting them. "I heard you were a good trainer, that you've done miracles with some of the recruits. You sure you want to give that up?"

"I lost three of my recruits, I don't know that makes me a good trainer." I made my peace with what happened to Amy months ago. Tevin and Nick? I still feel like I should have done something different.

"What happened to Amy was a freak accident. Tragic, but an accident." Mia stops in the hallway, and I stop beside her, waiting for her to continue. "For what I understand, Tevin was a loose cannon. He was a danger to himself from day one. And Nick just got his heart broken. Also, not your fault. You've kept nineteen of them and they're all shaping up to be decent soldiers. Oh, by the way, Maxim is due to be back any day now. If you want to keep an eye out for him."

Maxim, another sacred warrior, is also Tevin's father. He's stationed here at Pandora's Box, although he's spent the last weeks in New York on leave. I don't think he blames me for what Tevin did, but I'm not anxious to run into him. At the end of the day, I was Tevin's commanding officer when he died.

"How do you know all this?" I cock my head and look at her as we walk down the hallway. "Don't you have a job you're supposed to be doing?"

"Scholar-warrior-monk, remember?" She flashes a smile in my direction. "Sometimes I get tired of looking at ancient scrolls, so I wander the halls. It's amazing what you can find out just by watching and listening. On that note, be careful with Marissa. If my brother finds out you are doing anything that might even remotely hurt her, a demotion is the least of your concerns."

"I don't know what you're talking about." Dread washes over me. The last thing I need to do is upset the General of the Army by being accused of messing around with his stepdaughter. "Marissa and I are..."

"Friends. I get it." We must have reached her doorway because she stops. "You're different with her. She's different, too. I saw you two a few times at Hope, even before Tevin died. She's relaxed with you, confident. If there's nothing there, fine. But if there is? Go slow. She's been through a lot."

"I know she's been through a lot. I appreciate you looking out for her, but I'm her superior officer. It would be inappropriate." I struggle to find the right words because I know I'm lying through my teeth. I'm attracted to Marissa and have been for a while.

"Because that's stopped anyone ever." She waves a hand through the air like she's clearing away bad energy. Then she changes the subject so quickly that my head spins. "I know you don't have close friends here, except for Marissa. We're playing cards tonight in the common room and could use an extra player. Want to join us?"

The offer catches me off guard. The truth is I haven't had close friends anywhere in a while. Not since my injury.

A psychologist would probably say I'm keeping people at a distance because I don't want to get hurt again like I did with Natasha. I would argue that I'm enjoying solitude after living my whole life in a society that depends on physical and emotional connection. I'm around people all day to fulfill the physical need my body has for others of my kind. At night, a good book can keep me company.

"Sure. I'd love to." The words are out of my mouth before I have time to think about them.

"Great. Kurt and I are grabbing dinner in thirty down in the mess if you want to join us." She opens her door. "Game starts at seven if you don't."

"Give me a couple of minutes to put these things away." I hold up my shopping bag. "I'll join you for dinner."

"Awesome, then I can grill you about the assignment you did for the Division." She winks an eye at me. "See you in a few."

CHAPTER TEN

I grab dinner in the mess with Mia and Kurt; it's a comfortable, easy meal with a conversation dominated by Mia. She's something else. Talkative, observant, and bursting with positive energy. The last part I already know from my previous interactions with her. She's always got something good to say. Mia had been around a little bit while the recruits were stationed at Hope. There had been a class or two that she taught and a training session she'd led through Central Park.

Tonight, she dissects my trip to Jerusalem and all but guesses that I'd been offered a job by the Division, something I deeply deny. I'm not foolish. Options are good to have. Letting my current bosses know I might be on my way out the door? Something I know I should keep quiet. Especially because I'm not sure I want to take the job offer seriously. Deciding to move full time to Jerusalem is serious. Aside from knowing my mom will be home in Hope alone, I need to consider the danger of the area.

"I bet some of those ancient religious sites hold incredible mysteries." She takes a drink of water. "The riddles on the walls, written in plain sight for everyone to see? God, how I'd love unlimited access for a couple of months. I bet I could find all kinds of forgotten artifacts."

"I don't think everything is a mystery." Kurt spears a piece of broccoli and waves it at Mia. "Some of them are simply pretty buildings with pretty inscriptions on the walls."

"Some, but not all." She wiggles her eyebrows. "What if I could find the Ark of the Covenant? Or the Holy Grail? Oh! Or if I could track down a copy of the Q scrolls? I bet there are clues to all those mysteries in these buildings, if you know where to look."

"I thought the Ark of the Covenant was in Ethiopia being held by some group claiming to be the lost tribe of Israel." Kurt makes a face. "Or was in Nigeria? I don't remember, I saw a television show about it."

"You're talking about the Ethiopian Orthodox Church, they used to be part of the Coptic Orthodox Church. The Church of Our Lady Mary of Zion claims they have it, but I don't think they do. If they did, why would they keep it hidden? It could be one of the most venerated existing artifacts in Jewish and Christian mythology." Eyes sparkling, Mia looks ready to jump out of her seat and start off on a quest of her own. I wonder how someone my age could possibly know so much without looking it up. "The Ark holds manna, Aaron's rod, and the Ten Commandments. It would be earth shattering if someone found the Ark today."

"How does she know this stuff?" I know Mia is a scholar, but seriously? We may have been sent here by the God of

Israel, we might even have our own religion that reflects elements of Judaism that existed when we first Fell, but no one has these kind of details memorized.

"You get used to it." He sips from a bottle of cola that I gaze at enviously. I haven't had a soda since I left Hope, and I have no idea where he found one in the prison. They aren't readily available here in the mess and I haven't seen them in the commissary. "She's like this all the time. If she's not researching or fighting or training, she's looking for new things to research. It's kind of exhausting."

"Okay…" Interesting. She must have gotten along well with Amy. She was like that. One of the artifacts Mia mentioned comes to mind. "What is Q?"

"If it exists, it's an original text that some of the other texts are derived from." She produces a pen from one of her pockets and draws a bunch of lines on a napkin with the names of the four books of the Christian gospel. Then she writes another name, Thomas. "The books of Matthew and Luke seem to have common source material, Q. But that material isn't present in Mark, although parts of Mark seem to also be source material for Matthew and Luke. So, if you take Mark and Q together, you can get the books of Matthew and Luke. Of course, there is a little original material in both of those books as well, but that's not the point. Then, you take the Gospel of Thomas, which was discovered like eighty years ago, and you can find more of Q. So, if someone could find Q, it would be like finding one of the original gospels."

"You know a lot about the Christian Bible." Marissa would probably love this conversation. For a minute, I wish she were here.

"I know a lot about many ancient texts." Mia corrects me. "Our kind Fell about five hundred years before Christ, if you believe he existed. Many parts of our history are entwined with that of early Christianity because we came from the same area of the world and from a common background – the God of Israel. As I've done research on our own secrets, I've had to consider that some of our legends and mysteries followed the branch of Judaism that eventually became what we know today to be Christianity."

"That's a logical assumption." My talk with Marissa at the church comes to mind. She, too, had alluded to a common origin. That if God could send us, why couldn't he send Jesus?

"And…now you're cut off." Reaching past me, Kurt picks up the napkin, folds it neatly, and puts it into his pocket. "Your time is up until tomorrow, then you can have this back."

"I don't need that back; it was a diagram for Collin's benefit." Seemingly unperturbed by Kurt's interruption, she casually returns to eating her dinner.

"She has a time limit." He gives me the napkin. Unsure what to do with it, I put it in my own pocket. "When her time is up, she can't talk about lost scrolls or hidden texts any more until tomorrow. Otherwise, this is all she'll talk about all night long. And, no offense, it's not the kind of conversation I want to have while beating you at cards."

"Who says I'm going to lose?" He laughs and I realize it feels good to joke around and sit with other Fallen, instead of keeping to myself. Mia and Kurt are easy to talk to. Mia's basically a genius and Kurt has a great sense of humor. I could see myself being friends with them.

We finish off our dinners and head to the common room where Mia grabs a table with four chairs. Kurt takes a deck of cards off the game shelf, and we sit down. Mia directly across from me, Kurt waiting for his partner.

"You know how to play Euchre? Yes?" Mia grabs the deck from Kurt and starts separating the cards.

"Yes. Although, it's been a while since I last played." I'm sure I'll be fine, playing is like falling off a bicycle. Once you learn, you always remember. When it's cold and snowy in New York, Euchre had been a common way to pass an evening.

"As long as I don't have to teach you." She finishes discarding the cards we won't use and looks at the clock. "I wonder where Alain is. I didn't see him in the mess."

"I'm right here." Alain arrives just in time to hear his name. "Sorry I'm late. There were some issues with the cameras on the prisoner level. We got them sorted out, but it made me late for dinner. Do you mind?"

He has a bag of chips in his hand.

"Doesn't bother me, just don't get the cards greasy." Mia indicates the empty seat across from Kurt. "Collin, head trainer for the incoming Hope and Orasul recruits, meet Alain, IT specialist from Les Gens."

Alain shakes Collin's hand before he claims his seat. "You have some talented recruits coming up. Patrick, in particular, has a good sense for electronics and electronic surveillance. I've enjoying having him assigned to our department."

"Thank you, I do have gifted recruits, but you won't see Patrick for a few days. He's on assignment in Brazil." Marissa, Jenn, Brandon, Kaia, they're all talented in their own way. One thing I've learned in the last couple of years as their teacher is that they're all different. I think I expected recruits to all be the same, I hadn't taken into account their individual personalities. Now that I've gotten to know them, I see where they can excel. Like Marissa, she'd do an outstanding job working for the Division. Tevin? He would have been terrible at it.

"Brazil? Ugh." Alain makes an unhappy noise in his throat. "He's going to hate that. Marching through the jungle to track down some demon killing village pets? It's not the kind of assignment a guy like Patrick is going to enjoy."

"He got pulled onto that detail while I was in Jerusalem." I agree. There are other recruits I would have sent before Patrick, although it's good for him to go. Part of the recruitment process is to try out different jobs within the military structure. As a Fallen, we don't join the military for a few years; we join for life. He has the physical capabilities to complete the mission, and he should at least see what it's like to be a soldier on the ground instead of an IT tech tucked away in a control room. "You're right, I don't think he'll like it, but he'll survive the mission just fine."

"How did you end up the head trainer, by the way? No offense, but you're kind of young, aren't you?" He opens his bag of chips and pops one into his mouth.

"No offense taken." I'm used to this question. I got it a lot when I first ended up at the high school teaching. Even the youngest teachers were older than me at the time. Had I gone into Civil Service, I wouldn't have finished our version of college yet. Personal experience trumps book education in my case. I motion to my face and the scar that runs down the left side. "I took an injury in the battle with Discord and then wasted away in a hospital for enough weeks that they were tired of looking at me. General Keagan, the commander of Orasul and Hope, came and got me. He talked me into the job, telling me they needed someone more relatable to the students. Someone younger. Someone who'd seen battle. I'm with this class until they graduate. Then I can either go back and do it again or I can ask for a different commission."

"First, thank you for your service. I heard that was a hell of a battle." Alain glances at Mia who's shuffling the cards, ready to start. "You think you'll do it? Go back and start again with a new class?"

"I don't know." I shrug and avoid looking at Mia. "I've got a few thoughts about where I'd like to be in a few months, but I have time to decide."

"Enough talking, more playing." Mia interrupts the conversation and starts dealing the cards. "Collin, these are the rules. We play until we're tired or bored with the game. No set number of rounds. After each round, we change partners. Player with the most wins at the end of the night is the winner."

"Do play High and Low, or just straight Euchre?" I pick up my cards and start arranging them in my hand.

"Straight Euchre, always. Do you have room for one more?" A voice behind me sends a cold wash over my body. I dread turning around to confirm what my ears are telling me. This can't possibly be the way my night is going to go.

"Hey, Riley, sure, pull up a chair." Mia collects the card back to deal again. "We can play five handed. Anna working tonight?"

"She's on a plane to Brazil. We got wind of a village there that thinks they have a Curupira on the loose." He moves a chair from another table toward ours. "Discord is being quiet. There's nothing really for me to do but relax tonight."

The chairs all shuffle and Riley, General of the Army, commander of this prison, and stepfather to Marissa, takes a spot between Mia and Alain. No one stands up to salute him; I wonder what proper protocol is. I also wonder if it's appropriate to beat the General at cards.

"Oh." I realize Kurt is looking at me when he speaks up. "I think you're freaking out Collin."

The General turns to me in surprise.

"Relax." Mia shuffles and starts to deal again. "We're all off duty, no one has a rank right now, and Riley sucks at cards. We're just playing for fun."

"Okay…" I shift in my seat. "Am I supposed to salute you or anything? I'm at a loss for protocol at the moment."

Alain snickers and then returns to his chips.

"Notice I'm not in any kind of uniform. I'm off duty. Please don't salute me." The General motions to his off duty civilian clothes. "I live in this bubble and get tired of hearing my rank all the time. I know exactly what my position is, thank you very much. Somedays I like to hear my first name. Please call me Riley."

"Yes, sir." I cringe. I don't know what's making this more uncomfortable, the fact that he's the General asking me to call him by his first name, or the fact that he's Marissa's stepfather and I'm trying very hard tonight not to think about her. "I mean, Riley. This is a little bit uncomfortable. General Keagan is a lot more tied to protocol."

"General Keagan has a stick where it shouldn't be." Riley laughs at his own joke. "In all seriousness, he's a good commander. Just takes himself a little too seriously."

Things I shall never repeat out loud.

"We're a lot more relaxed here." Kurt takes pity on me and explains. "There's a limited number of officers and they're constantly coming and going on missions. We socialize with people we like, regardless of rank, when we're off the clock. If we dig our heels in and refuse to hang out with enlisted or with lower rank officers, we'd spend a lot of time alone."

"And you wouldn't have someone to fix your computer for you when it goes haywire." Alain arranges his cards. "I bid four. For the record, I'm enlisted. I never went to officer's training. Sergent, if it matters to you."

"Captain." I look through my cards. Even if I had a good hand right now, I don't think I could bid. My head is spinning too much. "I went to officer's training right after basic and took a promotion after my injury."

"First Lieutenant, Major, General of the Army." Riley points around the table, ending with himself. "Now that's out of the way, let's play cards."

All things considered, playing cards with Riley turned out to be fun, despite a fair amount of intimidation. Not that he did anything to make me feel anxious other than being in the room. At first, I was worried he'd ask me how Marissa was doing and my energy would get all out of whack and he'd pick up on what Mia already knows. I already feel like a creep for having feelings at all; I don't need her parent to make me feel worse. Or bust my rank. Or, even worse, remove me from my position to get me away from Marissa.

I might not understand how I feel or what I feel or even if I want our relationship to go any farther than friends, but I do know I don't want to lose the opportunity to figure it out.

Riley, it turns out, has a good sense of humor and is an easy guy to get along with. We talk about benign topics. Music. Television. How the next baseball season is going to go. Alain brings up something about the next generation of smart phones; that conversation doesn't go very far. Kurt declares it too much akin to Alain's job and we aren't allowed to talk about work while we're playing cards.

"You got some down time in Jerusalem." Kurt collects the cards for the next deal. "How was it?"

"We were in the Old City. It was quiet. Pretty empty, a little creepy." I glance at the score sheet. I'm down two games from the leader, Mia. Riley, who really is bad at cards, is last. I wonder how long we'll play. It's already past nine. "You've been here longer than me, surely you've had time off there."

"Not really." He shuffles and then starts to deal. "Work kept us busy at first and now it's not exactly the kind of place you want to go on your time off. Too much tension. You get a chance to see anything interesting?"

"The hotel we stayed in was kind of neat. It was an old building, like two-hundred years old, that had been nicely remodeled. To tell you the truth, I'd never stayed in a hotel before. I'm glad Marissa was with me, or I would've been lost." I collect my cards and focus, unhappy with myself for bringing up Marissa. "We ate dinner, and I found an English channel on the television so I watched some show on building houses until I fell asleep. It was uneventful."

"You went to that church." Mia looks at me across the table, raising an eyebrow. "You got to be a tourist for a little bit. And the Division called you in to help with a situation."

"Which is work, and we're not talking about work, right?" I close the topic off as quickly as I can. At some point,

I need to spend some serious time thinking about that little job I did with the Division, but now isn't the time. Not with my boss sitting at the same table as me.

CHAPTER ELEVEN

It's Monday and we're back at the Israeli base, preparing to run the obstacle course again. I'm so grateful their commanders have allowed us the privilege of using their facilities. The space around the prison is too small, too basic, and command lacks the interest in building it up at this time. There is a long-term plan to expand the prison, add more security and facilities for the soldiers stationed there, but that can't happen until the world knows about the prison. Right now, most of the world thinks it's a historic archeological site. If we start adding things like climbing walls and towers, someone is going to notice.

The first order of business it to take an easy warm up run. We'll do six miles through relatively easy terrain to get our cardio up. No weighted backpacks today, just a gentle run. It's a little chilly this morning, maybe seven degrees, but we'll warm up as we run.

It's nice to have an outside trail to run. While we were stationed in Hope, most of the time we were logging our

cardio hours on treadmills in Hope's training facilities. A few runners at a time could take a trek through Central Park, but a whole class of recruits? Twenty-three runners, including me, would draw unwanted attention.

Personally, I hate using treadmills. I would use my time off to take the subway to the park where I'd run the six-mile loop around the park on the paved drives. On nice days, I'd double it. I don't claim to be a runner, but jogging the path keeps me in shape and it's something I can do alone. Aside from the times lately when I've spotted Marissa, she has kept her promise and called me when she wants on the balance beams, I prefer to work out alone. I like the quiet.

But here? The sky is beautiful, the scenery inspiring, and the trail just long enough to get us started for the day.

The voice inside my head reminds me I can run this track indefinitely if I want to take the job offer. It's another point to put in the plus column.

I wonder if Marissa has thought about the job. Maybe I should ask her.

No, I shouldn't. I don't want to persuade her one way or the other. At the end of her recruitment, she'll apply for the position she wants and either she'll get it, or she won't. She has months before it's time to make that final decision.

Maybe she won't want to work for the Division. Maybe she'll want to work for her mom's unit, tracking down creatures in the jungles.

But she said she liked the Division, that working in an environment like that is appealing.

And besides, we were both offered the job. That means we should talk about it.

In addition, I'm her trainer. It's my job to help guide her toward the end of basic training. It's something I would do with any of the recruits.

"Collin, are we going to run, or just stand here?" Mia, who asked to come along on this training session, interrupts my thoughts.

Today, we're running in civilian clothes. She's standing there in running pants, a long sleeve shirt, and tennis shoes, staring at me like she'd said my name several times before she got my attention. I look past her at the rest of the class, and I notice they're all looking at me, too. Maybe she has been trying to get my attention.

"Sorry, running today's schedule in my head." Although I'm already stretched out and ready, I do one more standing quad stretch on each leg, mostly to buy myself time and get my head on straight.

"No worries, I think the class would like to get going, that's all." She rolls her neck and waits.

"Tasha, take lead, I'll bring up the back. Steady jog, we're running to get warmed up, not running for time." I give the lead out to our class leader. She replies with a solid nod and motions for the class to follow her onto the trail.

Mia falls in toward the middle of the pack and Marissa paces herself next to me at the rear.

"Are you okay?" We'll get winded soon enough, but right now she's got enough in her to ask a question.

"Just thinking." Tasha is taking the group easy, like I said. We gently move past a line of olive trees and down a sandy road. Before we reach a mile, the running trail will turn right, away from the road. We'll pass the Israeli barracks, a few other buildings, and then we'll be away from any kind of buildings for the rest of the run. It's a peaceful trail.

"Thinking about that job offer?" She keeps her voice down, understanding I probably don't want the other recruits to know about that. "Me, too."

"Yeah?" I hazard a glance her way. She's jogging even stride with me, her eyes forward on the ground or on the runner in front of her. I can't tell if she's avoiding eye contact with me or not; I return my focus forward, too. The last thing I need to do is take a fall.

"Yeah." She's quiet for a while, until we turn off the main road. "I know we're on duty tonight, but I was hoping… maybe we could talk about it afterwards? I need to talk it out and I don't feel like I should be doing that with Jenn. I mean, here I am playing catch up after what happened, and I'm the one with the offer. I would feel more comfortable talking to you."

Well, that answers that. Marissa wants to talk about the job offer. What she doesn't know is that Benjamin texted me early this morning. He wants to know if we can come back and have a couple more meet and greets with the locals. I haven't run it by command yet, but I can't see a reason they'll say no.

"Sure. We can cut out some time after duty." I wonder where we'll go. The common room is crowded most nights and there's no coffee shop.

"Thanks." I expect her to pull ahead of me in line, but she doesn't. She keeps pace next to me like we're on this jog together without the rest of the class. We're coming up on the incline of a hill so we can't keep talking; we'll need our full attention to push up the hill. I'm okay with that. I have to sort out my own thoughts about the Jerusalem Division before we talk tonight.

Over an hour later, we complete our jog at the obstacle course. Tasha had kept a solid pace throughout the track, neither slowing down nor speeding up. This is one of the reasons I like having her lead, she's steady and strong, mindful of the ability level of everyone in her unit. Tevin would have pushed the group harder, set a faster pace, and left behind the slower runners.

In retrospect, he may have had the top marks in class, but he wasn't a good leader. In truth, he was a bit of a bully.

"That's not a nice thing to say about a guy who can't defend himself." Tevin's ghost appears beside me, walking with me as I count to make sure we didn't lose any runners. I ignore him.

"Take fifteen minutes." I step away from Marissa to walk among the recruits, and Tevin follows. "Stretch out, catch your breath. Marissa will run the course twice because she needs to make up times from her absence. The rest of you will run it once. If you don't like your score, you can go a second time and I'll take the best score of the day."

"Generous." He's still talking. "Are you sure you want someone at your back that had to run an obstacle course twice to get a good score? I mean, really, how hard is it?"

I breathe in through my nose and start on my own after-running stretches. I don't know what triggers Tevin's memory, but it's consistent. Whenever I'm out here on the course, or working in the prison, he seems to appear. I'm sure my subconscious is trying to tell me something and I wish it would get it over with so I can move on.

At first, I wanted to argue with the ghost. I realized quickly that would land me in a hospital bed across the hall from Marissa's. Ghosts aren't real. Talking to Tevin is talking to myself, which would likely put me on a psych hold. So, I bite my tongue and do my best to ignore him.

"I bet I can run the course faster than you." Another voice, this time female, interrupts my thoughts.

Mia is strolling in my direction.

"Really?" I like a challenge. Well, a challenge that doesn't come from a figment of my imagination that manifests in the shape of a dead student. "When was the last time you ran one of these?"

"It's been a hot minute." She admits, her eyes scanning the course. "General Riley doesn't take training the warrior-scribe-monk as seriously as I wished he would. He tends to keep me locked up in the vault rather than out here on the training areas."

"We all have a job to do." I would hate spending all my time in the archives, also known as the vault. I prefer spending my time working with people, not scrolls. "We'll run the course last."

"You got it." She holds up her wrist, showing me her watch. "I'll track times for you. Sound good?"

"I appreciate the help." With her assistance, we can speed up the exercise. Grabbing my clipboard from the backpack I'd left on the field before the run, I flip to the page that holds last week's numbers. I raise my voice. "When you're ready, line up. We have a lot of runs to get in today before lunch. Let's get to it."

Marissa's first time isn't anywhere near what it should be. She struggles at the first wall, weeks of sitting in the hospital catching up with her. She might be able to keep up on the jog and gently walk the balance beams, but the strength in her arms is abysmal. Finally giving up, she takes the time deduction and goes around the obstacle. The second wall is a little better because there's a rope to help pull you over. At the end, the time is so slow that I feel bad writing it down on her record.

"I think I need to get into the gym and do some arms." I hear her tell Mia. "That was awful."

"You have a second shot; I'd just pass the wall without trying and take the time deduction. You already know you can't pull yourself over." Mia's advice is sound. This is a time trial, not a final. And on some of the other obstacles she picks up speed. She might not come in dead last if she skips the wall altogether.

Tasha finishes her run next and approaches Marissa. "That was a good try for being down a month. If you want, I can spot you in the gym and help you catch up on your arms. It won't take long to get back into shape."

"Thanks, I might take you up on that." Marissa watches more of her classmates cross the finish line with times well below hers. Finally, she jogs across the yard to the start of the course again, ready to run it again.

On her second run, she does exactly what Mia suggested, she skips both walls in favor of the time deductions. It's a dicey choice that could backfire on her, but then she double times it the rest of the course, sliding across the finish a whole minute under her first time. It's enough to keep her from the bottom, but nowhere near enough for her to retake her spot at the top.

As I watch the other recruits who want a second chance run the course, I wonder if she's even going to make a play for Tasha's position. In theory, she already has a job offer in a field she's interested in. She doesn't need to be at the top of the class to get first pick anymore. She might be perfectly happy spending the next five months in the middle of the pack; she wouldn't have to fight daily, nor would she need to take additional leadership training courses required of the top two recruits.

If she takes the job, that is.

I intend to wait for the recruits to head off to lunch before running the course against Mia; she has other plans. Once the last recruit crosses the finish, she raises her voice to get everyone's attention. "I need a line judge. Your Captain and I are going to run the course against each other. Who wants to call the winner?"

Sixteen hands fly into the air.

Mia picks two, seemingly at random, and places them on either side of the finish line. "What are the rules?"

"Gentleman's rules." One of the recruits' groans in disappointment. "No tripping, pushing, or knocking your opponent off any obstacle. Run your race to the best of your ability and the first to cross the finish line wins."

"Oh, you're not fun." Mia jokingly pouts.

"You're half my body weight; do you seriously want to make this a full body contact contest?" Even if she says yes, there's no way I'm giving in to that. Mia might not be tiny by any stretch of the imagination, but I'm not going to try and pull her off the ropes if she gets there before me. I'm sure the General would kill me if I accidentally hurt her.

"What's the penalty for skipping obstacles?" She taps her finger against her bottom lip like she's thinking, plotting her attack.

"I'm not planning on skipping any obstacles." My eyes narrow as I realize that would be a quick way to get around me if I pulled into the lead. "Are you?"

It takes a while for her to respond, and I realize my instinct is right. She's weighing a possibly penalty against an easy opportunity to take the lead. "No."

"Then no need to discuss a penalty." I shake hands with Mia. "Shall we?"

"I'll time you." Jenn volunteers. "Just for curiosity's sake."

"You want to see how my time compares to the rest of the class." I laugh.

"Maybe." She doesn't bother to look guilty. "Most of us haven't seen you run it before."

"Then go ahead, get your timer ready." I turn with Mia and we walk to the starting line, no rush.

We line up, side by side, at the start. Someone drops their arm to signal a start and we take off down the fifty-yard sprint to the first obstacle, the short wall. I realize halfway there that Mia is playing with me. She's fast. Really fast, especially as a sprinter. While I probably could have caught up to her on obstacles that require brute strength like the rope wall or the rope swing, Mia gets there first. Because of our rules, I can't knock her down or go around her. Had we run the course individually and compared times, I might have won. By running against her, she has a serious mental advantage.

She crosses the finish line fifteen seconds in front of me.

The girls in the class let out a shout and applaud her for her run, by far faster than any of the recruits. My time had been fast, but in line with the rest of the class.

"You set me up." My accusation is good natured and has no hostility. She has an advantage, and she used it. That's what I would have done, too, if I'd been in her shoes.

"I like to win." She lifts a shoulder and lets it drop. "I knew you'd be stronger than me and faster on some of the obstacles. I needed to take my advantage where I could if I was going to win. Nice moves on the balance beams, by the way. Twinkle toes."

I swear, the balance beams are going to be the death of me one day. Attempting to catch up to her, I'd done my best to sprint across them and nearly fell off. I can just imagine myself hitting the ground wrong and breaking my collar bone or displacing my shoulder. Thank goodness I regained my balance and finished. I never would have heard the end of it had I fallen.

"Alright, everyone head to the showers to clean up. I'll meet you in the mess for lunch." The class, including Marissa, takes off at a jog toward the shower house. "I'll show you where the officers shower is. Trust me, you're going to want to use that one."

"Thanks." We both pick up our backpacks with our change of clothes and walk toward the showers. "It felt good to be out here today. Have you liked doing the training thing?"

"It's a great day to be out here." Despite my considerations to change jobs, I *have* enjoyed training the recruits. "It's a fulfilling job. Why do you ask?"

"There's some talk of moving my job around so that I'm teaching more." She wrinkles her nose. "I like my solitude and my books and my scrolls. I used to like going out on missions with Kurt, but that doesn't happen much anymore. Mostly, I like isolation to study. I'm not sure how I feel about having a regular gig in a classroom."

"Is that really the best use of a warrior?" I'm surprised and can't picture her back in Hope or Orasul going to class every day. "I kind of pictured you as an Indiana Jones type of archeologist. I can't see you in one of the cities, you seem to belong in places like this. Where there are mysteries to be discovered."

"That's how I picture myself, too, and I enjoy being out here. But Riley and Maxim think it's a bad idea to have all the warriors stationed in the same place." That makes sense. One well-placed missile attack and it could wipe out the whole order. "They think if Kurt and I go back to the states, we can both train upcoming soldiers and help with the patrols we want to send out into North America. Scrolls and books can be transported. The only thing I won't have ready access to is building inscriptions, but cameras work, and I can always get on a plane to anywhere in the world. I'm just not sure about the teaching thing."

"We're all different, that's something you'll have to work out for yourself." I consider how I got roped into teaching. "I'll tell you, though, I didn't pick this career. I wouldn't have because I was worried the students wouldn't listen to me. We're so close to the same age. General Keagan picked it for me. He basically kicked me out of bed and told me to go be productive. I'm glad he did, I feel like I've done a lot of good here."

"And you met Marissa." Mia gives me the side eye and a smile.

"Not the topic at hand." I dismiss her comment, but in a lot of ways, I'm happy she knows that I'm struggling with that relationship. It means I have at least one person I can talk to. "If you try teaching and you hate it, don't you think the Generals would move you to another position. Do you really think they'd force you to do a job that makes you miserable?"

"That's a good point, I hadn't thought about it that way." We reach the shower house, and she stops outside the women's door. "Thanks for your perspective. See you in the mess?"

"See you in a few." I continue around to the other side of the building, deep in thought. If the command is considering moving Mia and Kurt into training positions, there may not be a need for me at all. The realization takes some weight off my shoulders. If they aren't depending on me, it will be easier to take a different position at the end of this. I can think about what's best for me and not about what's best for the program.

Starting over with a new group of students and recruits isn't necessarily a bad idea, but it doesn't make me feel as excited as working for the Division. And now that opportunity is within reach. Maybe not in the city I want, but it's a step in the right direction. Soon, I'll need to talk to General Riley. But first, I need to talk to Marissa.

CHAPTER TWELVE

Marissa and I agree to meet for duty at her barracks room. I knock on the door thirty minutes before we're supposed to be in the prison proper. I hear a bit of noise and then Jenn's standing at the door, a huge grin on her face. "Hi."

"Hello." An uncomfortable feeling washes over me. Jenn, while always polite and prepared in class, is a party girl. She's the center of the universe for the recruits. You want to know who's interested in whom? Ask Jenn. Looking for a hidden stash of cookies and potato chips from home? Talk to her. Bored and need to get out on your night off duty? Give her a call. And if she looks this excited, something is up.

"Marissa's coming." Her eyes seem to be watching me for some kind of reaction. I don't know what she's looking for; I stand perfectly still and wait. "She went to the gym this afternoon. She might be a little sore."

"Okay." I'm still not sure what kind of reaction she's looking for.

"Move." The door opens wider and Marissa pushes Jenn out of the way. "I've got to get to work."

"Have fun. At work." Jenn exchanges a look with Marissa, the kind of look that females alone are capable of. The ones that contain an entire conversation without saying a word.

I decide it's best to stay oblivious to what is going on and I ignore it. The less questions I ask, the less worried I need to be later. We're in a prison compound. It's not like there are that many ways to get yourself into trouble here unless you're going to try and sneak out. Surely Jenn is smart enough not to do that.

"Are you ready for your first prison detail?" I launch into conversation as Marissa falls into step beside me down the stairs into the belly of the prison.

"I'm a little nervous, after what happened during transport." I should have realized she would equate this assignment to the day Tevin died and Discord escaped. "It seems to me that more seasoned soldiers should be doing this."

"Discord is not going to get out of his cell, I can promise you that." We reach the ground floor, and I open the door. "We learned from our mistakes on that transport; it was a surprise to us that he could get inside your head by talking to you. We thought his powers relied on physical contact. We were wrong. Now, we change out guards daily, no one is with him for too long."

"And you're sure the cell is secure?" She pauses a few steps from the guard check-in window.

"Positive." I pass her and approach the window. The scanner accepts my palm print, the computer welcomes me to Pandora's Box, and the door slides open. "If he could get out, he would have by now. The food here isn't good enough to want to stick around."

Marissa shoots me a wry expression and then offers her own palm print to the computer screen. A moment later, it welcomes her, and she advances through the doorway.

Inside is the headguard for the prison. Ironically, he's never seen Discord, save in pictures and on computer monitors. As a precaution, his position has been kept a complete secret from the demon. This guard can throw the switch and trap anyone in the prison if Discord escapes.

"Weapons?" He glances away from the security screens on his desk. There's no sound, keeping Discord' voice at bay.

Marissa and I both show him the swords we're carrying on our backs. As far as weapons go, they're a little antiquated. The important part is they're defendable. If Discord were to get ahold of one, another soldier could defend themselves and possibly disarm the demon. Guns are strictly prohibited inside the prison. If Discord gets his hands on one of those? You wouldn't stand a chance.

"You have a two-hour patrol window. Set a timer and stick to it. If your relief doesn't arrive, turn around and walk out, locking the doors behind you." He presses another button, and the last door opens in front of us. "Have a good shift."

"Thanks." Marissa and I enter the cell block of the prison and I have to give her serious credit. You'd never know this is her first shift here, her back is straight and tall, her eyes forward, and her body screaming confidence. Many of

her classmates looked terrified the first time they stepped through those doors.

There isn't much going on inside the prison right now. Discord is our only resident and he's deep within the building, the farthest cell from the entrance. Our job for tonight is to allow him into the courtyard for his yard time. Because of his unique demon attributes, he needs moonlight the same way we need sunlight. That, and he needs blood to drink. Human or Fallen blood is his preference. Since his capture, cow's blood has had to do.

I hear the slightest intake of breath from Marissa when we finally exit the hallway and enter the maximum-security wing of the prison. What was once dirt floors and limestone brick walls holding iron bars is now reinforced with steel, bulletproof glass, and bright lighting that simulates sunlight. It's an unbelievable sight to descend into an ancient building only to find a state-of-the-art holding system for the most dangerous creatures to walk the earth.

We head up a short set of stairs to the guard room, a small room located above the cells where we will ultimately be able to watch all the cells at the same time. Two soldiers are sitting inside, playing cards at a small table. They look up as the alarm on their timer goes off.

"You're new." They stand, one with short curly hair noticing Marissa. "Recruit?"

"Yes." Moving to the window, Marissa looks downward. Discord is standing in the center of his cell, hands folded neatly in front of him, waiting. "Does he know it's time to go outside?"

"Probably. He's been quiet since we got here. Maybe you'll get lucky, and he'll keep to himself." The solider glances down at the prison cell. "He's a pain when he gets talkative."

"I'll keep that in mind." She turns away from the window to look at the soldier. "Thanks for the heads up."

"Have a great shift." They both descend the steps and leave maximum security.

"This is it, the great prison." Turning back to the window, she takes in the whole room. Thirteen cells, all built away from a common center like spokes on a wheel. Glass and steel panels can slide into place, allowing the prisoners to access a staircase that leads to a small outdoor courtyard where they can get sunshine or moonlight, and fresh air. This is a new addition, our forebearers didn't see any purpose in allowing the demons outside. Our current leaders feel a more humane system is necessary.

"It is." I walk to the window and stand next to her. Discord is still standing perfectly still, which is unnerving. "Impressive, yes?"

"Yes." Her eyes land on the prisoner again and I wonder what she's feeling. He's the demon that killed Tevin; it must be hard to see him. "When do we take him outside?"

"As soon as you're ready." I don't want to rush her. The moving cells are as safe as they can possibly be; Discord escaping isn't a concern. Him doing a job on her mentally is another matter. "No rush. He's outside for sixty minutes and we're only ten into our shift. We have time."

Her head bobs and I resist the urge to touch her arm. Something in this part of the prison dampens our ability to read energy; I can't get an impression of what she's feeling. If I touch the skin on her arm, I might be able to get an idea. Is this going to break her? Is she strong and angry?

"Let's go." With a quick turn, she's facing me. "He needs his yard time."

"You sure?" I don't know why I ask. I can see that she is.

"Absolutely. I'm ready for this." She waits for me to lead the way. "I need to do this."

"Face him?" I glance back at her over my shoulder.

"Yes."

We step into the central wheel of the prison, coming into Discord' view. His head tilts to the side as he studies us, looking for familiarity. He dismisses me immediately, I'm not new to him. Then, he looks at Marissa and smiles. "It's the girl."

I lock my facial expression down while a chill runs down my spine. He remembers her.

My instinct is to step in front of her, to put a barrier between them besides steel and glass. It's a foolish urge. What am I going to do that our engineers haven't already done?

My instincts aside, Marissa needs to walk through this trial on her own. If she's going to survive in this world, she should know how to face down her enemies. If she can't? Then she should go back to one of our cities and get a job in civil service. This is a tough test, but an important one.

Marissa, for her part, keeps walking with her head held high. She doesn't respond in any way at all, not with her eyes, and not with her voice.

We reach the edge of Discord' cell. Now, she speaks. "Please put your hands in the cube."

Discord watches her with hungry eyes, moving slowly toward the edge of his cell. Once there, he places his hands inside a metal cube that attaches iron cuffs and chains to his wrists. He hisses; the iron burns. "I thought you angels were the good guys. This use of iron is inhumane. It hurts. You should cuff me with steel."

Marissa doesn't react to his suggestion, and neither do I. We stay on task, adjusting the sealed walkway to reach the front of his cell. Once in place, we open the door. "You may go."

I expect a glare or an irritated comment at my dismissal. Instead, Discord straightens his shoulders and steps into the walkway. From here, he'll follow the narrow passage to a set of stairs and then upward to an arched doorway that leads to the outside. Once there, the door will close behind him, locking him into a steel and glass cell similar to the one he lives inside. This one, however, has outside ventilation, giving him the only fresh air he'll ever have access to again.

Marissa and I head up a separate set of stairs into an annex where we will be able to watch Discord. Escape will be almost impossible from the cell; command, however, requires eyes on him twenty-four hours a day. He's already proven himself capable of things we did not expect once, no need to take any chances a second time.

Before he moves too far away from us, Discord stops. "He was delicious, your boyfriend. My last proper meal."

I'm not violent. I have never been violent. I fought when it was necessary, and I train to be disciplined. I've never asked more of my recruits than needed. I never considered fighting someone over a girl or a game or any other reason. I can count the number of battles I've been in on one hand. I am not violent.

But at this moment, I want to rip Discord's heart out through his nose.

Still, Marissa doesn't react except for a barely noticeable stiffening of her muscles.

She waits patiently for him to exit the door into the courtyard and then closes it behind him. Moving forward into the annex, I notice her shoulders relax once Discord is out of sight. Although it's only momentary, it seems to be enough time for her to reset herself.

Once we reach the annex, we can see Discord through the window. Marissa pushes the button for the intercom. "You have one hour. The timer has started."

Discord starts to reply, but she releases the button, making his voice muffled.

I look at her now relaxed body and irritated face, wondering what she's going to do next. "You okay?"

"Yes, I'm okay." The annoyance in her voice matches her face. She looks at me. "He's an ass."

I struggle not to laugh. She's right, of course, although I doubt many people have called him that to his face. He's known for his eloquence and arrogance. Before his capture, he was wealthy and powerful. He liked his extravagances. I'd even heard he had been wearing a $4,000 suit when he was captured and arrested. He'd been so certain his minions would stop the Fallen forces that he hadn't bothered to evacuate the building.

"You know, he can probably hear you." I move my position to get a better look at him below me. He's slowly walking in a circle around the cell, his hands still cuffed in front of him. He doesn't seem to be paying attention to us at all. "His hearing is better than ours."

"I don't care if he can hear me." She crosses her arms over her chest. "He's mean and he's a bully. I understand that he's a super powerful demon that has brought destruction to countless lives. Despite that, he's not worth my time or my thoughts."

"Except that he's your job." I hate to point out the obvious. "You can't exactly forget about him."

"That doesn't mean I have to think about him, either. At least when I'm off duty." Turning her back, she looks around the control room. It's small, filled only with a few screens to help watch the father corners of Discord' outdoor cell, the intercom, two chairs, and a small table. There's an emergency rations footlocker under the table and I can see the door will shut and bolt. It must be built that way in case something goes wrong in the prison.

"That's true about any job." I grab the two chairs and pull them over to the window so we can keep a better eye on Discord. "You have to be able to disconnect when you're not working. Have other interests. You can't let your job define you."

"Do you disconnect from us?" Accepting the chair, she takes a seat backward so she can lean forward onto the back of the chair. Her eyes are focused on Discord. "Do you sometimes forget that you have a unit of recruits waiting for your next command? What do you do for fun?"

This response requires careful consideration. The truth is that for the weeks she was in the hospital, I unplugged from my job by visiting her. Some days sitting in the same room, reading a book while she rested, was enough. More recently, it's about spotting her on the beams so I can catch her if she falls. Isn't that an irony? I decide to go with a mundane answer. "You know I enjoy reading. And Mia invited me to play cards with her and Kurt and a guy from

IT named Alain. This week your stepdad was there, too. Although that was a little intimidating."

"You played cards with Riley?" She giggles. "He doesn't intimidate me because he's my dad, but that must have been terrible for you. Who won?"

"Not him. He's bad at cards." At that, she giggles again. I like the sound of her laughter. "It was fine once I got used to him being there. He was insistent that we all behave like normal people without ranks. I watch old science fiction television shows when I'm in Hope, I love Star Trek reruns. The original series with Captain Kirk. I like jogging to clear my mind. What do you do?"

"The balance beams, but you know that. It's the best way to clear my head." She thinks about her next response. "Kaia and I study. Jenn and I eat popcorn and talk about girl things. I used to spend a lot of time training with Tevin."

Unwilling to touch on that topic, I keep my mouth shut.

Marissa seems to run out of steam. She doesn't say anything else for a long time, maybe half an hour. We sit in silence, watching Discord walk around his cell. Sometimes, he holds his face upward toward the moonlight. It's barely eight o'clock, the sun sets early this time of year.

"Tevin was a jerk."

Her sudden words echo through the silence of the control room making me wonder if she said them out loud or if I'd heard them in the privacy of my own head. I turn my head to look at her.

She's still staring at Discord, her brow furrowed in concentration. "He was a jerk. The more distance I get from the night we brought Discord here, the angrier I get. Tevin was stupid and he was a jerk."

I'm completely thrown off by her statement. She doesn't talk about Tevin, not ever. At least, she hasn't since I started visiting her in the hospital. Nothing more than a passing reference here and there. "He was young, and he did what he thought he had to in order to save the rest of you. That doesn't make him a jerk."

"He was a jerk before Discord. He was a jerk because he didn't care about anything but himself." Marissa stands from her chair and paces around the room, stretching her arms above her head. I hear her back crack in protest. "He had this vision of what life was going to be like and he pushed me to accept it. He didn't care what I thought, or what I wanted. And he hated Aria and Sasha. He couldn't see past the fact they were demons. It didn't matter that they'd both dedicated their lives to making our world better. I like them both. I liked going out with them and spending time with them. It used to make him so mad."

"What did he want?" I ask the question gently, giving her room to talk without pushing too hard.

"He wanted to be on retrieval and kill teams." She returns to her seat and retakes her post. "He wanted to do what Mom is doing right now. Chasing down bad guys who need to be put down or brought to this prison. I don't think that's what I want. I understand that I've never done it, and I have a special gift that would be really useful, but I don't want to hate my job."

"You want to work for the Division." I know it's the truth. She may not realize it yet, but her path is clear to me. "You want to help people and make a positive difference in their lives."

"Yeah." She looks at me. "Tevin used to tell me working for the Division is a waste of talent."

"You're right, Tevin was a jerk." I can see how someone like him would see the Division that way. All your military training put aside, no defined enemy. He would have struggled in that environment. He was hard-wired to be a military specialist, a fighter. Nothing else would have made him satisfied. "Do you ever talk to Jenn and Kaia about him?"

"No." She shakes her head. "It's a forbidden topic. One time, Kaia told me Tevin was selfish. Then, the subject was closed."

I want to tell her that she needs to talk to someone, anyone, but the timer on the wall warns us it's time to bring the prisoner back inside. I figure this is a topic we can pick back up later. "You ready?"

This time, I can see her steel her nerves. She stands evenly between her feet and closes her eyes. I wait while she takes three breaths in through her nose that she slowly releases from her mouth. Her shoulders relax and when she opens her eyes again, she's ready. "Let's go."

Moving Discord back into his cell is uneventful. He doesn't resist and he enters the walkway without complaint. Once he's in his home, he places his hands back in the metal cube. The iron cuffs come off and he sighs with relief.

"I wish there were a way to do that with less pain." He rubs his wrists, red with irritation. "I understand the necessity, but no one seems to believe me when I promise I have no intention of attempting escape."

Neither Marissa nor I respond. We put all our focus in returning the walkway to its original position.

"You can speak to me, you know." Discord approaches the glass closest to us. "It gets lonely here with no one to talk to."

"I have nothing to say to you; you are a killer." Marissa turns to face him. "You can rot in here in silence for all I care."

She turns on her heel, our task finished, toward the guard room.

"You punish me for being what I was created to be." He calls after her, his eyes hungry when he looks at her. "Without darkness there can be no light, only the muddled half-light of twilight. You need me. You need my siblings. Without us, the Fallen are useless remnants of the bygone age of gods that have left us here to decay. Without me, you are useless."

She stops with one foot on the steps to the guard room, considering his words. Then she keeps walking away.

CHAPTER THIRTEEN

When our shift is over, Marissa and I head over to the common room to relax and talk, but we find it crowded. Discussing job options in a room full of other soldiers and recruits who might also be vying for the same job doesn't seem like a smart idea. I don't have an office in the prison and the classroom feels big and cold for this conversation.

"Do you care to come to my barracks?" I'm lucky, I have a private room, unlike Marissa who shares with Kaia and Jenn. "It's not big, but it's private."

"That's fine, if you don't mind me in your space." She looks a little hesitant, something I can only guess is because the last time she was in a male's room, it was probably Tevin's. But she doesn't think about me like that, so this shouldn't be a problem.

"It doesn't bother me. If it did, I wouldn't have offered." I lead her down the residential hallway until we stop at my door. I open it and gesture her in. "It's hard to find privacy in this prison."

My room is small, only meant for one person. I have a twin bed against one wall, but no bunk. A footlocker is at the foot of the bed and a desk with one chair is against the opposite wall. I do have a private bathroom, tiny though it may be, and I often wonder how the engineers ran water pipes through the ancient building.

Marissa looks around the room, takes off her sword and lays it on the desk, and then claims the bed. She positions herself so her back leans against the wall. I glance at her sitting there on the plain, gray blanket, and I wonder if it's going to smell like her when I try to sleep tonight. I push the thought away and take off my own sword to hang on the hook on my wall.

I consider taking my shoes off, but I don't want to freak her out by getting too comfortable. Instead, I grab the desk chair, spin it around, and sit down facing her. "Do you want to start?"

She looks at me, an odd expression on her face, and seems to reach for words. I try not to frown at her. It's not like Marissa to be at a loss for words. She always speaks her mind when she's ready and she's never been shy about telling me what's going on in her head.

"Can you sit next to me?" She finally seems to reach what's bothering her. "I went to the gym and overdid it before duty. My arms are killing me, and I could use a little borrowed energy."

"Sure." My body is moving to take the spot on the bed next to her before I have time to think about why this might be a bad idea. At least for me. To her, I'm just a friend she can depend on; one who can help her with my energy to help her heal. I settle in place, my back against the wall, my bicep touching hers to help with the transfer. There may be two layers of fabric between us; goosebumps still threaten. I swallow the feeling. I cannot be attracted to her like this. "Better?"

"Much, thank you." She slides over a little closer, so her hip touches mine, too. I pray to God that she isn't paying enough attention to realize how much my heart just sped up. "I want to know what you think. About the job."

I'd put some consideration in over dinner, now knowing what Mia told me about changes to the training program that might be in the works. If command doesn't need me, if my current job is going away, that makes this choice easy if I'm the only one to consider. Can I work in the prison? Yes. Do I want to? No. Same is true for the seek and capture teams. I'd like to be stationed in Hope; that job isn't available. Which leaves me with Jerusalem.

"I haven't talked to command at all yet. I don't know what they'll ask of me, and that could change my mind. But right now? The Jerusalem job seems like the best option for me." Beside me, Marissa nods her head. I hurry through the next part. "That doesn't mean it's the best choice for you. You shouldn't make your decision based on mine."

"I won't." Marissa's body remains completely relaxed. "There are some patrols I haven't gone out on yet. I might love hunting in the jungle with Mom's unit. I doubt it, but it's possible. I know I didn't love today's work. I can deal with Discord if I have to; I'd rather not. It's not even the Tevin thing that bothers me about him. It's that he's unredeemable. His purpose is purely to cause trouble wherever he goes. I want to make a positive difference somewhere. That's not here."

"Your logic makes sense." I can feel warmth seeping from my body into hers as her muscles heal. I wonder how much damage she did and how she managed her whole shift at the prison without letting me realize the pain she was in. "What drives you is making a difference. You want to touch lives in a positive way."

"Yes." She turns her head to look at me, making me appreciate how close we're sitting. I've never kissed anyone before. The thought grabs hold of my throat until I can't think of anything else until she turns her head away again. "It's possible I don't score high enough to pick my job. Maybe they'll just assign me where they want me, and this conversation is a waste of time."

"Don't worry about your scores." I can't tell her, but she's far above most of her classmates. She'd worked incredibly hard while in Orasul and Hope. Losing a month here in Jerusalem had put her behind, but not so far that she couldn't catch up. "Keep studying with Kaia when she gets back from Brazil, keep working out, and don't give up. Besides, you have a job offer. That's different than putting in a request for a position."

"Really?" She sounds shocked. "I can just accept the job in Jerusalem if I want and command has to approve it?"

"It's not quite that simple, but yes. If you have a job offer, all that needs to happen is that command approve it." I finally can't stand it anymore. I lean forward and pull off my shoes. Combat boots, while a great protection for your feet, are solid. There's no air circulation and my feet get hot inside them. "Sorry. I can't wait to take my shoes off when I get home. But back to the job; your situation is less complicated than mine. You're a recruit entering the military structure. You're not leaving a job behind."

She considers this for a while and then looks at me, alarmed. "Wait. You're saying they could tell you no."

"That's exactly what I'm saying. All I can do it put in for a position transfer." I try to explain to her the finer details of military placement. "Technically, my current contract is up at the end of your basic training – a little less than five months from now. At that point, I can renew, which means I go back and start over with a new class of students, or I can request a transfer to another department. To get a job in that new department, there must be an opening and both commanders must agree to the transfer."

"Just because Benjamin wants you to join his staff, it's not enough. General Keagan has to agree to let you go." I can hear the understanding in her voice.

"Technically, it's General Riley that I'm under now, he's the one who will have to agree to the transfer." Shoes off, I settle back against the wall, arm to arm with Marissa. "I reassigned to his unit when we moved from Hope to Jerusalem. But, yes, Keagan could also request my return. Like I said, it's not that simple."

"They could force you to do a job you don't want to do?" She makes a noise in her throat. "That doesn't seem right."

"Army Basics 101. We belong to them." Her disappointment is palpable. "I know it's a bit upsetting, but that doesn't mean the answer is no. It only means I have to make my case. It does help that Benjamin is asking for me specifically, and I understand there are other options for teachers. My point is you can't make your future choices based on what you think I'm going to do. If you want the job with Jerusalem's Division, go for it."

"But I like working with you." She picks imaginary lint off her pants. "I don't want that to stop in five months. You were the best teacher I ever had in school, and you've been an amazing trainer. And now that we're friends, I like that, too."

"We might work in different places, but that doesn't mean we can't be friends." I consider my apartment back in New York. Would I be happy there if Marissa were still here? Then I think of my office in Orasul. How would it feel to be back there? Has someone else been using it while I've been gone? It's almost been a year since I left it behind. "We're not a matched pair, Marissa. I know you're thinking about Tevin and his plans. You were as close to a matched pair as anyone in the program. You worked better together than apart. Chances are, you would have been assigned together. Fallen always work in pairs. Even if it's not me, you'll have a partner."

"What if it's someone like Kaia? Collin, I can't imagine working with her for the rest of my life." Her body gives a little shudder. "Ugh."

"I think you like Kaia more than you're letting on." I can feel her energy has stabilized; I should move to the chair. I don't. I like the feel of her arm next to mine. "You haven't missed a single tutoring appointment until she got pulled for patrol in Brazil. I'll bet you don't miss any once she's back, either."

"I need help catching up, that's all." I don't have to look at her to know she's grinning.

"You're a terrible liar, you know that, right?" Even though we're arm to arm, I bump her with my shoulder, making her laugh.

"Okay, she's gotten so much better since high school." Marissa begrudgingly admits. "It's easier to see around the chip on her shoulder and get to the real stuff. Part of me understands her true problem. We don't talk about it, or anything like that, but I get her better now and that makes it easier to ignore it when she gets an attitude."

"And what's her real problem?" I have my own opinions but I'm curious what Marissa thinks.

She replies right away. "She misses her mom. It's hard growing up without one. And I think she worries she isn't making her dad proud, too, but I think we all worry about that."

Kaia's mom had been killed in action when she was only five, the same age Marissa had been when she lost her real parents. The difference is that Marissa was then raised by her aunt Anna, who became a mom to her. Kaia had been raised by her single father. Tevin's mom had included her in their family, but it wasn't the same as growing up with a mom in the same apartment.

A lot of Fallen, especially the military families, have missing parents. For me, it was my dad. He'd been around most of my life, but when I was fifteen, just before I had to make a choice between military and civil service, he got sick and died. None of the medics or nurses could figure out what was wrong. They finally decided he must have been infected with something while he was on patrol in the city. It's rare, but there are a few demons who possess a natural poison in their bloodstream. It's not normally deadly to Fallen, but it can make them very sick. The medics decided that must have been what killed my dad.

I don't know what it's like to come home from school one day and find out your parent has been killed. I do know what it's like to watch a parent slowly waste away. It's horrible, but at least I had my chance to say my goodbyes.

My mom, for her part, kept things together like a champion. She made me go to school and sat by my dad's bedside until the end. Then, she picked her life back up and went to work as a civil servant after resigning from the army. Even though I was almost an adult by then, she didn't want to leave me without any parents. She supported me through my hospital stay and keeps an eye on my apartment now that I've been stationed in Jerusalem.

To me, she's basically a superhero.

"I think you're right. I miss my mom, too, and she's alive and working in Hope." I agree.

"You lost your dad, right?" I'm surprised Marissa remembers. I think I mentioned it once in class months ago. It doesn't seem like the kind of information that would stick. Or matter, for that point.

"Yes. When I was fifteen." I open up a little more. This conversation is supposed to be about future jobs, but somehow, it's become very personal. "My family was all military then. Now, Mom works a civil service job for command. It's a good way to retire from the army without actually retiring from the army. She's very supportive."

"And she lives in Hope?"

"That's part of the reason I'd like an assignment there, eventually." I'd asked her once if she wanted to move out of the city, maybe back to Orasul, where life is slower. She laughed and told me she enjoyed the city and didn't need life to be slower. "Aside from that, I like New York. I like the people and that you have so many cultures just a subway ticket away. It's like the whole city is a force of

nature. And I really like the way Aria runs her Division. It's a good department with good people that are doing excellent work."

"But that job's not available right now." Marissa rests her head back on the wall. "You'll take Jerusalem if Riley will approve it, won't you?"

"Probably." I change my tone to the best "stern teacher" tone I can muster. "But that stays between you and me. None of the other recruits can know. Or your parents. I'll talk to the General when I'm ready. Until then, this is a private matter."

"I get it. I don't tell them everything. I haven't told them about the job offer at all. I wanted to be sure it was something I wanted first." Her phone buzzes and she reaches into her pocket to pull it out.

"And do you want it?" I let the question out before she has the chance to look at her phone.

"Yeah, I think I do." She sighs, releasing her worries. "When I talk to Riley about it, I won't mention that you got the same offer. And I won't talk to him until after I do my patrol with Mom's team. Just to make sure there isn't something amazing about hunting killer demons I'm missing."

I smile. There's no way Marissa is going to want a job sleeping in the jungle or on the side of a mountain while tracking Kinderfresser or some other child eating demon. "That sounds like a plan."

She reads her text. "Jenn's looking for me. I gotta go."

I expect her to jump up from the bed and head for the door. Instead, she reaches across her body with her free hand and gently grabs my arm. I look at her in surprise.

"Thank you for being a good friend." Her eyes hold onto mine. "I lost myself for a while. I knew it the night we went into the sewers, the night Amy died. I'd become a person doing things that I didn't even want to do just to keep things with Tevin okay. I didn't know how to fix it. And now I'm starting to feel like myself again; I'm making decisions based on what I want and not what he wants. You've been so supportive through all of this, and you've shown me how strong I can be. So, thank you."

I open my mouth, not sure what to say. Marissa saves me the trouble. She jumps up from the bed and leaves without looking back at me.

As the door shuts behind her, I stretch out on my bed, staring at the ceiling.

I like her. A lot.

There's a chance we won't get assigned to the same place in five months.

Right now, I'm her superior. She's off limits.

We're friends.

She was friends with Nick, look how that turned out. She might not like me the same way.

I think about the way she touched my hand at the Church and the way she held my arm just now. She must feel something. She doesn't act that way with anyone else.

Then I remember I didn't tell her about this Saturday's patrol. We'll be going back into the city to meet with another family for Benjamin. "Crap."

I consider texting her, then decide that would be foolish. She literally left this room a few minutes ago. She's probably not even back to her own room yet.

Then I figure, who cares. I grab my phone and shoot off the text. "Saturday's assignment back in Jerusalem. Civ

clothes appropriate – less intimidating. We leave in AM, no overnight."

Immediately, I receive a response. "Awesome."

CHAPTER FOURTEEN

Marissa and I patrol the prison again on Thursday evening. This time, we're kept well away from Discord's cell. Instead, we check the perimeter to make sure the fences are intact. With two rows of perimeter fences, this takes up most of our time, leaving us just thirty minutes to visit the control room.

The prison's control room is state of the art. Whichever entities, Fallen, American, or Israeli, paid for the technology spared no expense. The video screens are crystal clear and intercoms throughout the prison can pick up conversations or dictate instructions in case of an emergency. Bulletproof glass is everywhere and, like the guard room in the maximum-security wing, the room holds reserve rations and water in case of a situation in which the prison is forced to go into emergency shutdown.

As we finish up our shift with a tour of the control room, Alain is admitted through the locked doors. He's carrying a bag of tools and looks ready to work.

"Collin, good to see you." He pauses to shake my hand.

"Alain, likewise." I return his greeting and introduce Marissa. "This is Marissa, Mia's niece. We're just finishing up our shift."

He holds his bag up to show us. "Working on the com system. You playing cards on Saturday?"

"I'd love to If I'm back." I hadn't seen Mia in a couple of days. I wasn't sure if the card games were a regular thing or if I'd be invited again. "I'm on duty in Jerusalem for part of the day. I'll let you know?"

"Send us a text if you're going to make it." He keeps moving toward the control panels. "It's not often we get to play two weeks in a row. Usually, Mia and Kurt are out on some kind of mission. They started the game; we only play when they're in town."

"I'll do my best to make it. See you later." I enter my thumb print into the scanner and the exit door clicks open. We make our way back to the main entrance of the prison to clock out.

Once outside the main gate, a feeling of relief washes over me. Like Marissa, I'm not a fan of this job. Inside the prison is the feeling of oppression and barely maintained control. I trust the protocols and technology; I trust the engineers who reinforced the cells. Yet, there's a feeling of unease that permeates the facility thanks to the power of the demon held inside. I wonder if it will get worse when we capture his brothers and place them within their own cells. I hope I'm not here to see it.

"I know this is part of my training, but I'll be happy when it's over." Her body shudders as she releases some of her tension. I have an urge to squeeze her shoulders, instead I stretch my own arms as a distraction. Then she rolls her neck and I hear a crack.

"That didn't sound good." I wince. In truth, it sounded painful.

"Just tension. Too much bookwork today and not enough time to get outside and exercise." She looks at her phone. "Sun's going down, it's too late now. I hope I have time tomorrow afternoon when tutoring is done. Kaia will be back and I'm sure she'll keep me busy in the evening."

Fridays are days dedicated to practicing gifts. Because no one else can do what Marissa can do, levitate objects, she gets passed from one tutor to another.

"Who are you with tomorrow?" Our internal pressure released, we start the short walk back to our barracks rooms.

"Actually, I'm with Riley." She grins. "He's always been the best teacher. When I was still in high school, he'd work with me at home, which would make Mom mad because we'd end up breaking things."

I smile. It's odd, thinking about the commanders in such a domestic way. It's hard to picture that they had an apartment with lamps that could get broken and a fifteen-year-old daughter just learning her skills.

"How's the work going?" I haven't been to one of her sessions since Hope and tomorrow my schedule is full. "I won't be in to check on you again until next week. Making progress?"

"Oh, yeah." She stops in the hallway and turns to look at me, a bright excitement in her eyes. "The stay in the hospital didn't slow me down at all. I can move almost anything small; I have enough control to move a glass of water without spilling it. If it's less than, say, ten pounds, it's not a problem. Now we're working on larger items. And myself. I'm trying to see if I can make myself float above the ground."

"That would be impressive and take an immense amount of power and control." I can't begin to imagine how much internal strength it would take to levitate a human body. Marissa probably weighs one-thirty. Although I'd say one-twenty if asked out loud. It's a lot of body mass to move. "Any luck so far?"

"Not yet, but I'm not giving up. Last week's teacher said that if I'm going to do it, the best opportunity is now because I'll be my strongest at the end of basic with all the workouts and obstacle courses and cardio you have us do. I'm really pushing myself." Turning toward the barracks, she starts walking again.

"I'm looking forward to the next time I visit one of your sessions." At the other end of the prison, the mess is open for the evening. Fallen are making their way to dinner, my stomach reminding me I skipped lunch today. My doorway comes into view at the end of the hallway. "Good job today. I'll see you Saturday morning?"

"There's something else." Now, she looks unsure of something, and I wonder what's up. "I know it's dinner time, but Kaia has been out all week and I need to catch up on the tests I missed. I think I can be ready to take the first test I missed in Jungle Tactics if you can help me a little bit tonight after dinner. Can you help me study?"

Okay, not what I expected. "I'm the one who grades the test, I don't know if that would be appropriate."

"Please?" She pleads, her eyes begging mine. "I really want to get that work caught up and Jenn's awful to study with. Kaia's good, but she won't be back until tomorrow, and then we're back on duty. And you might be the one who grades the test, but you also teach us every week. Just pretend we're in class and I'm asking questions."

I know this is a bad idea. Every time I spend time with Marissa, my confused feelings get more confused. Which is really bad because she's still off limits. Plus, she's probably still grieving for Tevin. She just went through a major traumatic experience and lost two of her best friends, Amy and Nick. She's still under my command. I'm not even sure how I feel about both of us taking the Jerusalem job together because what if she finds someone else? It would be like Natasha all over again.

"Let me eat dinner first." I look at the time and do some calculations in my head. "Meet me back here in ninety minutes."

"Thank you!" A look of relief floods her face, and I wonder if it's because she wants the help so badly, or if it's because I'm letting her come back here to spend more time together. I wish, not for the first time, that I was better at reading females. "Have a good dinner. I'll see you later."

She all but skips down the hallway toward her own room.

"What was that about?" Mia is approaching from the other direction. "Did she move back ahead of Kaia in ranking again?"

"No, I told her I'd meet her later to study. She really wants to get caught up." I use my key and open my door.

"What class?" Mia follows me but stops in the doorway before she enters my space. Leaning on the doorjamb, she watches me hang my weapons up for the evening.

"Jungle Tactics. She missed two tests, and she wants to make the first one up next week." I'm considering changing into more comfortable civilian clothes when I hear Mia snort.

"She's not that excited about Jungle Tactics." Mia's wry tone is almost enough to make me blush. "She's got a crush on you. And...gee, I'm pretty sure you have a crush on her. Convenient."

"Back off and please don't try to play matchmaker." I decide to pass on changing clothes. If I have time, I'll change after dinner. "She'd been seeing Tevin for a long time. Months. And it's not like they broke up. He was killed in action. She needs time."

"You right." Crossing her arms over her chest, she gives me a hard look. "But don't wait too long. In five months, you'll be heading different directions if you're not careful."

I think about Jerusalem. "It will work out."

"I hope so." She backs out of the room and points toward the mess. "Let's grab some food, I'm starving."

"Me, too. Skipped lunch." We match each other's stride down the hallway. "I haven't seen you around the last few days, where've you been?"

"Quick trip to Les Gens. I wanted to observe their training program."

"Did you see Nick? How's he doing?" I know he isn't my responsibility anymore, but I feel for the guy. He was collateral damage to Tevin's arrogance. All Nick did was fall for the wrong girl and then he lost his friends, his unit, and ultimately, he gave up his job to start over in a new city.

"He's good. I checked in on him; it wasn't weird or anything because he'd been around the apartment when he was still in high school, so we know each other." Mia pulls open the door to the mess and gestures for me enter. "He's made friends and is settling into the new training program. He lost a couple of weeks by making the transfer, but he seems to like his new home."

"I'm glad to hear that." And, truly, I am.

My study session with Marissa was uneventful, other than we got off topic and talked more about the things we miss about New York than anything else. She understands most of the material and shouldn't have any problem passing the first of the two tests she missed. I get the feeling her need for tutoring is a bit exaggerated, which is fine with me. I enjoyed having the evening with her. There, I said it.

Friday is filled with book classes in the morning and study of born gifts in the afternoon. I check in on a third of the class to make sure they're making progress as their tutors see fit, then I have the rest of the afternoon and evening off. Kaia is back; I don't expect Marissa to want to study again. Instead, I head outside for a run.

I stop when I see Kurt setting up archery equipment on the flattest part of the grounds. Nearby, some of the human enlisted who help guard the complex are watching with curiosity.

"Target practice?" I approach him carefully so that I don't startle him. The last thing I want is to be the cause of someone going to the hospital wing with an arrow through their shoulder.

"That's the plan." He arranges several bows and buckets of bolts. "Some of the other enlisted are coming out to work on accuracy. We get stuck here for too long without using our skills and we get sloppy. Care to join us?"

"Absolutely. I haven't had a chance to practice archery since I left Orasul almost a year ago." His words float back through my head. "You said stuck here. Does that mean some of the staff are unhappy with their jobs?"

"Maybe stuck isn't the right word." The targets are large. I help him carry each one out seventy meters. "Stationed? We aren't out hunting every night unless we get pulled away on one of Anna's teams. The local Division isn't open enough to ask us for help yet, and with the fighting to the south, we can't get real R and R, either. I put together some friendly little competitions to keep up our skills and to kill some boredom."

I don't mention my assignment for tomorrow; the local Division is willing to ask for help, just not help in the manner of a whole company of Fallen.

"I guess some of you have been here a while." I try to do the math backwards in my head. How long has the prison been here? We just moved Discord, so it couldn't have been that long.

"A couple of years." Walking back to the buckets of bolts, we grab another target to place. "We're close enough to Jerusalem that day trips helped until the war started. Now, we're more or less stuck here. Command doesn't approve trips into the city unless it's on official business. Safety concerns. You can only play so many rounds of cards before you feel like you're going stir crazy. That's why there's always plenty of soldiers volunteering for Anna's missions. It's not fun to track a demon in the jungle or the desert, but at least it's a change of scenery."

"Command really doesn't approve visits into Jerusalem?" I'm honestly surprised. Why would they allow Marissa and I to go?

"Nope, not since October." Kurt looks at me over the target. "I hear you're heading back tomorrow. Official Division business. You're lucky."

"Marissa and I helped them out with a situation when she was doing her Division meet and greet last week. My understanding is that we're doing something of a follow up on that circumstance." I don't add that I bet Benjamin is also going to continue to try and woo us to work for him. As far as I know, he hasn't filed any official paperwork with the Fallen army yet requesting two Fallen to take positions within his Division. I'm sure I would have heard about it, especially if he includes our names on the request.

"Man, I wish I could tag along on that gig." After placing the last of the targets, we pick up bows and start testing their bowstrings. "Hey, and while you're there, if you have a chance to pick me up some cola, I would be extremely grateful. My supply is almost out."

"Be happy to if we have a chance to stop at a store." I look at the targets and wonder if I'm even going to be able to hit one. Archery isn't my best sport, and these targets are Olympic distance away. "Is there a prize for this, or just bragging rights?"

"I secured two four-day passes to Paris." He nocks his arrow and lets it fly. I watch it land and realize hitting the target will not be a problem for him. "It gives the winner two travel days and two days to relax. It requires a flight out of Tel Aviv, which isn't any safer than Jerusalem, but it's the only way out of the country unless you want to drive. And those aren't borders anyone wants to cross right now."

"That's true." The doors behind me open and a few enlisted come walking toward us. A couple are carrying their own bows. "Looks like you've got some takers."

"I always have takers. Especially when R and R passes are up for grabs."

Security for Benjamin's building is even more impressive on Saturday than it was the last time we visited. There are more armed guards and more questions at the check-in desk before we're given our visitor badges.

Benjamin is apologetic when he meets us in the waiting area. "I'm sorry, there's a threat of terrorist activity today, so security is a little amplified. Thank you for coming despite that, I appreciate your assistance."

"You were a little vague about what you needed. Can you explain in more detail, other than its another meeting with some of the locals?" We follow him into the conference room where he shuts the door behind him.

Constance is already at the table, flipping through pages in a folder. She smiles and stands, shaking Marissa's hand and nodding toward me. "Thank you for coming back, you made quite the impression on my sister and her family."

"I'm glad we were able to help." Marissa takes one of the seats and spins to face Constance. "What more can we do to assist?"

Listening to Marissa talk, I'm impressed by her professionalism. You'd think she was a seasoned officer and not a recruit with the rank of Private First Class. She can't even qualify to move up to Corporal until she graduates from basic.

"We've secured a location for the afternoon. A few other demons would like to talk to you, to hear what you have to say. They're unwilling to show you where they live so we'll be on neutral ground." Here, he hesitates, which makes me nervous. There's something about this conversation that's more complicated. "There will be several families, and I don't think any of them are dangerous. But, between the number of demons who want to talk to you, and the concern for terrorist activity today, we're going to be armed. We don't like doing that when working with the locals, it sends the wrong message, however, today seems like an exception to the rule."

"How many demons are we talking about? I've read the travel ban, I understand the concern for a human attack in the city, but you're being extremely cautious." I glance at Marissa and wonder if I should order her to stay in the precinct. No, I can't. She wants this job. We need to be realistic about the dangers.

"A few." Constance closes her folder. "I don't know exactly who is going to show up. We extended the offer to all concerned members of the community, so I can't give you background on any individuals. We'll be going in a little blind."

"Okay." Marissa looks toward me, questions in her eyes. She recognizes this is sketchy, especially when we can't carry any weapons as visitors.

I think of the Beretta locked in my gun cabinet back in Hope. I rarely carry it, but a big part of me wishes I had it now.

"Your safety is our first concern. We won't let anything happen." Benjamin does his best to assure us. "But, if you're ready, we need to get moving."

We're loaded into a car and driven across town to a nondescript building in a residential area. There are several cars parked in the small lot to the left of the building. Trees and a couple of picnic tables fill the small front yard. Benjamin leads us inside and I realize we must be in a school. Classrooms are positioned to the left and the right of the main hallway, lockers line the walls. He takes us to a set of double doors where Simeon is waiting for us.

He looks troubled.

Benjamin takes in his expression. "What's wrong?"

"Nothing wrong, just unexpected." He shoves his hands into his pockets. "We have a few more demons here than we expected."

"How many more?" Already wary of being pulled into a large group of unknown demons, now my internal alarms are really going off. I don't think all demons are bad. Aria is a great example of a good person and a great police officer who just happens to have some demon DNA. I've met plenty like her in New York and here in Jerusalem, I've met Constance, her sister, and Matthew. All good people. But a group of unknowns? Yeah, I'm a little nervous.

"You need to see for yourself." Simeon pushes the door open and motions us to come inside.

The room we walk into is a gym with bleachers on both sides. One side of the room is almost completely full of demons of various species, all of them talking amongst themselves. There must be over a hundred of them in the room.

I force myself to not reach for a weapon that isn't there.

Marissa's eyes scan the crowd, her jaw slightly slack.

"Some of them came from hours away to hear what you have to say." Simeon whispers to me. "I'm sorry, we expected maybe fifteen. We were going to use one of the classrooms."

"It's okay, we'll figure it out." I look at Marissa. "I hope you're comfortable talking in front of a large group."

"I guess I'm going to have to be."

CHAPTER FIFTEEN

I'm not sure what I expected when Benjamin called me. Maybe another single-family meeting like we'd had with Constance's sister. I had not expected this. What had to be the entire population of demons in the Jerusalem area sat in the bleachers in front of me.

"Some of them drove overnight to get here." Simeon's voice is low. "Most of them are scared. They want to hear what you have to say about going public and about persecution of their kind. They're afraid humans and Fallen will join forces to eradicate their species from the planet; or that Pandora's Box will be used to contain them all. They need to be reassured."

"Okay, let me think for a minute." I look at Marissa, not sure what to do next.

"We can do this." Her eyes are taking in the group in front of us, moving from one to another. There are females and males, some appear human, others don't. "We can do this."

"We're not official representatives of the Fallen." I rack my brain, trying to decide what we can say. It's one thing to extend a hand of friendship to a single family. We're in a whole different world giving reassurance to a community. The realization that I need further permission hits me. I touch Marissa's shoulder. "Can you call the General?"

"What?" Confusion clouds her expression. "Why?"

"Because I bet you have a direct line to his cell phone. I'll have to go through channels. Something of this size is outside my authorization. I need an okay before we can continue." I turn to Simeon. "I need a few minutes to confer with my superiors. I'm sure we'll be okay, but I can't speak on behalf of Pandora's Box or anyone else without permission."

"I understand. We should have given you a heads up when we realized how big of a meeting this would be. My apologies." The crowd behind him had started to quiet as they noticed Marissa and I standing here. "Step into the hallway and make your call, I'll keep them focused in here."

I nod and listen to Marissa while she sends the call. Only a few moments later, Riley picks up. She advises him of our situation and hands me the phone.

"General?"

"Collin, talk to me about what's going on." I can't believe I'm talking to the General on Marissa's personal cell phone. I feel like I'm breaking rules.

"I've got about a hundred civilians here looking for some reassurance." Simeon's words run through my head. "Mostly, I think they're scared. They're afraid we'll ally with humans against them and kill them or put them in prisons like Pandora's Box. This is not what I expected when I agreed to come into the city and talk. I thought it

would be one family, maybe two. I would have referred this to someone higher up in command if I had known. Simeon said some of them have driven overnight to get here. I don't feel comfortable telling them to come back on another day when someone with more ranking can come."

"I understand, it's not an ideal situation for you, but it's what we've got right now." He pauses. "Out of curiosity, why is Marissa with you?"

"She helped with a situation involving a family when we were in Jerusalem last time. Benjamin requested both of us come back to talk to a couple more families." For a moment, I panic that I didn't file the report from our last visit, but I clearly remember sending it to my superiors. "He requested we both come back. She was good with them female and her baby and is adept at calming worried demons. I filed a report on it."

"I'm sure you did; my question wasn't a condemnation. I'm behind on my paperwork." I can hear Riley clicking away at a laptop. I wonder if he's in the office. "Okay. Listen up, I'm going to tell you what you're cleared to say."

A few minutes later, when I hang up the phone, I'm a lot calmer. I know how to handle the crowd, and I know I'm not going to get busted down to Lieutenant for bringing Marissa back into Jerusalem. Because, honestly, it hadn't occurred to me that while my superiors might have approved this patrol, Riley didn't know about it. I assume he knows everything that happens at Pandora's Box. It turns out that he doesn't.

I give Marissa the run down. After a minute, she nods.

"We're ready." Turning to Benjamin, I take a deep breath. All I need to do now is stay calm.

This time when we enter the gym, the crowd quiets, watching us closely. Constance is moving along the front of the group speaking with a female in the front row. A familiar face stands from his seat and approaches us.

"I thought you could use a friendly face." Matthew shakes my hand. "Sara stayed home with the baby."

"It's good to see you." Awareness of the rest of the audience washes over me. They're watching Matthew, considering his act of friendship. I wonder if it will change any feelings.

He retakes his seat, the crowd around him rumbling with low voices.

"Thank you all for coming." Benjamin raises his voice, speaking as loudly as he can. The rumbling slowly dies away. "I'm sorry, we weren't prepared for this many of you, but we'll do our best to talk loudly for you to hear us and we'll answer as many questions as we can. Please let me introduce Captain Collin Smith and Private Marissa Cazut. They are among the Fallen stationed at Pandora's Box and have given us their time this afternoon."

No applause or welcome from the crowd. They continue to stare at me and Marissa like we're specimens in biology class waiting to be dissected. I'm willing to bet that besides Matthew, no one in this crowd has met a Fallen face to face. To them, we're the boogeymen they tell stories about in the dark of night.

I wonder how I'm going to start. I didn't come prepared to make a speech, and while I'm happy to stand in front of a classroom of recruits and teach, I'm not a big fan of public speaking. Having Marissa standing there looking at me doesn't help matters.

While I'm fumbling, Marissa turns her attention back to the crowd. "Good morning. Like Superintendent Benjamin said, we're here to answer your questions and help you feel more comfortable with the changes that are here now and the ones that are coming. I hope at the end of today, you'll be a little less afraid, and you'll see that we aren't that different from you. Even Collin here, as you can see, is a bit nervous talking in front of such a large audience."

There's a smattering of chuckles from the gathering which gives me a boost of confidence. I look at the faces. They're scared yes, but also hopeful, and I realize these demons could be my responsibility in a few months. If I get the transfer, I will have a chance to get to know each and every one of the creatures in front of me. Talking to them will be like talking to my recruits. I was nervous the first day I taught a high school class; look where I am now. I can do this.

"It's true. Right now, I'm a lot more scared of you than you should be of me." I squeeze Marissa's arm in thanks. It seems I need a push to get started. "You can feel free to call me Collin. I grew up in New York, in the Fallen city called Hope. I'll be honest with you; I was part of the unit that captured Discord. The scar you see on my face is my constant reminder of what that day was like. After that, I went on to teach high school and eventually became the head trainer for the current class of army recruits. That's how I got involved with the Division, first in New York, and then here. Benjamin offered Marissa and I the opportunity to see how their department works and that led to my introduction to Matthew and his wife. And now, I'm here talking to you."

My mind wanders. Should I talk about the things Riley advised me, or take questions? Marissa jumps in, giving me the answer. "The first thing you should know is that we're afraid, too. There are so many humans and so few of us. When I first heard about the Five-Year plan, I was terrified. What if the humans turn against us? What if they capture us and lock us away? And then I met Aria. She's like you and she works for the Division in New York. I like her. She's smart and confident. You'd never know she was different from the humans unless you really look at her eyes. That's when I realized how dangerous this could be for her; yet she works with humans every day in their police department. She's made me believe this is possible. We can live out in the open. You'll be able to go to regular grocery stores and movie theaters."

"That's easy for you to say. You can blend in with humans. No one would think you were anything different unless you told them." A male with blue skin stands from his seat. "What about those of us who look different? You expect humans to embrace us?"

"Let me show you something." Marissa takes her phone out of her pocket and scrolls to a picture. She approaches the audience and shows it to the male. "This is Sasha. She's my friend. We go to a demon theater together sometimes to see shows. I can't wait until we can go to a regular theater and see a regular show. She works for the governing body of demons in the New York area, which means she's on the front line of integration. She'll be one of the faces you see on television in New York when this all happens."

"She looks like me." He stares at the picture, his expression one of amazement. "She already works with humans?"

"The ones who know about us, yes." I take back control of the conversation. Marissa is so good at dissolving fear and making others feel heard. I am, however, the higher-ranking officer. I should be the one leading the discussion. "And there are more than you realize. High ranking politicians and community leaders. Members of the police force and the military. They know because while we're making the plan to enter the world, they're making the plan to accept us. They will have the job of preventing mass hysteria and panic. Little by little, they're preparing their people."

"Aren't you afraid someone will leak the information too early, before we're ready?" Another male, this time one sitting next to Matthew, speaks up. This is a tricky question because, yes, that is a real fear.

"Very, but that isn't something I can control. I can promise you the humans who know, at least the ones I've met, are selected very carefully." Riley had mentioned concerns about lists, a registry of demons in each community. "We've heard concerns about a registry. We're doing everything in our power to make sure that doesn't happen. Once our world becomes known, you have a choice. You can come out into the light, or you can continue to live life as you do now. There will be nothing instituted that forces you to tell your neighbors."

"You said you have a friend who is demon, this Sasha." A blue skinned female sitting next to the male who'd already spoken stands up. She wears long sleeves and a scarf over her head. I can see she's used to hiding her appearance. "Is that…normal in New York? I've never seen a Fallen before today; I've only heard the stories. That you hunt and kill my kind."

The difficult question. I knew it would come. Riley had reminded me that I can't atone for over two thousand years of actions by our people. I can only talk about here and now. "I will be completely honest with you. Do all Fallen have close friends who are demons? No. Are there Fallen who are resistant to this change? Yes. But, Aria, the demon who works for the Division? She teaches in our schools. Every week, she finds the courage to walk into Hope and talk to us about your cultures and your people. She's pretty awesome and most of the kids love her."

"Should you be afraid of us?" Marissa smiles kindly at the female. "No. The brave demons who came to us and helped us capture Discord showed us that things can be different. This is hard for me. I lost both of my parents because of a battle with a demon when I was only five. I'm sure many of you have lost family or friends because of us. I'm asking you to put that in the past. Let us have peace now, we have so much to learn from each other. I, for one, would like to be friends instead of enemies."

And just like that, with a few words spoken directly from Marissa's heart, the energy in the room changes. As I watch, bodies relax. On some faces, I see the ghost of a smile. Off to the side, Benjamin looks pleased. The meeting isn't over by a long stretch. We stay for almost two hours, answering the questions we can, getting to know each other. Eventually, there is even laughter.

One hard question is posed by a half demon named Abigail. "Why are there no Fallen in the Division here? I understand you are visiting us from the prison in the countryside. Why can't you stay here and be a part of our community like you are in New York?"

I hesitate before I reply. We must live in a hive to survive. I don't know if that's secret information. Not to mention the job offer. I certainly can't talk openly about that.

Benjamin saves me by speaking up from the side of the room. "Until now, I haven't had the funding to put in a request for two more staff members. However, I do agree that having Fallen as part of our community would go a long way toward goodwill. I will be filing the paperwork with my people and be reaching out to Captain Collin's people in the next few weeks about getting a more permanent relationship with the Fallen."

"Does that mean we get to keep them?" The blue female shouts the question. Laughter echoes through the building.

"Our current duties here in Jerusalem are up in a couple of months." No reason to let anyone know Marissa is only a recruit. Benjamin knows, and if that's good enough for him to offer us a job, that's all that matters. "At that point, we'll be available for reassignment. If Benjamin likes us well enough, he can request us. If not us, there are other well qualified Fallen who would be happy to work here."

When the meeting finally wraps up, Marissa and I have no less than five invitations to dinner, all of which we politely decline for now because we need to get back to the prison before dark. Promises are made that we will return before our time in Jerusalem is up, a promise that I hope we'll be able to keep.

"You must be hungry, let me take you to a late lunch before we rendezvous with your driver Nathan." Benjamin, who seems very pleased by the outcome of the meeting, leads us to his vehicle.

"That would be nice, thank you." Marissa slides into the backseat with Constance and I take the front. "You have a good community here."

"It's a community that would benefit from having you as part of it. Both of you." He pulls into the street. "Have you given my offer any thought?"

"I've given it a lot of thought." Buildings slide past us. They're mostly made of limestone brick, sandy colored. Between modern buildings, you can catch glimpses of ancient structures built hundreds of years ago. It's so different than New York; I wonder what it would be like to know these streets and these people. How would it feel to work here daily and have regular restaurants and shops that I stop at? "I've put in for a job in New York, but it is unlikely that will come through. Like you, their budget is limited. But I like this job. Your offer is very appealing."

"I make a good second choice?" He laughs.

"My mother is in New York, and I don't think I'm going to get her to move here. I'd like to have her a little closer than halfway around the world." I think about mom living in Hope. She has her friends and her hobbies and her job. She'd hate to pick up her life and move here. "I'm thinking about it enough to discuss it with my superiors. They will ultimately have the final say as to where my next assignment is. You will have a better chance of getting me if you ask for me by name in your request."

"Then I'll ask for you both." Benjamin looks at Marissa in the rearview mirror. "What about you, Marissa? Have you considered becoming a resident of our city?"

"I have one more major training mission abroad, then I'll be able to make a decision." She watches a human woman with a toddler outside the window. They seem to be on their way to the market. "I like it here, the history and the people. I could see myself staying."

"Good." He seems satisfied with our answers. "Then I won't bother you any more with my questions. Marissa, I hope your last training mission is one that bores you to tears and, Collin, I hope your superior officers see the value of having you stationed here. I believe we can build a good community with Fallen and demon and human all living together in peace."

CHAPTER SIXTEEN

The office chair I'm sitting on isn't comfortable. The back and the seat are hard and serviceable, but not cozy. Like most everything inside the prison, it's designed to get the job done. In the last couple of weeks, I'd started to notice that about Pandora's Box. Chairs, tables, desks, beds, nothing is more than what is necessary. Even my barracks room contains only the most basic of items. I'd brought next to nothing from home to make it my own save a few paperback novels I intended to leave in the common room library.

Pandora's Box is a building, not a home, and here I am considering making it mine.

In the four weeks since our meeting with the demons Jerusalem, Marissa and I have been called back twice. Once to meet with a Shedim, which impressed me because I'd believed them to be extinct. These creatures are not a result of Pandora's Box being opened; they were created with the

purpose of guarding sacred spaces and were sent to the world long before the Fallen.

The second time had been to discuss setting up a governing agency for the demon population, made up of demons, like the one we already have in New York. Thankful for technology, I'd been able to teleconference in Sasha and her team.

These opportunities have given me the chance to see what working in Jerusalem would really be like, and I like it. Because the Division is still getting established, there's a lot of room to help direct its foundation and build relationships with the locals. And, while the community has been small enough until now to patrol itself and work together, they seem excited at the prospect of having their own governing agency to work with humans once we reach the end of the Five-Year plan.

There's a lot of work to be done.

Meanwhile, Marissa has been catching up with her classes. She meets with Kaia whenever they aren't on duty, and on the nights Kaia isn't available, she usually convinces me to study with her. I realized early on that studying isn't her main priority when we're together. She sits quietly reading her textbooks and doing homework while I read my own books. Often, we don't talk much, but the companionship is enough for us to be comfortable in silence. I asked her once why she bothers to come see me when she can study just as well in her own room, and she told me it was because she's been working harder in the gym to build back her strength. She wants to borrow familiar energy to help heal her muscles faster.

I don't question her explanation.

We have been out at the balance beams a few times, me doing my job of spotting her while she walks, runs, and jumps on the beams. She seems to be fearless, and she never falls, making me question why I insist on being there. I assure myself it's so that I can get help if she tumbles.

The truth is, we've spent a lot of time together in the last few weeks. Or months, if you want to look back that far. Mia enjoys pointing out how much time; I ignore her. Even if she's right in her assumption that Marissa likes me and I like her, it doesn't matter right now. I'm still her superior officer, she's still just a recruit, and even thinking about this is completely off limits.

But time is winding down. At the end of May, Marissa and I will both be done with basic training. If I do things right, I won't be her superior officer anymore. That thought gives me a wave of relief every time I think about it. Doing things right is going to require a level of honesty I hope I'm ready for.

"Captain, the General will see you now." General Riley's assistant interrupts my thoughts and sends an impulse of nerves through my stomach. I don't have to imagine what this summons is about; command needs to plan for the next recruiting class. They need to know if that class will include me. If it does, I'll be packing up and heading back to Orasul come June first. I hope it doesn't.

I'm led into the General's office. It isn't as stark as the waiting room. His chairs, although still serviceable, at least have cushions on them. The desk looks like something surplus from the 1960's, grey and metal. Matching filing cabinets line the walls to the left of the desk and his weapons hang on the wall to the right. The photo from his wedding day to Marissa's mom is framed and on his desk. A very young Marissa looks out from the picture. She must have been only fifteen.

I sincerely hope he realizes how much she's grown up in the years since that picture.

"Thank you, you can go ahead to dinner." The General addresses his assistant. "I'll lock up when we're done here."

"Thank you, sir." He leaves the room.

"Have a seat, Captain." The General motions to one of the two chairs in front of him. My personnel file is on the desk. It's open, a copy of my recruitment photo on top. God, that was so long ago.

"Thank you, sir." I echo the assistant's words as I slide into the chair and my nerves kick into overtime. There are too many unknowns right now. I'm going to have to be honest in this conversation about things I really don't want to be honest about. At least not with this man.

"I understand teaching high school and leading this class of recruits wasn't your idea." He pages through the file, no doubt looking at my service record. I find it interesting he's using paper. Most records are electronic now. "You'd taken an injury? How did that happen?"

"Yes. In the battle for Discord." The memory is always there, right below the surface. My team had been clearing a stairwell in the building and we'd been ambushed. Demons came at us from the floors above and below, intent on killing the whole team. Natasha had been there with me. Instead of trusting her to fight for herself, I turned from my lead position to check on her. She was fine, taking out the enemy that targeted her without trouble. But I, being distracted, didn't notice the demon coming at my back. His cut across my face had been a missed attempt to slice my throat. A second jab with his blade tore into my shoulder, disabling my left arm. One of my teammates incapacitated and killed the attacker, but the damage had been done, and I was evacuated out. "I allowed myself to be distracted because I didn't trust my team. It isn't a mistake I will make twice."

"Why didn't you trust your team?" He lands on the page he's looking for and skims over it with his eyes. I'm sure he's read it before. "Maybe I should word the question this way: why didn't you trust your partner?"

Because she was female and I didn't want her to get hurt doesn't seem like the best answer, albeit a true one. I take a deep breath and think about what I'm going to say. "I was young and probably didn't have enough experience to be leading that team. Nathasha hadn't been my partner for very long; I struggled to read her location and emotional level. When the attack came, it was my first instinct to turn and make sure she was okay."

"Would you do the same thing now?"

"No." I don't have to think about this answer. Marissa would kill me if I didn't trust her to take care of herself. "I have a better feel for Marissa and her abilities. I think if we were ever put into a dangerous position, I'd be more confident. I'd trust her to do what I trained her to do."

"That's the right answer, Captain." The General flips one more page and looks at the last record in the file. It's a commendation from my time in officer's training. "You completed officer's training right after basic and graduated with honors. You've done well teaching and training this year's recruits. Yet, you haven't put in a request to train the next batch. You haven't put in a request for any position

other than one with the Division in New York, which I know you realize is unavailable at this time. So, tell me, what do you want to be doing when this program is over?"

For an eternity of seconds, I pour through my thoughts and make sure I want to say what I practiced. I try to picture playing cards with the General and then I try to remember what it was like to talk with him like he was just another soldier. He holds my future in his hand. If I handle this wrong, I could be shipped off to anywhere he likes.

"I'm not sure what to ask for yet." The blood feels like it's rushing out of my head as I say the words. "Marissa's the best partner I've had, and I'd like to keep working with her. She hasn't gone on her training run with Major Cazut yet, and she isn't sure what she wants to request. I'm waiting on her to decide."

"Superintendent Benjamin of the Division certainly sings your praises." He closes my file, and his eyes focus on mine. "I'm sure you know he's requested both of you be assigned to him."

"I am aware and it's a job I'd be grateful to have. They're just getting started and because of my good relationship with the Division in New York, I think I could be useful to them in establishing their programs." I plunge forward. "Marissa and I both. She's a natural; talking to people and demons both come easy to her. She's calming and personable, and she's good at getting them to trust her."

"Then why don't you advise her to go ahead and make the placement request?" Tilting his head to the side, the General looks at me with curiosity. "Why wait?"

"I don't want to push her. Tevin pushed her. He tried to mold her into what he wanted, which was to be on Major

Cazut's team. He wanted to hunt and kill. Marissa needs see for herself what she wants." I force myself to hold his curious gaze. I don't want to look away.

"Then you've talked to her about this?"

"Yes." I hesitate. "If she decides she wants assigned to Major Cazut's team, I'll reconsider my options."

"That's highly unlikely. Marissa is a city girl at heart. Marching through the desert isn't something I expect her to enjoy." He chuckles and I'm reminded again that he's her stepfather. "I'll tell you what, I am going to confidentially inform command that we'll be expanding the Fallen presence in Jerusalem. I want to put together a unit of four that will work directly for Benjamin's team. I think we're going to need more people trained to work for the Division in the future and this will be a good location to start that. I'll be assigning you command."

"Thank you, sir, but I have to decline command. You need to find someone else to lead the team." And here goes the hard part. I wonder if he'd take it personally if I threw up in his trash can right now.

"Why would you turn down a command position? It would mean better pay, better benefits. An increase in rank." He seems baffled.

"I can't be her commanding officer anymore." His eyes widen and I know he understands. "I like her in a way that's inappropriate as her superior officer. I have not acted on it, nor do I plan to unless she gives me reason to think she feels the same. I'm not Tevin. I would never sneak around and put her in danger the way he did. But I cannot be her commander."

"Hmmm." The General makes a noise in the back of his throat and continues to look at me. I wonder exactly how

far back he's going to bust my rank when he starts to shake his head. "Damn. I owe my sister an apology."

"Pardon?" I'm not sure I heard him right.

"Mia." He chuckles once. "She tried to warn me, and I told her she was imagining things. Okay, you won't command the unit, that's fine. I'll assign command to someone here at Pandora's Box. You'll have to work out of here anyway since there is no Fallen city inside of Jerusalem. You will be a unit of four, two pairs. I have other requests for work with the Division. Like I said, this will be a good place to train the officers we'll eventually send to other cities."

"Any idea who else you might add to this detail?" My body finally relaxes. The hard part is over.

"Jenn and Kaia come to mind. They're both looking for that kind of position, they're grades are in the right range, and they both seem to have the right temperament for the job." The General opens his laptop and pulls up the files on the recruits. "Patrick might do a good job, but I think there are better placements for him."

"Kaia?" I frown. I must have missed something important if he thinks Kaia wants a job with the Division. "She's been very vocal against the Division and about the alliance with the demons."

"She made the kill on her training run in the jungle. It changes you, once you see a sentient being bleeding out at your feet." He seems startled. "She didn't talk to you about it?"

"Not at all. In the debrief, she mentioned that she'd made the kill, but she didn't mention anything about the creature being sentient. I can understand how that might change her outlook." I realize that with all the time I've been spending with Marissa, I haven't met with the other recruits as much as I used to. I need to make the time again, starting with Kaia. If she wants to work for the Division, that's a huge change of heart. "I'll make some time to talk to her, make sure she's not just reacting."

"Sounds good." The General stands, a sign that I'm about to be dismissed. "And I'll find someone else to lead the training program starting in June. Oh, and you and Marissa will be on Major Cazut's detail in two weeks. You'll be flying back to the US; we'll be hunting in the Colorado Plateau."

"Can I ask what we're hunting for?" A hunt in the United States is unusual. Most training missions are in less densely populated areas like South America or Africa.

"We think it's an Incubus who is trafficking women." He closes his computer screen. "A serial killer."

I see Mia sitting at a table alone in the mess with her phone in her hand and I head her direction. Almost to the table when she looks up, I'm greeted with a happy expression. "Hi, how's your day been?"

"I've had worse." I set my tray down and sit in the chair next to her. "I've also had better. You told your brother?"

"Oh, that. He wasn't supposed to tell you that he knew. He also thought I was exaggerating." Setting her phone down on the table, she picks up her fork. "Did he get all wacky on you and come find you for a talk? Or did it just come up in conversation? He does much better with these things if he has a warning and I didn't want him to reassign you somewhere silly because he was surprised."

"He didn't come looking for me, at least not for that reason." The chicken and potatoes on my plate suddenly look less appealing than they did a minute ago. There hasn't been enough time for the stress of my meeting with the General to sink in. Now, it seems to be hitting me hard. "He wanted to discuss my record and whether or not I'd be returning to train the next batch of recruits. It came up."

"I assume that means the request from Jerusalem's Division came through?" Her eyes scan the mess hall. "Oh, I'm listening to you, but I'm also keeping my eyes open for Riley. Anna is on duty tonight and he said he might come join me for dinner."

"Should I leave?" I start to pick up my tray, sure that I don't want to be anywhere around, but she stops me with a hand on my arm.

"No." Mia looks at me and rolls her eyes. "You males, I swear. You've played cards with him and survived. He's just a person with a high stress job. Cut him a break. Now, before he gets here, tell me about your conversation. Did he freak out?"

"No, he was calm about it. Mostly, he seemed disappointed that going back to Orasul to start the training program over again wasn't an option. I mean, he could order me to do it, but I don't think he will." I take a bite of the baked chicken and my stomach grumbles. "Right now, we're tentatively expected to head to Jerusalem and take the job there in June. We'll confirm after Marissa's last training mission."

"I know she hasn't done her training run with Anna yet but there's no way that job changes her mind. She's not built for chasing rogue demons and sleeping in the jungle." She shakes her head. "But you're right, she won't submit her paperwork request until she's absolutely sure she's ruled out all the other options. She's very thorough that way."

A tingle runs down my spine. I turn toward the mess hall door and watch Marissa walk through with Kaia. She has her backpack, which means they must have been in the classroom studying. Although she's caught up on the classwork she missed, the two of them have continued to use the room for study sessions on new material. With finals coming in six weeks, other recruits had begun to join them. Academically, the recruits' opportunity to impress me and Command is running out.

The two females laugh together as they join the mess line.

I hear Mia snicker and I consider making a rude gesture in her direction. "Exactly how much time have you spent helping her study?"

"Nothing inappropriate has happened." I turn my back to Marissa and purposefully ignore the tingle. "We're just together a lot between class and patrols and gym time. And, yes, she likes to study with me when Kaia isn't available, but she says it's mostly to use my energy to help heal up after the gym. I'm serious. Nothing inappropriate."

"I believe you. You're too much of a rule follower to let anything happen between you." Her eyes scan the room again for the General. "What, exactly, did he ask you that made you fess up? I'm curious."

"He didn't ask anything. He offered me command of the Jerusalem unit he wants to put together. I told him no; I can't be her commanding officer." This time, I take a larger bite of my dinner. I need a reason to stop talking.

"You gave up a command?" Mia exclaims. Then she lowers her voice. "You don't even know for sure she's into you and you gave up a command without talking to Marissa? Are you crazy?"

I chew my food slowly, quietly hoping the General will show up and stop the conversation. No such luck. "I'm not going to say or do anything that could redirect her choices. I want her to pick Jerusalem because it's what she really wants to do. Not because of me."

"Isn't that what you're doing?" She raises an eyebrow and nods toward the door. Her brother is getting into the mess line. "Do you mean to tell me you won't change your mind about Jerusalem if she decides to join up with Anna's unit?"

I don't bother to answer. We both know what I'll say.

CHAPTER SEVENTEEN

The metal building waiting at the end of the road in the desert is non-descript, worn down, and buzzing with activity. Night has already fallen despite the dozens of vehicles parked alongside the motorway. Inside the building, we're breaking into our units. We've had three days of hunting in the desert at night with temperatures dropping into the thirties.

It's not as bad as the jungle here, at least we have a run-down motel to sleep in with its diner next door. And there's a promise of a couple days off in Hope before we head back to Pandora's Box, once the mission is complete.

Crowded inside the building, we're all dressed in SWAT team style tactical gear. Sandy colors with bulletproof vests, night vision goggles, and helmets. Our traditional weapons have been left behind in favor of handguns. Incubi are perfectly susceptible to a gunshot wound as are the humans who might be working with our target.

Major Cazut steps to the podium at the front of the room and all twenty soldiers inside quiet down.

"Tonight, we're searching this area." She uses a laser pointer to circle a section of the map hung on the wall. "We have FBI support; we're getting closer to the national park and there are humans in the area. If there is a possibility of human interaction in your quadrant, you have already been briefed on what to expect. Agent Ramirez."

An FBI agent dressed like we are steps to the podium. "Officially, you don't exist. If you run into the human population, flash the FBI badge we've given you and move on. If you find our target, detain, but do not kill. Any kill you make goes on my record as the agent on this case."

He smiles, his white teeth bright against his tanned skin.

"In all seriousness, we want to capture the incubus and any humans he has with him." Major Cazut retakes the mic. "The incubus will be transported with us back to a prison cell in Hope until we can figure out what to do with him. Humans will be handed over to the FBI who will deal with them according to their own laws. Not us, nor the incubus, will be included in the official record. We're ghosts, Fallen, let's make sure we get in and out silently. Be ready to move in five."

We're used to this drill now after the three previous nights of hunting, I adjust the straps on my uniform and hope that tonight I can keep warm. The terrain here is cold at night, thankfully the arid conditions keep snow away, unlike other upper elevations where there are still feet of snow on the ground. Daytime highs, not that we see them while we sleep, are close to seventy.

"Help me out." Marissa, struggling with her gear, is doing her best to attach her joey pouch to the back of her belt where she can reach it later.

I accept it from her hands and snap it into place. Between the bullet proof vests, extra rounds of ammo, helmets, and the emergency supplies each team is required to carry, this is a heavy operation. Marissa really struggled the first night out but has been getting better each night since.

The General was right, she isn't built for this kind of work. She's quick on her feet in a fight, something she uses to her advantage. With all the gear these hunting teams carry, she loses her best advantage, something she wouldn't have a problem with if she were on the streets of New York or Jerusalem.

Not that she's complained. She's geared up, loaded her supplies, and been ready to go each evening with a smile and a positive attitude.

If we're lucky, someone will manage to find the cave or hidden cabin the incubus is using to hide in tonight, and we can wrap this search up. If we're not? Well, then we've got one more night of this tomorrow before we're sent home. Recruits have a five-day maximum of being on this kind of mission. They haven't built the stamina to be away from the rest of their hive yet and will start to decline shortly after day five. With travel time, five nights of searching is already pushing it.

"You feeling good?" I tug at the joey pack to make sure it won't fall off. It stays in place.

"Yeah." Marissa looks back at me, her eyes roaming over my uniform. She notices a pocket that isn't snapped in place and fixes it. "I didn't realize how draining it can be to be away from the rest of the unit. Even with twenty of us here, I'm starting to drag a little bit at the end of the night."

"You've been working, it tires you. If you were on leave, sitting on a beach somewhere, you'd last longer." Glancing

across the room, I spot two other recruits assigned to this mission. They both look much greener than Marissa. They might not make it through the last night. "Two more nights, you can hang on."

"I didn't know before how hard my mom works. I need to give her a lot more credit." Marissa's eyes focus on Major Cazut working her way through the crowd of soldiers. It's one of her rituals; every night, she stops to speak to every Fallen on her team. When she reaches the other recruits, Thomas and Hannah, she hesitates, then speaks to the team next to her. I realize she's breaking them up to work with other, more seasoned Fallen. It's a smart move. They could be a liability if they're already starting to fade.

"Captain Smith." Marissa's mom approaches me with a discerning eye. "Private Cazut. How are we feeling this evening?"

"We're good." Marissa responds before I can. She puts some extra pep into her voice.

"Ready and waiting your orders, ma'am." I glance at Marissa. She's standing tall and strong.

"Good." Major Cazut's eyes run over Marissa, looking for tiredness or weakness. I feel like I'm intruding on a private moment. Then she lowers her voice and leans toward Marissa. "See me after the patrol, we'll grab breakfast."

"Yes, ma'am." A bright smile takes over Marissa's face. Being on a patrol like this one has kept us all busy and she hasn't had the opportunity to visit with her mom. Clearly, the idea of spending a little time with her gives Marissa the boost she needs.

Major Cazut moves on to speak to other soldiers.

Eyes on the two FBI agents waiting off to the side, Marissa whispers to me. "I can't believe all of this happens and more of the human population doesn't know about us. Military, government, FBI, it's crazy to me that we're still a secret at all."

"It hasn't been like this for long. We've been slowly integrating over the last few years." The doors to the building open and we move toward the transports that will drop us off at our hunting locations. "The Committee hopes early integration to the human agencies like this will help when the time comes to go public; that enough humans have worked with us to realize we're not a threat."

"It's still impressive." We join the line to load onto the bus waiting outside.

Pairs of soldiers move silently through the night, it's not quite eleven o'clock. We have six hours to scan our target area and make it back to the evac site. There isn't much talking on the bus ride, each team mentally preparing themselves for the hunt. Not only are we tracking a demon who has become a serial killer, but he has a team of humans working for him. Additionally, there are natural predators like scorpions, poisonous lizards, mountain lions, coyotes, and rattlesnakes. While most of those creatures won't be out at night, we'll need to be careful while sweeping cave systems.

The bus slows at our stop, and we jump off, the quiet, electric operated machine driving away immediately. The comm in our ear clicks to life. "Confirmed drop off team six. Your clock is running. See you back here in six hours. Good luck."

The link closes, leaving us alone in the quiet night. It won't turn on again until we reach our rendezvous time, or if someone finds the incubus.

I motion for Marissa to start moving. She shifts her position approximately ten feet to my left and we start the trek toward a nearby canyon with dozens of natural caves. Our job is to clear the canyon and confirm the caves aren't being used as a hiding place for the incubus and his stash of kidnapped women.

According to the dossier given each team, this incubus has likely been kidnapping women from the surrounding area for a decade. He brings them to a safe house that we suspect is here in the desert, where he uses them until he is bored of them. Then he either kills them off or sells them into human trafficking rings. In the last few years, a handful of women have escaped or evaded his capture.

We walk the mile to the canyon and then look out at the expanse in front of us. It's huge. I'm not sure we'll be able to clear every cave in the system before our time is up. I'm considering my options for approach when we both hear a voice echo up from below.

The voice is too muffled for us to understand any words; regardless, no one should be out here this time of night. There's no camping allowed in this area and no cabins or homes for miles. We should be in the middle of a seven-million-acre wilderness.

I signal for Marissa to move forward with caution. We need to find the source of that voice without giving up our own position. Determined to keep the high ground, we push along the top of the canyon away from the road.

With the echo of the rock face, it's almost impossible to determine if we're moving toward or away from the voice we heard. We can only trust our ears and our instincts.

We move another fifty feet west on the canyon wall when Marissa reaches out and grabs my arm, signaling behind us.

In the distance, I can see headlights driving along the edge of the canyon on the hard, desert dirt. They're coming straight for us.

We slip over the edge of the canyon, hugging the wall so that we don't make an unplanned descent to the bottom. Below us, we can still hear occasional voices, this time clearer and closer. Between the voices and the vehicle, it's obvious we've stumbled upon something.

I hold my breath as a white van slips past us in the night. It doesn't slow down as it passes; a good sign we haven't been spotted. But now we're in a tough spot. I need to call in the activity. No one should be out here; there's a good chance this is the group of men and the demon we're looking for.

At the same time, we haven't pinpointed their exact location yet. I don't want the rest of our team to come in blind.

I'm just about to suggest we head back toward the road and call in the situation when two distinct sets of footsteps come walking above us.

"What are we out here looking for?" A male voice is clear and close above us. The light from a flashlight flickers on the canyon wall across from us. Whomever is up there is searching for something.

"Ricky thinks he saw two figures walking in the desert a couple of miles over from here. Just shadows, but they made him nervous." A second voice answers. "We're making sure no one followed the van. Buyers should be here in an hour and a half, and we don't need any surprises."

"Looks clear to me." The first voice rasps before the sound of a match flaring. A moment later we can smell cigarette smoke. "Who'd be out here besides us anyway?"

"Heck if I know." I risk a quick look above the rim of the canyon. The two men are a dozen feet away from us and shining a light back toward the road. Both are armed with serious weapons, making me wonder if we've stumbled upon a drug drop off. I need to get the FBI notified right away. The men turn as I drop back into hiding. "Come on, I can see all the way to the road, and it looks clear. Ricky's imagining things."

Marissa and I wait for the footsteps to walk away and then we wait a few minutes longer. If the buyers are going to come soon, we've got a short window to stop whatever is about to happen.

"Team six, we think we've found them. Over." I open the channel back to main command and pray no one walking above can hear it.

Marissa's mom answers my call. "What do you see, Six? Over."

"A white van coming in with a delivery and two males, heavily armed, checking to make sure no one is following them. Someone noticed one of our teams working a couple of miles away. They're nervous. Over." I glance at Marissa and consider volunteering to pull out. She's technically still a recruit and has never done a patrol like this before. Now I'm expecting her to face down an unknown number of men with guns?

She'd kill me if she knew I was thinking like this.

"We're redirecting the teams now. Hang tight, help will be there as quickly as possible. Over." Major Cazut puts all her authority into her voice. She's not about to put her daughter in unnecessary danger.

"You have less than ninety minutes before their buyers arrive." I look around. There's so little cover out here that, short of hiding in one of the caves below us, there isn't anywhere for us to go. "I'm going to drop a little lower into the canyon with Marissa. I think we'll have better cover down there and I might be able to get eyes on the operation. I don't know how many males or victims are up there. My GPS locator is on. Over."

"Move only if it's safe. We're coming to you. Over."

"You got it. Over."

The comm clicks off but our tracking system activates. It might take thirty minutes, but we should start seeing more team members coming in soon. They'll have a plan of action. My job now? Get Marissa and I out of here in one piece.

I motion for her to drop lower on the wall, heading toward a cave I can see about twenty feet away. She follows me silently, much more comfortable at these heights than I am. Careful not to knock any rocks loose, we make it to the entrance and disappear inside.

The cave is small, but deep enough for both of us to fit in the back, hidden by the dark. I cross my fingers there aren't any dangerous creatures making this space their home for the night, we can't risk turning on a light to look. A rattlesnake bite is just as deadly to a Fallen as it is to a human.

Marissa's voice is barely more than a breath of air. "What now?"

"We wait." I lean my head on the wall, wishing there was more I could do, but it doesn't make sense to risk both our lives when we have an entire team in the vicinity.

Forty-five minutes later, the comm clicks on again. "Collin? Marissa? Over."

"We're here." I answer, wondering how Marissa is feeling with her mom on the other line and a very dangerous

situation above us. She seems rock solid. No tears, no anxiety that I'm picking up on, just a mask of resolve on her face. I put my hand on her cheek, the only place she has skin showing, and look at her. She nods once, accepting my request to check her wellbeing. Nothing but determination comes back at me. I resist the urge to kiss her check and instead give her arm a squeeze.

"We've got eyes on you now, a pair of snipers on the edge of the canyon wall, opposite your side. The camp with the men is approximately thirty yards west and above you. We have four teams in place, you're going to be the fifth. First, you're going to scale the canyon wall until you're just below the camp. You're going to click your comm once when you're in place. Marissa will follow behind you at that point. You'll click twice when she's in place. Then, on my signal, all teams will breach the perimeter. Our goal is to save as many women as possible. Are you clear of the plan? Over." Major Cazut gives the commands carefully, methodically.

I mentally curse. Marissa and I are going to be in a dangerous spot. Thank God there's only a sliver of a moon. We'll be dangerously exposed on that climb across the canyon wall. If anyone looks down, there's a good chance they'll see us despite our desert tactical gear. If they decide to pick us off without asking questions? One, or both, of us could be dead before the sniper even realizes we've been made.

"Clear. I'm on the move. Over." I decide it's best to move as quickly as possible, I immediately step out into the faint moonlight, my eyes on the wall where I need to go. There is no sign of humans, or the incubus, anywhere. I say a prayer and start my climb.

Climbing up or down is relatively easy if you're in good shape, despite disliking heights. Climbing sideways? It's miserable, especially when your life depends on you being completely silent. One rock knocked loose could be a death sentence if the wrong person hears it and thinks to look down.

Marissa? I'm not worried about her. She's small and fast and lives to be up high. The side of this rock wall might not be balance beams, but they might as well be. I'm sure she'll all but dance thirty yards across.

Me? I'm bigger than her, bulky. I weigh more. I don't practice on balance beams every day. I'm starting to wonder right now if maybe I should.

My foot hits a rock that goes coursing down the incline. I freeze, waiting. After a few minutes, no one comes, and I'm satisfied they didn't hear me. A few minutes after that, with a rush of adrenaline, I reach my destination. I can clearly hear the males talking above me. It seems all the women are alive right now, five of them. Their buyers will take the ones they want, any leftovers will be shot and buried nearby. Why bad guys insist on talking about their plans out loud, I'll never know.

I reach to click my com as a hand grabs the back of my jacket and pulls me over the ledge.

CHAPTER EIGHTEEN

There's a gun in my face before I can react. I hold my hands up, aware my weapons are now all out of reach. Three human men stand in front of me, each of them pointing a gun my direction. Behind them is the incubus.

Unless you know you're looking for an incubus, you might miss him. They live normal, human lifespans, and integrate well into modern society. Over the centuries, their looks adapt and change, always appearing to be the perfect, handsome, human male. You know the man you passed on the train that seemed too perfect to be real? He probably was.

This one stands just over six feet tall with perfect brown hair, a full beard, and piercing blue eyes. His coloring is tanned enough to make it seem like he's recently been to a beach. That's all I can see while he's wearing a dark jacket, jeans, and boots, but I'm willing to bet he's got a six pack under that clothing, too, well-manicured hands, and maybe a couple of tattoos.

"Well. And what are you doing out here?" His eyes narrow as he looks me over. There are no identifying markers on the outside of my uniform.

"War games, I thought you guys were my target." I let the lie roll off my tongue and hope backup arrives soon. We already know this group is burying bodies out here and I don't want to be added to their most recent count. "We didn't realize anyone else was out here."

"Who are you with?" His eyes linger on my gear, the Beretta on my hip. "FBI? CBI? Local police?"

"Independent, we're not part of any government institution." I realize I'm probably being too nice. "Who are you, anyway?"

"I'm the guy with the gun pointed at you and I'm the one asking questions. You're well-funded if you're independent. That gear's impressive." Turning toward the closest man to me, he issues his orders. "Disarm him and we'll put him with the girls until I can figure out what to do with him."

"Why don't we just kill him?" The guy asks, not lowering the gun. "He's militia, no one is going to be looking for him until his mother realizes he's missing; and then none of his friends will admit to being out here dressed up for war. What's one more body?"

"It's a mess I don't want to clean up before our buyers get here." The incubus must not realize I'm Fallen. He'd be taking more precautions if he did. He's also trained his team to be professional; it hasn't gotten by me that no one is using names that can be remembered. "And don't forget to take his communication device, I don't want his friends showing up looking for him."

While all the men are watching me, I catch a glimpse of another Fallen team in the dark near a cave entrance a few yards away. They're using my capture as a distraction to get closer before taking down the men. Including the incubus, there are five men in front of me and I'll bet there's at least one or two more guarding the women who are probably housed in the cave.

Four teams, five if I get free and Marissa gets here, against five or six humans and one incubus. The odds are in our favor, but the number of guns I see certainly could even things out. Ultimately, we don't want to kill anyone if we can avoid it. Especially me. I'd really like to walk out of this situation.

The man closest to me finally lowers his weapon. "On your knees, hands on your head."

I comply at the same time I feel Marissa's energy brush up against my back, making me curse again inside my head. She'd positioned herself to come over that canyon wall like planned, even with the attention of the men looking straight at her. I wonder if she's lost her mind. She should have stayed in place when the plan started to go haywire.

He tucks his own gun in the back of his pants and reaches for my Beretta when a very calm, loud voice echoes through the darkness. "No one move."

Of course, that never works.

All four men turn to look toward the voice, reaching for their weapons. The incubus hisses and backs away from the sound, realizing right away that I'm not alone. His eyes meet mine across the short distance and he shakes his head. "Fallen. Kill him."

The man closest to me makes a grab for my weapon, but I roll out of the way, figuring I'm already in trouble. My eyes focus on him, watching him reach for his own gun, at the same time my peripheral vision takes in the incubus disappearing into the night. I consider what I want to do. Getting shot? Not what I want.

A shot rings out in the night, changing the scene entirely.

Two of the men, the smart ones, reach their hands into the air in surrender. Fallen soldiers swarm into the area to take control of them, handcuffs at the ready. The third man takes off at a run, heading farther west along the canyon wall. Two more Fallen are close on his heels, it's unlikely he'll be able to outrun them. I dismiss them from my immediate concerns.

The man closest to me is on the ground, his shoulder bleeding from a bullet wound. I turn my head and see Marissa standing on the edge of the canyon wall, her Glock drawn and pointed at the man who had been ready to shoot me only moments earlier. She speaks to him in a low voice. "They said, no one moves."

"You're just a girl." He wheezes on the ground, moving in pain. I remember the weapon tucked in his belt; I reach over and grab it, although he seems to be right-handed, and she nailed him in the right shoulder. He won't be handling anything with that arm for a while.

"Trust me, I'm a lot more than just a girl." Marissa takes a stance over top of him, her weapon solid and sure. Hands aren't shaking, no nerves are coming off her. It's like she's done this a dozen times before. Without turning to look at me, she changes her attention. "Collin, you okay?"

"Injured ego, but just fine." Pushing up from the ground, I get back on my feet. Instinct is to chase after the incubus, but protocol requires Marissa and I stay with the man she took down. I have to trust someone else on the team is able to intercept him. "If we're going to do work like this more often, I should practice my silently crawling across a rock wall skills."

Marissa's eyes narrow, but she doesn't take them off her prisoner. I realize I may have made an error in the comment. She doesn't know my plan to stay partnered with her after basic. I hurry and change the subject. "Help me roll him and we'll get him cuffed."

"Can we cuff him with that wound?" The wound is bleeding a lot; Marissa's nine-millimeter did a fair amount of damage. I don't want to do more.

"You're right, that's probably not a great idea." I notice he's wearing jeans. "Let's zip tie his wrists to his jeans through the belt loop. That should keep him still enough until the FBI get here."

The man groans. "God, that hurts. Can you do anything? I'm going to bleed out."

"I doubt you'll bleed out from a shoulder wound but let me see what I can do." We secure his hands and then I take out the emergency medical bag from my joey pouch. Memories of Amy flash through my mind. I ignore them and go to work bandaging the shoulder to stop the bleeding.

"Hey, I need a female. The women in the cave are terrified." Another soldier, one of Major Cazut's regular team, approaches us, his eyes on Marissa. "I'll stay with him if you go."

"On it." She waits until the new soldier is in place, wrapping the shoulder, then she lowers her weapon and holsters it at her side. On the way to the cave, we both take off our helmets. When you have hostages, you want their rescuers to seem as human as possible. While we can't do much about the tactical gear we're wearing, we can at least let them see our faces.

Standing at the entrance to the cave, I give Marissa space to approach the women. I might be a good guy, but the scar on my face will probably scare them. There's no reason for me to get too close when another female soldier, Hannah, is there already.

The four women are clearly terrified. Tears streak their cheeks, their eyes are puffy, and they're visibly shaking. A male soldier hands Hannah and Marissa some blankets to wrap the women in, hiding their bodies from view. They'd been dressed up for the sale, showing off their attributes to their potential buyer. It's cruel and sadistic, probably a way to remind them of what they're being purchased for. It's disgusting.

Marissa is holding the hand of one of the women, speaking to her softly, when I feel a tug on my sleeve. Turning, I see Major Cazut standing next to me. She motions with her head for us to step out of the cave.

"How's she doing?" The Major looks past me to her daughter.

"She seems solid enough, but the adrenaline is still running. We'll see what happens when she has a minute to slow down." Holding my helmet loosely in my hand, I wonder what else to say. Should I say I'll take care of her? Should I promise that she'll be okay?

"She'll need to talk to a debriefing counselor tomorrow. You both will." Debriefing counselor? I've never heard of anything like that before. "It's something new we've established since you took that injury. It's just to make sure you're processing what happened tonight."

"Yes, ma'am." Nodding my head, I know there's no room to argue.

"You surprised me tonight, Captain." She gestures away from the cave, indicating I should walk with her. "I didn't expect you to follow my orders on the wall. I thought you'd disobey and stay put."

"It was a dangerous move, but we follow orders." It's hard to separate the Major who led this hunt from Marissa's mom, a female I know cares for her daughter. I saw it every day at the hospital. She'd come in after her shifts and sit with Marissa, even with her daughter begged her to leave. "Can I speak freely?"

"Of course." We're a short distance from the rest of the teams now; our steps slow to a stop. "Why? You could have taken that team without us on the wall. Stealth operations would have worked just as well as a direct assault. Why choose that route?"

"There were too many of them for us to use a stealth attack. Someone would have gotten away, maybe in the van, maybe by slipping away into the night. We needed you in place to stop them from going over the side of the canyon wall as an escape route and we needed you to help balance our numbers." A tactical van pulls up outside the cave and the FBI agents get out. By morning, we'll all be gone, and this crime scene will be in the hands of the federal government. Our presence here will be erased. "Did I like putting my child in that kind of dangerous situation? No. But I can't think of her that way when we're out here. If I make decisions based on keeping her safe, then I'm a bad commander and I need to step aside."

"Besides, she'd hate it." I smile, unable to help myself.

"She would." The Major laughs, then her face gets serious again. "Riley talked to me before this mission. He told me about your meeting."

My mouth opens, but no words come out. I'd hoped that would be kept private. I guess not.

"Don't say anything." She raises her hand to stop me from talking. "You're a good team, I've been watching you this week. Sometimes you need something, and she responds before you say it. I picked this mission for her because it's not that different from something the Division would be involved in. Look at her in there, talking to those women. She calms them, helping them through what has happened. She's good at this. You're good at this. Don't let her try to join my team out of misguided loyalty."

"I don't know that any of us can stop her if she puts her mind to something." Inside the cave, I hear the sparkle of laughter. The woman closest to Marissa, against all odds, is laughing. "I'll do my best."

"Thank you." The look in the Major's eyes changes; it's obvious she's switching gears from mom back to commander. "One last thing: she's going to bottom out when we get back to the motel. The first time you fire your weapon can be traumatic. Please sit with her. She's going to need your support."

"Yes, ma'am." There's no way I'm turning down that order. My mind races through the night's events. "Did we catch the incubus? I saw him slip away but I couldn't do anything."

"Yes, one of the other teams secured him before he got too far away. And we picked up the buyers as soon as they turned off the highway. Everyone was human except the incubus." The com on her uniform clicks. "I need to take this."

Walking back to the cave entrance, I watch Marissa with the women. I've thought it a hundred times before, but she's a natural at the people part. Can she handle a gun? Absolutely, she proved that tonight, but it's not the most important thing she can do. Anyone can be trained to kill. Not everyone knows compassion like she does. Right now, I see it. It's the same magic she worked with the community in Jerusalem. The same kindness she showed Sasha that made them friends.

The Major's right, her not being part of the Division would be a waste of talent.

"Hey, they're going to the hospital and I'm going to ride with them that far. Then the FBI will bring me back to the motel." As if she'd been called by my thoughts, Marissa appears at my side. "I'll catch you in the morning?"

"Knock on my door when you get there, I'll still be up." I wonder how far the hospital is and if I should go with her. No, she should do this one on her own. There's blood splatter on her uniform I hadn't noticed before. I'm sure she hasn't noticed it either. "Grab a change of clothes before you come. We both need to decompress, and I think it's best if we're not alone."

"Okay." She frowns. "You good?"

"I'm good. See you in a while." There's a light squeeze on my arm and then she climbs into the FBI van with the women. One reaches out immediately and takes her hand before the door closes.

There's a soft knock on my door. The clock reads four in the morning. I've changed into sweatpants and a t-shirt, my tactical gear stacked neatly in the corner of the room to deal with tomorrow. The Beretta is unloaded and on the side table.

I set down my tablet and move to open the door.

Marissa is waiting on the other side, still dressed in her gear, holding her helmet and a change of clothes in one hand, a bag from an all-night drive through in the other. She steps past me and into the small motel room, handing me the bag as she goes. "I stress eat. A cheeseburger sounded good after we dropped the women off. I brought you something in case you were hungry."

"Thanks." I set the bag on the small table in the room. She's feeling it, the tension of what we just went through. Her first hunt, the first time she's fired a weapon at a bad guy. I can feel the anxiety coming off her in waves. "Let's get you out of that gear, it's heavy."

I turn her around and start working on her vest. She doesn't fight me or insist she can do it on her own, which is a good indication of how close to exhausted she must be. This is how it works for most of us. We survive on adrenaline while we're on the mission and then our bodies crash when it's over.

I remove the vest from her shoulders and set it down. She looks at it in surprise. "There's blood on it."

"Yes." I keep my voice calm and even. "It's blood spatter from the gunshot."

"Oh." Her eyes train on the tiny droplets of blood and I wonder if this is it, the moment that she falls apart. Instead, she shakes her head and sits on a chair, her fingers working at her boots. "Can I take a shower? I feel like I need a shower."

"Sure." I nod toward the bathroom door. "Clean towels are on the shelf above the toilet. Use anything else you need."

"Thanks." Marissa disappears into the small room and closes the door. A moment later, the water turns on. I know what she's doing, she's washing off the mission. It's a technic a lot of Fallen use to detach from whatever trauma we just went through. A little soap and water go a long way toward mental health.

I stack her gear in the corner next to mine, wondering how much time she'll take. I don't have to wait long. Less than five minutes later the water turns off. I don't want her to think I've been pacing the room waiting for her, so I take my spot back on the bed, my legs stretch out in front of me like I'm relaxed, my tablet back in my hands as I scroll through Mia's reports on the recruits during my absence. The updated grades and times from runs barely register while I worry about Marissa on the other side of that door.

The door quietly opens, and Marissa emerges from the bathroom, hair damp, wearing yoga pants and a New York t-shirt, the clothes she'd taken off piled neatly in her hands. The energy coming off her body is scrambled, chaotic. Major Cazut was right, Marissa shouldn't be alone right now.

I stand up and take the dirty clothes from her hands, adding it to her already discarded pile of gear. "You're not okay."

"I shot someone today." Her body starts to sag. "I didn't know it would feel like this. Collin, I shot a human man."

"You did. Don't mistake the truth. He may have been a human man, but he would have sold those women to the highest bidder. And if he couldn't sell them, they would have been killed and buried in the desert." It's a struggle to keep my voice calm, but I manage to do it. That man, all those men, deserve any pain they get. "He's as dangerous as the incubus he was working with. You did what you had to do, and you didn't kill him. He was armed and he wasn't backing down. If you hadn't acted, someone could have gotten hurt. It was a good shot."

"I know. And I know what they did to those women, even before they brought them out to meet the buyers." She makes a face. "The FBI agents I was with were talking after we left the hospital. It's…unthinkable. I shot a man."

And here come the tears.

I expected this. Heck, I played out the scenario in my mind. The problem? I'm not sure how to comfort Marissa without crossing any lines. A pat on the back doesn't seem like enough. Maybe a side hug? My mom told me once that sometimes a female just needs to cry out whatever is bothering them. Should I just let her cry while we sit in the chairs at the table? Maybe I should hold her hand like the nurses do in the hospital, but even that seems too intimate, too close.

In the end, Marissa makes the decision for me. One minute, she is standing across the room from me, tears silently falling down her face. The next, she's got her arms wrapped around my chest and her face buried in my shirt.

Completely shocked, I tentatively lower my arms around her, holding her close while she cries. With my right hand, I cup the back of her head, her damp hair making my own hand wet. I realize she smells like the motel's soap, the little packet that they leave for guests. It's citrus, like grapefruit and tangerine. It makes me think of warm places and beaches, of the ocean.

We could have stood there for minutes or hours, I have no idea. I just know the feeling of her in my arms is so right that I can't think about anything else. It's like everything in my life has come to this point and now I can't go back. I need her to be okay. I need her to see me for who I am. I need this.

"You must think I'm a terrible soldier." Her voice is muffled against my shirt, my shoulder wet from her tears.

"Of course not." I rest my chin on her head, breathing in the scent of the sea. "I think you're a humane soldier. You remember what I told you, back in Orasul? Do no more harm than necessary. This is what makes you good."

"I never thought about what it would feel like. To hurt someone. To see their blood on my clothes." Her body shudders and I hold her a little tighter. "It wasn't like killing a Rattus or an ugly creature that eats babies in the jungle. He looked like us."

"Just because he looked like us, that doesn't make him any less evil." Reluctantly, I release my hold on her to tilt her head back so that I can see in her eyes. "What you're feeling is normal. What happened was traumatic. The important part is knowing that you're not alone. I'm here and I'm not going anywhere tonight."

"Thank you." Her hands come up to rest on top of mine, holding me in place. Before I can stop myself, I lean forward and rest my forehead against hers.

"Come on." After a minute, I pull back, knowing that I'm too close. "You need to close your eyes for a few minutes. You must be exhausted."

She nods, sniffling. When I let go, I grab a tissue so she can wipe her eyes.

We sit on the bed, her close beside me. Sensing she needs comfort more than I need to maintain a healthy distance, I drop my arm around her shoulders and pull her close. "Just relax. Everything is going to be fine."

CHAPTER NINETEEN

The alarm on my phone blares too early the next morning. I reach toward the nightstand to hit snooze and realize someone is with me on the bed. My heart jumps and I sit up suddenly, remembering the night before.

Marissa is making an unhappy noise, reaching for her own phone on the opposite nightstand.

At some point, she must have crawled under the blankets. I'm still laying on top of them, a good thing. Fallen do not take sleeping together lightly and I'm sure this is not what Major Cazut had in mind when she asked me to sit with Marissa.

The truth is, I hadn't intended to fall asleep. I'd meant to let her sleep and then I was going to continue working on the files from home. It seems the stress from yesterday got to me, too.

Her hand hits the snooze button, and she relaxes back on the bed. "Why is my phone going off so early?"

I look at the time. It's eight in the morning. We've been asleep for about four hours. I think back and try to remember why we're up so early. "Your mom. You're having breakfast with your mom in thirty minutes."

"Crap, I forgot." Her voice is a little gravelly from sleep and her hair is messy. She looks up at me. "I'm sorry, are you mad I fell asleep?"

"I'm the one that told you to close your eyes, remember?" I want to reach over and smooth down her hair where it's sticking out, but I don't. Whatever passed between us last night has to be locked away again. "I'm sorry if you get busted by your mom. I didn't mean to fall asleep."

"It's okay." She smiles sleepily and squeezes my arm. "I feel so much better this morning. Thank you."

The way she's looking at me? I'm afraid for a minute that she's going to try and kiss me, but then she swings her legs around on the bed and stands up. She stretches her arms over her head, her shirt riding up so that I can see a flash of skin. I drop my eyes so that I won't stare. "We've got to debrief with the FBI and Major Cazut at ten, then we meet with the counselor. Do you want me to bring your gear, so you don't have to come back here?"

She gives me a funny look. "A minute ago, she was my mom. Now she's Major Cazut again?"

"She's your mom in our time off." I stretch, too. I should get up and grab some breakfast of my own. It's going to be a long day. "She's Major Cazut when we're working. Heck, to me, she might be Major Cazut on our time off. She kind of intimidates me."

I hear a snicker. "We'll see if she still intimidates you a year from now. Maybe you'll get a chance to get to know

her as something other than an officer. Yes, please bring my gear. I'll meet you at HQ at ten."

The door opens and shuts and she' gone.

I fall back on the bed. What the heck did I let happen last night? My eyes close and I remember the feel of her arms around me, the smell of her soap, the almost kiss when my hands were on her face. We have almost six weeks left of basic training. I can't let any of this happen. It doesn't matter if she's feeling the same way, and I think she is. I've got to get control.

"Rumor has it Marissa took out one of the men on the mission." Mia props herself up on the wall next to where I'm doing bicep curls in the tiny weight room. "True?"

We've seriously been back in Pandora's Box for all of an hour and a half, just long enough for me to unpack, stash my gear, and come down here to work off some internal tension. It's raining outside so a run is out of the question, although I'm sure Mia would find a way to track me down out there, too.

"It wasn't a kill, she just wounded him." I continue lifting, keeping count in my head. "How do you find these things out so fast?"

"Told you before, I'm very observant." Her eyes sparkle, then she turns more introspective. "How's she doing? I've heard the first time you make a shot is the worst."

At that comment, I put down the weight and give her my full attention. "You've never made a shot like that?"

"No." Her answer surprises me. I assumed that all the warriors are like Major Cazut, ultra military and handy with the weapons. "I mean, I've taken our Legion and Rattus, but nothing humanoid. Nothing sentient."

"How did you manage that?" I'm baffled. The battles before Discord was captured, the missions Major Cazut takes, the trouble caused by Chaos before he disappeared, how did she miss all of it?

"Like you, I'm young. I missed the early battles with Discord's army and by the time we went after Discord himself, I'd been picked to be the scholar for the warriors. It drives Kurt crazy, I know he wants to get out there with Anna and hunt some of these predators, but most of the time he's stuck here with me." She gestures around the weight room. "I stay in shape and I'm good with my sword, but it's all left to theory at the moment."

"Do you want to kill people? Or demons?" The door to the weight room opens and another soldier comes in. He climbs on a treadmill and sticks his earbuds in.

"No." She considers herself, then shakes her head. "Not really. Sometimes I feel less useful than the rest of my team. Riley's this great commander. Anna is out there tracking things that go bump in the night and Kurt goes with her whenever he can. Maxim is working with the scientists to see if we can set up smaller Divisions in more cities. And I'm…just studying old scrolls."

"What about the teaching?" From what I could see in the recruit notes, she did a good job while I was gone. Classes continued, her training sessions were different from mine, but still very challenging. I'd been told she even gave Tasha a run for her money. "Isn't that more?"

"It is, and I'm looking forward to it, although I'll miss being in the same city as my brother and his family." She joins me on the workout bench. "I assume you're going to stay based out of Jerusalem. You and Marissa."

"There is no me and Marissa." I correct her, then gently add. "Not right now, anyway."

"Again, not what I heard." She raises her shoulders in a shrug; Mia makes me exhausted.

"Can you just say what you're dancing around, please?" I want to finish this conversation before anyone else joins us in the weightroom. No extra ears are needed.

"I just heard you two work well together. Anna said you can practically move in tandem without talking first. She said you'll make a good team. Now we're just wondering where you'll be."

"Unless your brother has different plans, Marissa doesn't want to go back to Orasul and the job we both want in Hope isn't available." I set down the weights and wipe my hands on a towel. "My expectation is we'll be here in Jerusalem for a while. We didn't talk about it on the way home, and she has no idea I've held up my assignment to wait for her to make up her mind. I'd appreciate it if your family discussions can keep that little secret for me."

"Collin, she assumes you're going to be stationed together." Mia rolls her eyes. "She all but said that when we talked about it before last week's assignment. You had two days off together in Hope, what did you do there? You should have had plenty of time to talk about it."

"Not that it's any of your business, but she spent the first night with Sasha and Aria. They went to dinner and shopping, and I don't know what else. The second day?" I can't believe I'm about to admit to this. "We went to see the matinee at the theater. She wanted to go, and I didn't want her to go alone. We saw a musical. Then we had dinner with my mom. No big deal."

Eyebrows shoot upward on Mia's forehead. "I'm going to forget about the musical. You had dinner with your mom? And you don't think that's a big deal?"

"No. Mom knows her whole family is here in Jerusalem, and she didn't want her to be alone for the evening, so she invited her to dinner. It's not a big deal." Okay, even I don't believe that. Mom never invited Natasha to dinner. I don't know how Mom picked up on my feelings for Marissa, but she did. Must be Mother's Intuition or some nonsense.

After dinner, when I'd been back at my own apartment and Marissa was settled in the barracks, Mom texted me. *She's beautiful. And smart and confident. I see why you like her.*

I'm her superior officer, Mom. I do my best to shut that door before Mom walks through it any farther.

Only for a few more weeks. Yeah, Mom's smart.

"Whatever." She shakes her head and pushes up from the bench. "Cards tonight? Riley's coming and he said to make sure you were there, too."

A shudder of dread races through my body. "Are you serious?"

"Yep. I think he wants to get to know you better. Seeing as you're about seven weeks away from dating his kid." She turns on her heel and walks a few steps away. "See you at seven?"

"I'll be there." I may as well embrace it. If things work out the way I hope, Marissa's family will be part of my life, too.

"Good." She smiles at me over her shoulder. "Now I'm going to go pester Marissa and see what she has to say about her days off."

"Please don't." The words come out with a whine I'm not embarrassed to embrace. "I don't want her to know that I've been talking about her."

"I'm just going to ask her how her vacation days were. See what comes up." Mia winks at me and walks out before I can protest any more.

With a sigh, I return to my dumbbells and focus on my biceps.

Mia might tease, but I'm confident she won't break my confidence. She would never do anything to hurt Marissa, which is why I know she's being truthful about the way Marissa feels. She's going to do anything in her power to make sure Marissa is happy, healthy, and loved.

Love. Not a word I'm ready to contemplate yet. I like her a lot. There's time for the rest.

I just settle into my routine again when my phone vibrates. Irritated, and wondering who is bothering me now, I pick it up. It's a text from Command summoning me to the General's office in one hour. My heart skips a beat. I reply that I'll be there and put the weights back on the shelf.

Did he find out about the night in the motel room? Surely not. I hadn't told anyone and I'm sure Marissa wouldn't go tell her stepdad about it. Hopefully, it's something benign like after basic placements or that one of the recruits got caught doing something they shouldn't.

I grab my sweatshirt and pull it over my head before I head out the door and toward my room. I need to shower and put on some real clothes before I meet with the General.

I'm just about to head to the General's office when there's a knock on my door. I open it to find Marissa, no longer dressed in civilian clothes, but in her everyday military garb. "I'm just about to head over to the General's office. I've been summoned."

"Me, too." She steps through the door without my invitation; I don't say anything. I like it when she's in my space. "He texted and said he wanted to see us both."

"Then you know more about this meeting than I do." Finished tying my shoes, I stand up again. The need to touch her is so strong that I have to fight it. "Any idea what this is about?"

"I assume it has to do with the guy I shot. Maybe an update or something?" We step into the hallway, and I shut the door. She walks beside me. "I can't think of any other reason Riley would want to see me on an official matter."

I can think of one or two, but I keep that to myself. I don't know enough about their relationship to know if he'd interfere with her personal life and my place in it.

As we're waiting outside of the General's office for him to see us, I look around and wonder if this is the future Major Cazut imagined for Marissa when she was young. A job where you carry weapons every day because you're dealing with deadly creatures who would kill you at the first opportunity. Long periods of time living in a country that is at war. Training to fight and understanding how to put together or dismantle bombs. I wonder if it's what my mom wanted for me.

The door to the office opens and Tasha emerges. She looks happy, like she'd just won the lottery. "Thank you, sir."

Riley pats her on the shoulder and gives her a file folder. "You can take this to HRC, they'll get you settled."

That's when I realize what we're here for. The General must be handing out post basic training assignments. With only six weeks to go, the new soldiers will need to update their uniforms and acquire the proper gear for their next homes.

Looking back, it's been a long road here and I'm sad to know that in a few minutes, I'll be the outgoing trainer. The identity that brought me back from that hospital bed won't be who I am anymore. The hours I spent in the classroom, in the training rooms, talking to the recruits, it's all going to be in the past. Am I ready for the future? I hope so.

"Collin, Marissa, come in." He holds the door open for us and we take our seats in the small space across from his desk. "I see your last patrol was a success and you were instrumental in bringing in the incubus and his cohorts. How did you feel about the mission?"

We look at each other. I should respond as the higher-ranking officer, but I want Marissa to answer. It was her first hunt. The thing she's been preparing for since high school. I meet her eyes nod my head.

"The hunt was okay; I can do that if I need to." Her voice sounds tentative at first. "Although the idea of doing something like that in the jungle or Siberia or somewhere remote is kind of terrifying. But what we did last week, I could do that. What I liked best about the mission was helping those women. I was sad that I couldn't go with them into the hospital. They needed someone to help them feel safe, someone they could trust. Thankfully, there was an FBI agent that was able to go with them."

The General takes some notes on a legal pad. Then he looks at me. "Collin?"

I'm startled. I figured this meeting was about Marissa. I've already put in my requests in, what more does he need to know from me?

"That mission is an example of the Division could be responsible for once we become public knowledge." The General nods, confirming what Major Cazut explained to me in the field. "Like Marissa, I like the people part of the job more, but I'm trained for that part. I've served, I've fought, and I can hunt. The world is going to need Fallen in their cities. Not in *our* cities like Orasul that are too far from human civilization to be of help. The world needs us to be in places like New York and Jerusalem and Paris and Chicago and Los Angeles. When our world becomes public, I'd like to believe all the demons and all the Fallen and all the humans will be able to live together in peace, but you and I know that won't happen. The Division will be needed to stop creatures like the incubus from destroying lives. To hunt down Nightwalkers like the one that killed Amy. To keep the peace and foster communities that coexist. I'd like the opportunity to do that. *We'd* like the opportunity to do that."

The General sets his pen down on his desk and folds his hands together. For a long time, he looks at Marissa like I'm not even in the room and I wonder if I'd overstepped. "Is that what you want? To stay partnered with Collin and work for the Division?"

"Yes." I feel a rush of relief to hear Marissa say the word. She'd already said it in a dozen ways over the last

few months, but to hear her definitive confirmation that she wants the same thing I want? Such release.

Unthinking, I take a breath and let it out quickly, a sigh of relief. The General looks at me and I catch the shadow of a wry smile on his face. It's gone in a second, but I know it was there. I have a feeling card night is going to include some teasing later.

"What about you?" He tilts his head toward Marissa. "Are you comfortable continuing to work with Marissa?"

"Within the parameters we discussed, yes." I look at her. "Please."

The General chuckles this time, and I realize he's getting some humor and satisfaction out of my situation. I'm sitting in his office asking permission to date his daughter and she doesn't even realize it yet.

Marissa, not knowing what exactly is going on, is giving the General an irritated look. When he notices, he immediately wipes the smile off his face. What an awesome trick. That could come in handy.

"Okay." He reaches into a pile of folders and takes off the top two. "Effective immediately, I'm taking you off patrolling in the prison. You will be working in Jerusalem on weekends and commuting back here for your regular living situation. Because we've agreed with Benjamin's team that situations may arise that would require you to stay overnight in the city, we'll be securing an apartment for Fallen use, but that will take a little time. For obvious reasons we don't want you to stay in the apartment for more than three or four days at a time. With only two of you there at a time, you'll need to return to the hive regularly. Collin, you'll finish teaching this semester. Mia and Kurt will shadow you as they will be taking over your position in June."

"Really?" Marissa's face lights up. "I'm being assigned to the Division? Collin and I both are?"

"Along with Jenn and Kaia, yes, but they won't start until they finish basic and take their two-week furlough." He pulls two sheets of paper out of his top desk drawer and signs them, putting them in the folders he'd already retrieved. "You're starting earlier because the Superintendent has been overwhelmed with requests for meetings and small issues since your last visit. We feel it would be beneficial to have Fallen involved sooner rather than later to build relationships with the local community. You'll both be given vacation time once Jenn and Kaia are settled."

"Kaia and Jenn?" Marissa looks at me and then back at the General. "I thought Kaia wanted to be on mom's squad."

"She changed her mind. A few nights in the jungle can do that." General Riley doesn't correct Marissa. This is going to be different, like Mia has been trying to get me to see, I'll need to see the General and the Major another way now. They're Marissa's parents, not just superior officers anymore.

I'm not sure which is more intimidating.

"That's it. We have our orders." Marissa's smile is so big. She's excited and relieved and probably feeling another thousand kinds of feelings I don't know about.

"Almost." The General smiles brightly. "At graduation, you will both be receiving a promotion for your work here. Marissa, your leadership skills with your classmates and the work you did on the incubus case showed command that you are ready to take on more responsibilities. You'll be promoted to Corporal. Collin, you took on a position you weren't trained for, and your work has been outstanding. You will be promoted to Major in six weeks. This does not mean you will be in command of the unit at the Division. All four of you will report directly to Major Chloe Laurent. She will be the command for the Division here in Jerusalem and she will report to Major General Maxim who will be overseeing all Division Fallen moving forward. As of six weeks from now, I will no longer be your commanding officer."

Marissa's hand grabs my arm and squeezes hard. I look over at her and can't contain my smile. It's not just the job or the promotion, being removed from the General's direct command means a lot. She can go back to being just his daughter.

A few minutes later, we find ourselves in the hallway outside of the General's office. Marissa turns around and throws herself at me, hugging me around the neck tightly. "I can't believe it! I thought for sure someone more advanced than me would get that job. This is so amazing!"

Aware we're drawing attention from passersby in the hallway, and a few covert chuckles, I give her a quick squeeze and then I pull away from her. "You're good at this. Of course you were going to get the job."

"And Mia and Kurt are taking over for you? I'm kind of sad to know she's going away." Her eyes focus on the floor, her expression strange. Shy, maybe? Since when is Marissa shy about anything? "You want to go celebrate? Find some ice cream or something?"

"Mia and Kurt have a good opportunity in front of them and I happen to know Mia's ready for a change." I drop my arm loosely around her shoulder, like a friend would, and start walking her away from the General's office door. "And I wish we could do something, but I can't. I still have a job here that I need to do, which means I need to spend some time going over the reports from my absence. Then I promised Mia and the General a game of cards after dinner."

"Oh." Her eyes get big. "You and Riley are playing cards tonight?"

"I think Mia instigated it." My voice sounds apologetic. "Either way, I can't hang out tonight."

"That's fine, I should probably spend some time with Jenn and Kaia anyway." We stop in the main corridor that leads back to our respective barracks rooms. "Can I meet you for dinner instead?"

"Sure." Knowing that she wants to spend time with me makes me feel warm inside. Counting the days until we can make it something more official will be torture. "I'll meet you at your room a little before six."

CHAPTER TWENTY

"I can't tell you how happy we are that you'll be joining us permanently." Superintendent Benjamin meets us at the front desk of the department and gives us our visitors badges. I guess we'll get real badges sooner or later, officially making us part of the police force. "I think having you on board will go a long way toward quelling the concerns of our local community."

"Welcome to the team." The woman behind the desk smiles at Marissa and I, much more friendly than she'd been on our last three visits, this time speaking to us in heavily accented English.

"Thank you." I add another mental note to the logistics of this new job. Somehow, we're going to have to keep track of which humans know about the Fallen. It's also imperative that Marissa and I both get our driver's license. We can't count on Nathan to be our driver indefinitely, although he doesn't seem to mind. This job allows him to drop us off until we need to go home. He then heads off to spend the day with his parents.

Living in New York and Orasul, neither of us needed a license. We had what we needed and could walk to all the shops. Now the whole world is open to us.

I wait until we're in the familiar conference room with the door shut before I broach the topic of the woman at the desk. "Who knows what we are? The receptionist at the desk?"

"No." Constance shakes her head. "Just our team know what you are for now. Well, our team, the Commander we report to, and the Commissioner. We've been cleared by government officials for the information on who and what you are. No one else."

"What does the receptionist and everyone else think?" Marissa, pacing slowly around the room to take a closer look at the posters and maps, turns toward Benjamin. "And I have questions about uniforms and whether or not we're supposed to carry side arms and probably a hundred other things, too."

"I have many questions for you, as well, but first we'll discuss the logistics of the job." He gestures to a seat. "This will take some time and then we'll make some house calls."

"House calls." Shaking my head, I pull out a chair and take my seat. "In New York, police making house calls is a bad thing. It means someone has died or you're going to be arrested."

"With our community, you'll find it different." Constance pushes a file toward us. "Many of our kind can't leave their home unless it is under the cover of darkness because of their skin color or appendages humans do not have. Going

to them is a sign that we respect them and their opinions. We can move around in the daylight, they cannot."

"That makes sense." Marissa finishes her trek around the room and sits beside me. "Do you think that will change when their world opens up?"

"It will depend on the local humans." She leans back in her chair. "If they embrace us, then yes, I think you will see more of my kind living their lives more freely. If humans rally against us, then no. We fear death, just like you."

"To go back to your first question, most of the unit here believe you're Americans on loan to our staff to help with relations between Israeli police and American soldiers and tourists." Benjamin glances at the door as Simeon joins us. "Our cultures are different enough that sometimes Americans find themselves in uncomfortable situations here. Officially, at least for now, you are a liaison between our cultures."

"That leads me to the next question, or two questions, really." There's so much to cover that I barely know where to start. "What does the rest of your department think you do? And neither Marissa nor I speak Hebrew. I don't believe Jenn or Kaia do fluently, either. Is that going to be a problem?"

"We're a community building unit." Simeon sits next to me at the table. "The rest of the department believes our job is to help quell arguments and disagreements between the many cultures here. And we do work with non-demon citizens from time to time, but for the most part, our Commander deflects requests for us to work outside our purview. There's a second unit that addresses most human needs."

"As for the language, I think you'll be fine." Constance points to a sign on the wall. It is written in three languages, one of them being English. "Most everyone speaks some English, and you'll find it on all our official road and directional signs. Over time, you should pick up on some Hebrew and you can always ask us for clarification if needed. We won't send you out on your own until we're comfortable that you know the area and the community. Think of us as your training wheels."

"You will also hear Arabic from a portion of our community and Russian. Many Jewish people have immigrated here from the former Soviet Union. I believe it's the third most common native language here." Simeon reaches for a book on the table. It's a Russian to English dictionary. "You may struggle at first because these languages are so different from English, but I'm sure you'll pick up words here and there. And, like Constance said, almost everyone speaks English."

"Conservative street clothes will be appropriate to wear. You can see that we do not wear traditional police uniforms although there may be times when it is deemed appropriate, so I suggest you keep one or two of your uniforms handy." Simeon gestures downward at his jeans and black button-down shirt with the sleeves partially rolled up. "It makes us less noticeable when we come and go from homes. Just remember that our culture is very conservative. Apologies to Marissa, but I would advise against short skirts, short shorts, and sleeveless tops during the summertime. Especially around religious sites."

"Not a problem, and I'll talk to Kaia and Jenn before they get here. The Fallen have a conservative culture as well." Suppressing a smile, I'm grateful the Division put so much thought into this sit-down session. While I don't think I've ever seen Marissa in a short skirt, dresses in general wouldn't be appropriate for our jobs, it's good to start on the same page. "What about our weapons? I know we don't expect there to be trouble, but I can see you carry one."

"You will be issued a handgun as soon as I get clearance from the Commissioner. You will be permitted to always carry it, even when you are off duty. We all carry nine-millimeter, I hope that will work for you." Simeon removes the magazine from his Glock and sets it on the table. It's just like the kind of gun Marissa prefers and I wonder if I'll be able to get a Beretta. "Each vehicle has a rifle in the trunk, usually an M1 Carbine for serious trouble. I'm sure you've noticed Border Patrol carry larger rifles like the M16. I don't see you having the need for anything with that kind of power."

"I think that's the basics." Benjamin gestures to the folder Constance had placed on the table. "Our department is almost completely paper driven. We don't want to have an electronic database that could be hacked, too many lives depend on our ability to maintain anonymity. That is a list of our current community. It is not to leave this building. Actually, it's not to leave this hallway. The sooner you can commit to memory the families on that list, the easier your job will be. If you'll follow me, I can show you to your office."

Office? That's a perk I wasn't expecting.

"Unfortunately, due to space constraints, you four will be sharing this room." Benjamin opens a door to a small room. It has a window that faces the parking lot, and two desks have been crowded into the space. There're already two laptops waiting, one on each desk, and in-box is attached to the wall. As far as I'm concerned, it's perfect. "Your General explained your living situation with me, that you must return to your unit regularly, so you cannot live full time in Jerusalem. I assumed that meant it would be a rare occurrence that all four of you would be here together. If you are, you are welcome to use the conference room as added space."

"Thank you, this is more than enough." Being here now, going through the basics of a new job, it's settling in that this is real. In a few weeks, I'll teach my last class. I'll put on my civilian clothes and go to work creating a better future for demons and Fallen alike.

"Oh, and one more thing." He lowers his voice and checks the hallway to see if we're alone. Whatever he needs to say seems to be making him uncomfortable. "Your General also explained that many work partners marry. This is… unusual for our culture. Honestly, it's frowned upon and often forbidden in some workplaces. I understand it is the norm in your culture. I just wanted to let you know that we will adjust our…expectations accordingly if needed. That is all. I'm going to leave you to get settled into your new office. I'll come back in little while and take you to get your new credentials made."

"Wait." Marissa, who is blushing furiously, picks up a flowering plant from one of the desks. "What is this?"

"It's a gift from Sara. Constance told her you would be coming here to work, and she thought you could use some color in what must be a very dull government building." Noticing the walls, I can see she's right. Everything is painted a flat, off-white color. The floors are tan tile, and

the desks are standard issue metal with a fake wooden top. To him, it might be a plain, government office, but to me, it's a future of possibilities. "Constance promises to keep it watered and healthy when you are not in the office."

"Please tell Sara thank you." Marissa sets it down on the desk closest to the window where it can get sunlight. "It brightens up the room."

"You can tell her yourself, she's one of today's visits." Benjamin tips his head to us both and leaves us alone in the room to get settled.

The cards in my hand are basically worthless so I pass before I take a drink of one of Kurt's sodas. The sugary sweetness slides down my throat, nice and cold. I'm mostly a plain water kind of guy, but this indulgence is welcomed as we celebrate the end of an era. "What's got you handing out your sodas tonight, Kurt?"

"Cleaning out my stash before I ship out next week. Figured I'd bring them where they'll be appreciated." Add in the chips, popcorn, and the homemade cookies Sara sent me this week, and we have a small party. He grins in my direction. "Two weeks from now, I'll have all the soda I want without pestering you to pick it up at the store on your way home from work. I bid three."

The bid passes around the table and the hand starts to play. Mia, who seems to be playing only half-heartedly, tosses a card onto the table. "I can't believe this is our last night of cards."

Riley reaches an arm around her shoulders and hugs her tight. "Think about it this way, in a couple of weeks, you can be beating Keagan at cards."

"I know. It's just that I've gotten to like this." She gestures around the room. "Not the part where we can barely leave the prison, but the part where we're all here together. You and Anna and Marissa and me and Kurt and Collin and, heck, even Alain has been a great friend. I'm going to miss it."

"Thank you for including me." Alain salutes her with a potato chip and then rakes in the cards on the table.

Me? I find myself at a loss for words that she'd include me, although I'd become a regular at their card nights and Mia had become a good friend. I didn't see myself as part of their club, but more of a guest brought along to complete the table. Being with Marissa's family hadn't become any less intimidating, either, but with the time I've spent with them I've learned they are caring, supportive, and very close.

"Don't look like that, you're a part of us now." Kurt, who treats Mia like he's her second brother, gives my shoulder a gentle push.

I meet his eyes and nod once. "Thanks."

"Come on, let's not get too depressed, you all have a whole week left of finals, and then graduation. You need to keep your spirits up." Riley takes in the cards to deal. It's taken a while, but I'm finally comfortable calling him by his first name when we play cards. For weeks, I'd continue to call him General, which would elicit laughter and a gentle teasing. "This class, despite a few bumps and bruises along the way, has done very well. It's the first combined class for Hope and Orasul, and the largest class in a long time for any Fallen city. You have a lot to be proud of."

"For a job that I was resentful to be assigned at first, I'm going to miss them." Like Mia, I'm feeling a little nostalgic tonight. When I first started this path, it felt like it would last forever. A year of high school. A year and a half of basic training. Two and a half years of my life tied up teaching a team I wasn't the least bit interested in. Now, those high school kids are almost as old as I was when I started this path and I'm handing the reigns over to Mia and Kurt. "Tasha's going to do great in Officer Training. After Tevin died and Marissa dropped behind her in ranks, she bloomed. I'm so impressed by her, and I could have missed it. Mia, make sure you watch for those ones, the soldiers who are ready to shine if the louder ones would get out of their way."

"You know Nick's doing well, too." Riley deals the cards in Alain's direction. "Going to Les Gens was a good move for him. It's a smaller program, only four recruits there. Five, now that's he's joined them. He seems to have found a solid team to be a part of and gotten his footing back. It might have cost him a few months, but he'll be fine. He hasn't requested any transfers back to our units when he's done, either, I think he plans on staying in there indefinitely."

"There are worse places to land." Mia breathes in deeply like she can smell the memories of her time there. "I'd give anything to wake up and eat the pastries from that patisserie every morning down the street from the Arc de Triomphe. Macaroons and croque-monsieurs, and the Eiffel Tower. Oh, and the Louvre."

"And Mom and Dad." Riley smiles. Their parents retired to Les Gens several years back. "It sounds like you know where you want to be one day, too."

"Maybe." She shrugs her shoulders. "Mostly, I like to visit. I'm afraid I'd gain too much weight to fit into my uniform if I lived there too long."

I doubt that. I've seen her on our training runs for the last six weeks. For someone I once teased about being a scholar, she pushes herself as hard as anyone to be physically fit. Mia puts everything she has into her work, which is how I know the recruiting program will thrive under her care.

We play cards for a few minutes quietly, each of us in our own thoughts, munching on snacks and calling out our bids. That's something else I've found here, quiet. It's okay to sit in silence with these friends; to enjoy their company without words or worrying about keeping up unnecessary conversation. It's a lot like it was with Marissa months ago in the hospital. Sometimes the silence can be as fulfilling as a deep conversation.

Mia suddenly laughs, we all look at her with curiosity.

"I'm sorry." She sobers when she notices us all staring at her. "I was thinking about how absurd it is that Kaia and Marissa are not only going to the same command, but that they asked for it. Oh, how Marissa hated Kaia in the beginning."

"I have to admit that I was a little shocked by that myself." I might have put them together to study; I never thought they'd end up good friends. "As hard as they pushed each other in sparring classes I was surprised that neither of them ended up at the top of the class. I honestly thought I'd spend two and a half years watching them push each other to the top. Maybe, if it hadn't been for Tevin…"

"They both deferred to him as the leader of their class. I don't think it occurred to either of them that if they worked together instead of against each other that they could lead better than he did." Riley watches a soldier come into the common room and grab a book off the shelf. He smiles

and nods in our direction before he leaves us alone again. "Maxim is shipping back to Hope after this term; he can run the Division from there and he misses his family. Tevin's death really affected him, which I understand. He wants to be closer to his daughter and his wife."

"So much change." Alain shakes his head. "It feels like the end of something."

"For some of us. But I'll be here in three weeks to play. So will Collin." Riley's eyes meet mine across the table. "Right? You're not going to bail on me once Mia's gone, are you?"

"No, I'm not going to bail." It's my turn to deal the cards, so I pull them all toward me. "But we might need to find another player or two unless you plan on changing the game to rummy."

"Not my plan, we'll find someone." Riley's face becomes serious. "It's a pity that Marissa didn't make it back to the top of the class. She worked so hard for so long to get there and stay there."

"Don't feel bad for her." Brushing off the sentiment, I consider the Marissa I've gotten to know so well. She changed a lot after Tevin died, being at the top lost its luster. Instead, she focused on how to be happy and fulfilled. "She's finishing just fine in the middle of the pack. Her body took a beating, and she lost a lot of muscle while she was in the hospital. It took time to get back into shape. And look at the bright side, she's got a job she loves, and she'll be getting her Corporal stripe at graduation. She's just fine."

"I'll have to trust you on that, in the last few weeks she's stopping coming to visit my office as much. Most of what I know about what she's doing comes across my desk in the form of reports." He raises an eyebrow. "It seems she's got someone else to talk to now."

I resist squirming in my seat, not sure what to say. It's true, she comes to my room a lot of evenings. At first, she'd bring her tablet and use the excuse that she needs to study or that we need to go over something for work. There was always a reason for her visit. Now, sometimes she brings a book, and we'll sit quietly and read, or we'll come down here to the common room and watch American television.

"Oh!" Alain's eyes widen. "I didn't know that was a thing."

"It's not." I downplay, I am, after all, sitting at the table with Marissa's stepfather and aunt. "Maybe one day when she isn't under my command."

"Right." Mia snickers. "Now, are we going to play or are we going to gossip like old women?"

"We're going to play." I gesture toward the cards in her hand. "It's your bid."

CHAPTER TWENTY-ONE

I walk the hallway from my private barracks room to the recruit barracks not sure what I'm feeling. It's over. Two and a half years spent with these talented recruits and in a couple of hours, they'll all officially be soldiers. I was so resentful when it first started. Until they grew on me. Until Jenn's humor and Marissa's determination and Tasha's gentle leadership cracked that shell of bitterness.

The day Nick and Tevin got into a fight over Marissa brought it all home. I saw myself clearly, saw what the resentment was doing. I realized then I needed to make some changes, or I'd end up a bitter, lonely man. God, that was so long ago.

I opened up. For the first time since my injury, I was honest. Honest about Natasha, honest about my own part in my injury. I was honest with a high school kid who was heading down the same path I'd already walked down.

Taking this job changed everything. I have no idea where I'd be if it hadn't been for General Keagan. Maybe working in this prison, bitter and lonely, without friends. Without a future in the Division. Without Marissa.

Today's graduation ceremony will be different than ones of days past. There will be no formal uniforms, those are tucked away in our closets back in Orasul and Hope. Instead, we'll be wearing our regular desert-colored uniforms. We won't be in the large auditorium in Orasul, we'll be under the sunshine outside the prison where bleachers have been set up for anyone who wants to watch. Since our families won't be able to join us, a live stream will be sending the ceremony back home.

It will be a subdued celebration, but a celebration all the same. For many of the recruits, they'll be saying goodbye to friends they've had since childhood. Some will stay here and work in the prison. Others will join Major Cazut's team to hunt down killers and the rest of the Thirteen. A couple will be heading home to be defenders of Hope and Orasul. And my new team will begin our work at Jerusalem's Division. Nineteen different recruits heading nineteen different directions.

I turn the corner. There's a lot of activity in the main barracks hallway. Doors are open, I can hear laughter and see smiles everywhere. Some of the regular soldiers assigned to the prison are here, too, congratulating the recruits they'd gotten to know over the last six months. It's a happy, chaotic mess of people.

"Hey." Marissa appears at my side, her voice full of excitement and something else. Anticipation? "I didn't think we'd see you down here today."

"I wanted to come down and say goodbye and good luck to some of the recruits. The first batch ship home in the morning." Knowing what they probably have planned, I give Marissa a stern look. "Please remember that some of your friends need to load up the bus before dawn tomorrow. Try not to overdo it tonight."

"It's up to them to get their backsides into bed, I got nowhere to be tomorrow." Her grin is infectious, and I find myself smirking back at her. We officially start work on Monday with only the weekend between then and graduation, which is fine by me. We'd had a couple of days off in Hope a few weeks ago. I'm ready to focus on our new mission.

"Hey, keep an eye on Kaia tonight. Tevin used to take care of her. She misses her mom at big events like these and could probably use a friend." I'd tried to get Kaia's dad flown in as a surprise, but red tape got in the way.

"Jenn and I got it, but you don't need to worry, she stopped drinking when Tevin died." Down the hallway, Tasha is shaking hands and handing out hugs. She's finishing top of the class, a surprise to just about everyone, including me. Like everyone, I'd been so impressed and frustrated with Tevin that I hadn't seen her potential until he was gone. Marissa's hand gently touches the rank insignia on my bicep. Today will be my last day as a Captain. "Do you and Mia and Kurt have plans of your own tonight? Playing cards or whatever you guys do?"

"We haven't talked about it." Her hand drops from my arm before anyone in the hallway can notice. "I assume they're busy packing, they leave on Monday and, according to Mia, have accumulated too much junk to take back on the airplane. I think she's trying to ship back a trunk of things she's collected. Figuring out what will be cleared through customs is a bit of a challenge."

"I imagine they won't let her bring in old manuscripts without previous clearance and proper documentation." I hear her sigh when someone calls her name. "I need to go talk to some people. I'll see you later?"

"Yeah." I touch her back lightly to stop her from walking away. "Swing by my room later, after the party or before the party gets really crazy, whichever. I've got something for you."

"Oooo, a present?" Eyes light up.

"Don't get too excited." I wave her off down the hallway. "But come see me."

"I will." Backing away from me, her cheeks redden. After the ceremony, she won't be Private Cazut anymore. She'll be Corporal Cazut, and, more importantly, she won't be under my command anymore.

And we both know it.

Marissa turns and disappears into the crowd of Fallen in the hallway as I watch her.

"Honestly, can you be more obvious? I don't think the cook in the kitchen has figured out that you like her yet." Jenn, leaning in a doorway to my right, must have watched our whole exchange. She rolls her eyes and pushes away from the doorjamb. "Please tell me you're going to do something about that tonight."

"I'm not having this conversation with you." Scanning the hallway to make sure no one else can hear us, I stick with my usual response. "I'm still your commanding officer."

"For, like, another hour and a half." She snorts. "Come on, we're coworkers now. That means we can be friends."

"We'll be coworkers in two weeks, and for the next hour and a half, we're not going to talk about this." I step

away from her, ready to work my way into the crowd. "Congratulations, Jenn."

"You're no fun!" Her words ring out over the rest of the voices.

I turn around and smile. "You're stuck with me now. Get used to it."

Leaving Jenn behind, I push into the group of recruits and friends, shaking hands and wishing good luck. There are pats on the back and a few hugs. A few of the guys staying to work in the prison ask if I want to hang out and grab a drink later. I decline, I have other plans.

On the periphery of the crowd, Tevin's ghost tips his hat to me. I'm taken aback. Although he's never far from my mind, I hadn't conjured his spectral image in weeks. Yet there he is, dressed like the rest of the graduates in their desert camouflage pants and jackets, his beret in place on his head. Perfectly shined boots are on his feet and he's smiling like the rest of his class.

I make my way through the crowd until I can lean on the wall next to his image. He looks away from me, his eyes focusing on Marissa and Kaia talking across the hallway. "They're going to be okay, right?"

They laugh together, Marissa leaning into Kaia, as another recruit named Brandon cracks a joke. They seem completely at ease, there's no more challenge between them.

"Yeah, I think they are." And I'm sure I'm right. They might be venturing into uncharted territory, taking up jobs Tevin probably never would have approved of, but they have nothing to be afraid of. They're going to blaze a path for others to follow. "They're both fighters. It's been a tough few months and they miss you, but they're going to be just fine."

He nods, completely silent as we stand side by side, watching the pre-graduation party continue without us.

"We'll recognize you in the ceremony. You and Amy both. There will be a moment of silence." Sadness settles in my chest. Two young lives cut short. Two futures we'll never get to see.

"I figured." He finally looks away from the females, down to his feet. "She used to say she wanted to make a difference in the world. I'm glad she found her way to do it. I always knew she'd be spectacular. That shot she made in Colorado was remarkable."

"It was." Listening to Tevin's voice, I wonder how real this moment is. Has my mind created his ghost to help me deal with his death? Or is Tevin's phantom really haunting this prison and his classmates?

"Yes, I'm real." His eyes meet mine, but they're sad. "Your imagination isn't this creative."

"Did I say that out loud?" I wonder.

"You didn't have to." His eyes find her again, Marissa, like he's studying her for the last time. I'm glad he can see her joyful, happy. Jenn comes up behind her and squeezes her in a bearhug. Then he pushes away from the wall. "It's time for me to go. I…uh…I had to see her get this far."

I'm surprised to see him wipe at tears in his eyes and I feel the need to comfort him. "She's amazing. She's going to change the world, just like she's always wanted."

"I know." He wipes his eyes with the back of a hand and takes a breath like he's steadying himself. Moving directly in front of me, he stands at attention and then salutes me. "Goodbye, Captain."

Tevin turns on his heel and fades away into nothing as he walks toward the door.

I don't know how long I stand there, my eyes trained where Tevin should be, but Tasha's voice reminds me I'm in the middle of a crowded hallway. "Captain? Are you okay?"

"Sorry, lost in thought." I shake away the sadness and focus on her. "Are you ready for a two-week vacation?"

"I am, and my parents are excited to have me home. I ship out first thing tomorrow morning." Her bright smile pushes away the last of the sorrow. "It's been so long since I've been in Orasul. I never realized I'd miss it so much."

"Sometimes you have to go away to find the thing you miss the most." Tasha is a tall female, her brown hair braided neatly and tucked up at her neck, like most of the females wear their hair. It's hard to tell in her uniform, but she's lithe and fast on the field, and a deadly shot. She had easily beaten the rest of her class in the range. "You'll be under General Keagan's staff for Officer's Training, correct?"

"Yes, I wanted to thank you for your letter of recommendation. It helped me get placed back in Orasul and I really appreciate it." At the top of the class, Tasha qualifies for Officer's Training, something Marissa and Tevin had both been striving for at one time. Truthfully, this is better. Tasha is a born leader. I can see her with her own command one day. "I knew that I'd made the cut, I just wasn't sure which staff I'd be placed on. So, thank you."

"Keagan's a good commander, one I'll always owe a debt of gratitude to for pushing me into this job." Down the hallway, I can see Mia approaching. We must be getting close to time. "He's going to push you hard. You'll be angry with him sometimes and you'll probably think he hates you a lot of the time, but you'll end up a better officer for it. Trust his methods."

Graduation seems to be over before it even begins. Nineteen recruits, classes completed, training complete, now full-fledged members of the Fallen Army, the Orasul-Hope unit. There were moments of silence for Amy and Tevin, a speech from General Riley, and prayers from the priests. Ten promotions, including Marissa's to Corporal. The installation of Mia and Kurt as the next commanders of the recruitment program and, finally, my promotion to Major.

There were cheers and laughter, a few tears, and the excitement of starting something new.

And then it was over.

Two and a half years, gone.

"Are you coming to the party down in the mess, Major?" Mia's shoulder bumps into mine, breaking into my thoughts. Her hands are stuffed into her pockets, and she looks contemplative herself. She's leaving on Monday for Orasul.

"I don't know." My eyes scan the horizon, my mind wandering to Natasha for a moment. I banish her image from my mind. She's from a lifetime ago and a world that isn't mine. "Do you think the new soldiers want to party with their former commander?"

"Of course they do." Grabbing my arm, she gives it a tug. "Besides, I'm pretty sure the real party won't start until the brass all leave. This party is too official. There's food and music. Although I should tell you Riley and Anna told me to come get you, they might expect you to hang out with us."

Oddly, I'm not intimidated at the idea of spending part of my day with Marissa's family. I'd established a friendship with Riley over cards and Mia has proven to be a better friend than I could have expected. I'll miss her when she ships out. Anna still scares me. She's tough and determined and strong willed. I can see where Marissa gets those traits from.

"Alright, let's go." I release the memories I'm holding onto and turn toward Pandora's Box.

Mia slides her arm through mine, a friendly movement, as we follow the crowd inside. "You're going to miss this."

"I am." I look sideways at her. "You're going to love the new position."

"I am." Our eyes meet and hold. Then she looks away. "I'll miss the people here, but I'm excited about the job. Kurt is, too, which shocked me. I thought for sure he'd try and trade me off for a new partner."

"No way he's letting you go home alone." We shuffle through the doors and Mia drops my arm. I remember Kurt's improvised archery tournament. He'd taken time to help those of us who weren't as accurate as others. He'd been patient and thorough in his instruction. "You'll both make good trainers."

"Thanks." We stop at the doors to the mess. It had been decorated and music played from hidden speakers. Tables are draped in black, plastic tablecloths with army themed centerpieces. There are even balloons and streamers hanging from the ceiling. The food line is serving pizza and hamburgers and French fries and who knows what else. Someone has dug a popcorn machine out and the smell of fresh popcorn fills the room.

"Congratulations, Major." Too soon, I'm looking in the face of Marissa's mom. She holds her hand out, waiting to shake mine. I hesitate before I can think better of it, and she laughs. "I can't read you if I have my gloves on. Besides, you should see your face when you look at my daughter, what you're feeling is obvious to everyone."

Anna Cazut, Marissa's adoptive mom and biological aunt, is a sensitive. When she touches your skin, she can read your emotions. Raising an eyebrow, she presents her hand to me again. This time, I shake it firmly. "Thank you, Major."

"Anna, please." Her grip is as firm as mine. "No reason to be formal."

"Anna."

Mia grins at me from next to her.

"Come on, let's grab some food. I had to skip lunch to get ready for the graduation." Stepping in front of me, Anna leads us toward the serving lines. "My flight back from Warsaw was delayed. I swear, I spend more time on an airplane than I spend in my own bed lately."

Riley reaches an arm around Anna's waist and pulls her close, whispering something into her ear. I do my best to ignore them, but Mia pushes Riley in the shoulder. "Quit with the PDA. You're not being very General like."

"I'm off the clock." Kissing Anna on the cheek, he releases his hold on her. "And I miss my wife when she's gone."

"Well, hopefully in the next couple of years more cities will be able to set up their own Division and I won't have to travel as much." Returning the kiss, she grabs a tray from the stack at the front of the food line. "I would love to have thirty days in a row without needing to fly anywhere."

We find a quiet table away from the loudest part of the party where we can eat and talk, Marissa fluttering by from time to time, usually with Jenn or Kaia in tow. I try not to let my feelings be hurt, I really want her to sit down and spend time with us. No, that's not true. I want to spend some time alone with her, but there will be time for that later. Today is the last time her class will ever be together. They should enjoy their time.

After a while, the older Fallen start drifting away, leaving the former recruits to have the mess hall for the evening. I take my cue from Mia when she slips away to spend some time with her brother. With one last look back at the class that changed my life, I let myself out the door and head to my barracks.

A change of clothes later, and I feel more like myself, the melancholy that threatened me all day suddenly gone. Paperwork from my new job is stacked on my desk, a good distraction for the evening. I flip open my notebook. Marissa and I have lunch scheduled with Matthew and Sara on Monday. I consider the clothes in my footlocker and realize I need to go shopping. I only brought enough civilian clothes for a day or two at most. Now I need enough to make a life here.

Thirty minutes later, I'm sitting on the floor, going through everything in my footlocker, when there's a knock at the door.

There's only one person it could be, I call out. "Come in."

The door opens, but Marissa doesn't cross the threshold. She looks uncomfortable. "Hey. You didn't say goodbye."

"I figured I'd see you tomorrow." I try to sound casual and calm. In reality, my heart is racing. "Or later tonight if you remembered."

"I remember." Her eyes sharpen, I can see she's made a decision. She steps into the room and closes the door behind her. Leaning to the side, she looks at my clothes on the floor. "What are you doing?"

She's been in my room more than a dozen times. My heart still kicks it up a few notches. "I'm going through my clothes. I think I need to go shopping; I didn't bring enough civilian clothes for the new job."

"I like shopping." Marissa's eyes light up; she notices the small chocolate cake I have sitting on the desk. "Are you hiding food in your room?"

"That's for you. I've got Kurt's last two soda's chilling on ice in the bathroom, if you're interested." There needs to be an explanation. "I'd heard they weren't going to be able to make a graduation cake today, so I brought this back from Jerusalem for you."

"I do love chocolate." She takes a step toward me and then stops again. I wonder why she's acting so strangely. "I have to tell you something first."

"Okay." It's easy to see something is really bothering her. I get up from the floor and sit on the bed, hoping she'll sit next to me. Instead, she pulls out the desk chair and sits facing me. "What's wrong?"

"I overheard you when you were talking to Riley." Her brow furrows at the confession and I'm more confused. I can't think of anything I've recently said to Riley that she doesn't already know. "Weeks ago. I was coming to see him, and his assistant had already left for the day; I was going to knock on the door, but then I heard your voice, and I'd overheard too much before I realized it was a private conversation. So, yeah, I've known for a while why you were giving up your command."

"Oh." My brain freezes up and I can't think of anything else to say. It's not that I didn't realize she knew something. The way she touches my arm; the time she would spend sitting on my bed studying quietly. The night in Arizona when we were hunting the incubus. She'd been telling me for a while. "I'm sorry if I was at all inappropriate, but I'm not sorry for how I feel."

Tentative, her fingers touch my arm. I can feel her tugging at my energy, just like I taught her months ago. "You're nervous."

"Aren't you?" I pull her hand from my arm and place it against mine, palm to palm, then I close my fingers around hers. "This could change everything."

She seems to consider this for a few moments. Then her eyes meet mine. "When do our transfers go through? Is it tonight, or does it happen on Monday?"

"Five o'clock local time tonight." I wonder why that matters.

Marissa takes her phone out of her pocket and checks the time. It's a little after eight. Her eyes close for an instant before she sets the phone on my desk. "Good. I like you a lot. I'm not nervous, I'm excited. I feel like I'm part of a team when I'm with you, like we're equal. We like some of the same things and we have goals that make sense. You don't want to kill everything and you're okay that I have a friend who's a demon. I…like you."

"I like you, too." My free hand brushes against her cheek, her energy radiating out and enveloping me.

A message alerts Marissa's phone. She groans. "That's Jenn looking for me. She's such a mother hen."

The moment we were having has passed, but I don't move my hand. "Go to your friends. We can talk about this and eat that cake tomorrow. We have time."

Eyes narrowing, I can see her thinking hard, considering her choices. Her body slides forward on the chair until she's sitting on the very edge, me still cradling her face, our hands still joined. At that point, I don't know who moved first or if we both did.

It's the softest, gentlest kiss I can possibly imagine. Brief, tender, a promise for tomorrow and more tomorrows after that.

EPILOGUE

I open the door to my room, already knowing what to expect. I can feel her all the way out into the hallway, relaxed and satisfied after a successful few days in the office. We'd settled into a comfortable routine of four days on, three days off with Jerusalem's Division. The Fallen apartment that had been rented down the street from the office is a happy oasis from the bustle of Jerusalem and a place for us to crash when we can't make the drive back to Pandora's Box.

Kaia and Jenn make wonderful additions to the team. They've grown into confident members of the Division able to handle even the most complicated of issues. When the time to go public comes, an event that is getting closer by the day, they will make outstanding representatives of the Fallen to the rest of the world.

Sitting in the middle of my bed, Marissa is dressed in her black cargo pants and a black t-shirt, indicative of what she's planning for the evening, which is dinner with her parents. About the only time we wear any kind of uniform is when we're at the prison. She's towel drying her hair, it's long dark tresses damp from the shower. I watch her for a minute, until she reaches for her hairbrush sitting on my desk. Effortlessly, it sails through the air toward her.

I hear someone coming down the hallway and I hurry to shut the door.

"You're going to get caught in my room one day and we'll both be in trouble." In truth, I don't really care. I'd love a reason to keep her here all the time, although as an unmarried couple, Fallen culture frowns on the crossing of certain…boundaries. The priests, and her parents, probably like the illusion that we sleep separately.

"I'm not scared of Riley. Besides, do you know how terrible it is sharing a bathroom with a dozen other women?" She drops her brush and starts the process of braiding her hair back, her nimble fingers folding it into a simple plait she can wind into a bun at the back of her neck. "You shouldn't be back by now, either. Did you get your errands done?"

"I did." I drop the envelope I'm carrying on the desk and pull out the chair to sit. I want to see her face when I tell her the news. "I just left Major Laurent's office."

"Is there a problem?" She moans, her face falling. "Do we have to go back to work? Mom will kill me; we haven't been to dinner with them in two weeks."

"There's no problem." Excitement runs through my body like adrenaline. "It's good. We got the transfer."

The words sink in, her face changing from confusion to surprise. "What?"

"The transfer. We got it. We're going home." I grab the envelope and extract the paperwork. Transfer orders back to Hope. "We're being reassigned to the Division in New York, effective the end of the next month. We'll be here long enough to train our replacements and get Kaia and Jenn up to speed on our cases, but then we're heading home."

Marissa's body sags, a breath escaping from her body. While we love our team here in Jerusalem, we both want to return to the states. Now, after waiting for over a year, we have the opportunity. "Who's leaving the Division?"

"No one, they're adding two positions, and we got them." I lean in and kiss her carefully so that I don't make her lips red and swollen before dinner. "The Committee wants to train more of us, more members of the Division. Now that we know teams of ten Fallen can live independently of the hive, they hope to put us in more departments and more cities. More positions are going to be opening up."

"Oh, this is incredible." She finishes with her hair and takes the envelope from my hands. Once she looks over the paperwork, she carefully returns its contents. "I hate leaving Mom and Riley, and I love our team here, but I miss home."

"I know. That's why I took the assignment without asking you. I knew you'd want it." Turning in my seat, I place the envelope carefully on the desk. That was the easy part. "There's one other thing we need to talk about before we head to your parent's place."

Now, she looks suspicious. "What else?"

Out of my pocket comes the tiny box I'd picked up a few days ago. I give it to her.

Suspicion turns to shock; the lid opens to show a white gold band engraved with scrollwork and set with tiny diamond chips. It's simple, nothing too showy or big, it's exactly what she would have picked out if she'd gone with me to the store. My name is breathy when she says it. "Collin."

"Let's get married. Here, before we go back to New York." I pull her closer to me so that I can touch her. "We can invite the guys from the office, and Matthew and Sara, and your parents are here."

"But what about your mom and Mia?" Hands touch my face, holding me still while she speaks. "They can't be here."

"I'm sure they'll be happy to have a party when we get home." I lean my forehead to rest against hers. "Just say yes."

"Of course, yes!" She leans in and kisses me, not worried about how hard or how long. "Yes!"

She slides onto my lap, and I hold her close, grateful for everything that went wrong so this could go so right. We sit there for several minutes before I kiss her lightly on the neck. "We're going to be late."

"Yeah, probably not a good idea." Sliding off my lap, she holds the box in her hands. "This is for the ceremony?"

"Yes." The tiny diamonds sparkle in the light. "I didn't think you'd want an engagement ring, but I wanted to get you something. If you don't like it, we can take it back to the shop and exchange it."

"It's perfect." Smiling, she kisses me and slides the box into my pocket. "I think it's traditional for you to keep it until the wedding. Did you talk to Riley before you asked me?"

"Are you kidding?" Leaning back, I make a face. "We get along just fine, but I wasn't about to not ask for their blessing. Your mom would have killed me."

"You're right." Wrinkling her nose, I can see when she realizes what this dinner is about. "They know about the transfer, too, don't they? And this dinner is going to be a surprise engagement celebration."

"Guilty." I hold my hands up in an indication of surrender.

"Ugh." Tucking her hair into a bun, she uses two pins to hold it in place. "My mom's going to make such a huge deal of this."

"It is a huge deal." Pulling her close, I hold her next to my body. A thought occurs to me. "Jenn's got a pool going, doesn't she?"

"Yep."

I chuckle. It's a crazy family and I wouldn't want it any other way. "Let's go face your parents."

"Collin?"

"Yes?"

"I love you."

"I love you, too."

About the Author

Anne Schlea was born and raised in Northwest Ohio where she spent much of her childhood on her Grandparent's farm. She graduated from Woodmore High School and then went on to study music at Berry College in Rome, Georgia.

Today, Anne lives in the northern suburbs of Atlanta, Georgia, a short drive from the Appalachian Mountains, with her husband and her cat. She loves visiting wineries, making music, running her business, and hanging out with her Siamese cat, Rosanna.

Anne has written the adult series, *Retribution,* and the stand alone novel, *The Fallen.*

In 2022, she took a break from writing while she battled cancer. The treatment was focused and intense, requiring long stays at the hospital while she received almost 100 hours of continuous chemotherapy. She's in remission today, but the experience taught her to make the most of each moment.

www.ingramcontent.com/pod-product-compliance
Lightning Source LLC
LaVergne TN
LVHW020707110826
845149LV00012B/2145

* 9 7 9 8 9 9 1 0 3 9 9 4 9 *